EATEN BREAD

ANGIE ROWE

POOLBEG

This book is a work of fiction. The names, characters, places, businesses, organisations and incidents portrayed in it are either the product of the author's imagination or are used fictitiously. Any resemblance to actual persons, living or dead, events or locales is entirely coincidental.

Published 2021
by Poolbeg Press Ltd.
123 Grange Hill, Baldoyle,
Dublin 13, Ireland
Email: poolbeg@poolbeg.com

A catalogue record for this book is available from the British Library.

ISBN 978178199-420-7

www.poolbeg.com

About the Author

Angie Rowe has lived all her life in Dublin, firstly in Artane and for the last 40 years in Ballymount.

She is a qualified librarian and works in a psychiatric hospital and in a child and adolescent mental health service in Dublin. She has co-authored several academic articles on mental health and on librarianship.

Reading has always been part of her day. She particularly likes to read works by John Boyne, Colm Tóibín and Liane Moriarty, and loves the way Graham Norton writes such entertaining stories with seeming ease.

She began writing fiction in 2017 when she was given a voucher for a writing class. It was a revelation. The first building blocks of how to write a story led to more classes and more attempts. Until finally she finished writing her first book and was delighted when Poolbeg Press showed an interest in publishing it.

She is currently working on her next novel and loving every minute of it.

Angie is happily married to Chris and they have two sons, Graham and Darren.

Acknowledgements

Settle down, Reader, this could take a while. I'll start with you. Thank you, whoever you are, for reading this book — I never thought I'd see the day.

Thanks to Poolbeg Press for making it all happen — to Paula Campbell who said 'Yes' and to Gaye Shortland, the all-seeing editor, who is enthusiastic and wise in equal measure.

Robert Doran, an editor who pulled me out of many a pitfall — without his guidance and the confidence he gave me I'd never have had the nerve to approach a publisher.

Information sources were wide and varied but these books were essential:

Indian Removal: The Emigration of the Five Civilized Tribes of Indians (Volume 2) (The Civilization of the American Indian Series) Grant Foreman 1953.

The Irish Famine. Vol 2. Diarmaid Ferriter and Colm Tóibín 1999

The Great Hunger. Cecil Woodham Smith 1962.

The *Irish Times* newspaper archive provided details of the harvest of 1946 and the efforts of the volunteers who saved the crops.

Chantelle Standefer, Choctaw Tribal Member and

Instructor in the Choctaw Language School, Oklahoma, was an amazing source of reliable information. Chantelle's knowledge of her ancestors' way of life, names, jewellery, clothing and food were invaluable. She fully answered my very odd questions sent in emails in the middle of the night. Thank you, Chantelle.

Sarah Burns owns Knockanree. It's not a town — in real life it's a farm in Avoca. Abbeyfield Farm in the novel is based on her wonderful farm and house with the big inglenook fireplace and porch full of coats and wellingtons and a long lustrous history. Thanks for showing me the farm, and especially for introducing me to Henry and Sadie who remember the volunteers coming in 1946 to help with the harvest.

To the early readers, my apologies and thanks. Michael Jordan, always supportive, and my close friend Helene Forde who read the manuscript as many times as I did and was always there with wine and encouragement. Alison Campbell and Jacquie Kelly, who gave many hours to the cause. The inner circle, you know who you are, and Breda Wallace and Bernie Cadden who gave great advice on what to wear to a book launch and who never once yawned as I rehashed the storyline yet again. Special thanks to Carla Senf, who quietly listened and loudly supported me.

Great advice too from Mariana Linares, Foreign Rights Agent, Toronto, who is an extremely patient and kind person and good friend to my family.

To my Rowe family, Eileen, Brendan, Colette and Catherine. Couldn't have done it without you. Nor could I have managed without the support of the York Tribe, who always have my back.

Nearly there. Thank you, dear husband Chris, who provided endless cups of tea and chocolate but, more importantly, an amazing collection of books on Native American Indian culture. You shared the knowledge you'd absorbed over the years and helped me find the Kindred Spirits sculpture in Middleton. The tea and chocolate were good too. Honey, I couldn't have done it without you.

To my two wonderful sons, Graham and Darren, who listened to me going on and on about the extraordinary Choctaw gift and to Jennie, a woman of action, who went out and bought me a voucher for a writing class so that I could find a way to write the story. It worked! I'm so proud of you all and love you very much. I can say no more.

Dedication

For Chris, Graham and Darren —
and for Jennie, who bought the voucher

Author's Note

This book is a work of fiction, though based on facts. Matt O'Connell is a fictitious character whose story was inspired by the Armstrong brothers, Frank and William, of Scots-Irish blood. These brothers did everything in their power to help the Choctaw Indian Tribe in the 1800s and were held in high esteem by the tribe for their efforts. In actual fact, it was William Armstrong who chaired the meeting in Skullyville at which the $170 was contributed by the Choctaw to help the Irish during the Great Famine, and it was he who forwarded the donation to the Treasurer of the Memphis Irish Relief Committee.

Jim Ryan was Irish Minister for Agriculture at the time of the all-but-lost 1946 harvest and it is to his credit that the harvest was saved. However, the meeting between Minister Ryan and the characters in this book — Rivers, Connie, Jack and Fletcher — is entirely fictional.

'Eaten bread is soon forgot' is an old saying about unreturned favours or a forgotten kindness.

The gift of the Native American Choctaw tribe in 1847 was forgotten until the story came to light in 1989 when

Mr Don Mullen (Action from Ireland) came across it when arranging the 150th anniversary of the Great Famine. Records of the time verified the truth of the story and Mr Mullen invited members of the Choctaw tribe to the 'Famine Walk' in Mayo. The links between Ireland and the Choctaw Nation have become stronger with the passing of time and the Irish people are proud of those links.

A few years ago, I read an article from the *Irish Times* archives. Dated 1946, it reported on the heroic efforts of people throughout Ireland to save the harvest. Many businesses closed to allow workers from the city answer the call for help. Football matches were postponed, cinemas and dancehalls closed. Thousands were transported to help the farmers gather the drenched crops. I couldn't believe I hadn't heard about this before. Not only me – no one else seemed to have heard about it either. Another case of a kindness being forgotten.

CHAPTER 1

Knockanree

1946

Rosie leaned her elbows on the deep windowsill and watched summer raindrops dribble crookedly down the other side in jerky haphazard streams. She loosened the latch a fraction to let air into the humid kitchen. Another day. She had resigned herself to an eternity of days just like this one, a chain of them stretched from her distant past into . . . what? Could she even call it a future? More a sentence than a future, she thought. She wiped the steam from one of the small panes and leaned her forehead against the cool glass. It wasn't so much the waiting — no, she had no choice but to wait — that much she accepted. The thing that got her, that wrecked her, was hope. A good thing, hope, that's what people seemed to think. But she knew better.

From the corner of her eye she caught a movement. Something was slowly approaching the farmhouse, hugging the tall hedgerow. Something black and bent and shiny. She squinted at it, recognised the shape of the postman on his bicycle and tried to ignore that dreadful feeling of hope that crept into her soul.

'*Maguire's coming!*' she called.

'I'm not deaf,' said her grandfather. He heaved himself out of his chair beside the inglenook fireplace, shuffled as far as the wireless set and turned it on. A warm glow and gentle hum emanated from the brown box. 'What's he doing coming at this hour? It's nearly dinnertime. The news will be on. I hate visitors coming when the news is on. He'll talk all the way through the weather forecast. Feckin' eejit.'

'He must have something for us.' *Please have something for me*, she thought. A letter from him, even a postcard will do. A small tremble started in the pit of her stomach. She frowned into the pot at the piece of bacon simmering in a sea of green cabbage. I just hope Maguire's not hungry.

The door to the back porch opened and Michael Maguire stepped inside. A small man, barely taller than Rosie, thin from cycling the roads. He hung his glistening mackintosh on a wooden hook and, rubbing his hands together briskly, came into the kitchen.

'Is it raining out, Michael?' Rosie ignored the evidence from his dripping cap and forced an overbright smile.

Maguire turned to her grandfather. 'Shocking weather, Seán, eh? I don't ever remember an August as bad. If this keeps up, it won't matter if the land labourers stay on strike — there'll be nothing left to harvest, eh?'

Old Seán reached slowly for his unlit pipe and tapped it off the side of the fireplace. 'August can be a treacherous month to be sure, but the harvest will be got in, Michael.

Don't you worry your head about that. Sit down, will ya? What are you looking out for?'

'Not a thing.' Maguire settled at the large oak table which would easily seat ten. Today only three places were set. He removed his official cap and smoothed his greased widow's peak, then looked for somewhere to place his hat, finally settling on the bony old knee of his crossed leg.

Rosie put a cup of tea in front of him. He gave the tiniest nod of acknowledgement.

Never a word of thanks from the oul' shite, she thought. She pulled the tea towel taut in her hands and considered a sharp slap to the back of his head. I could say there was a fly on him, she thought . . . but she knew she wouldn't. Maybe a few years ago, she'd have risked it. But not these days.

He sipped his tea. She pressed her palms together and prayed for him to hurry up and give her the letter.

He lit a cigarette and plucked a stray flake of tobacco from his tongue, examined it briefly, then flicked it into the fire. The smell of tobacco mingled with that of damp clothes and cabbage. The wireless began to crackle.

She looked around for his postbag. He'd left it in the porch. Her heart sank with the dreaded certainty that there was no letter. No hope. Maguire stood and glanced out the window again.

'What the hell is wrong with you?' said Seán. 'Have you got worms or something? Sit down, for God's sake!'

Rosie followed Maguire's gaze out the window. Her father, head down, was striding toward them across the mucky yard. Maguire sat, eyes on the door, like a greyhound waiting for a hare.

The door was flung open and her father headed straight for the wireless. She watched the trail of mud track across the grey slate floor, her fists clenched behind her back. He'd never have done that when her mam was alive.

'Rosie, was this on all morning?' He fiddled with the wireless knobs, snatching voices and static from the outside world. 'I've told you before you'll run down the battery.'

She caught Maguire's smirk out of the corner of her eye.

The postman cleared his throat and smiled up at her father. 'Jack, I was just wondering—'

'The news will be starting,' said her father. He let out a sigh, leaned both hands on the back of a chair then asked, 'Wondering what?'

'If you're expecting a visitor?'

'No. Why?'

'Well, now.' Maguire drew on his cigarette. 'There's been someone asking for you.'

'Who?'

'A soldier.' Maguire leaned back in his chair and watched their faces.

'A soldier. Looking for me?' Her father shook his head. 'Must be a mistake.'

'Well, not you by name, exactly,' said Maguire. 'He rang the post office looking for Abbeyfield farm. Mother answered the phone. I wasn't talking to him myself.' His eyebrows came together for a moment. 'He should have arrived by now. I thought I'd let you know as I was passing.'

'What kind of soldier?' said Rosie.

Maguire raised his shoulders. 'Gave his name as Sergeant Rivers, and Mother said he sounded—' He twisted his head sharply to the window.

4

The unmistakable noise of the priest's old Ford hitting the potholes in the laneway filled the room. Maguire scurried to see.

'It's Father Geraghty,' he said, his voice high, 'and he's not alone!'

Rosie hurried to open the door.

A tall young man in uniform emerged from Father Geraghty's car and made his way towards the shelter of the porch. The portly priest seemed undecided between running and dignity as he waddled quickly after him.

'Good day to you all. I've brought your visitor.' Father Geraghty ushered the young man into the kitchen. 'He was going to walk from the town, but I wouldn't hear of it.'

The meal was forgotten. The one o'clock pips echoed around the silent room. All eyes turned to the stranger. Rosie thought she had never seen anyone quite like him before, even when she lived in Dublin. His uniform was not Irish army issue, nor English. American possibly, she thought.

Father Geraghty continued to smile as he made the introductions. 'This is Rosie.' The soldier quickly removed his army cap. 'And that's Seán, her grandfather, there. And this is the postman, Mr Maguire. You're very late today, Michael? You're usually home and having your dinner by now.'

Maguire shrugged.

'And this is Jack O'Connell. He's the owner of Abbeyfield.'

The soldier stood to attention. 'Sir.'

'Who are you?' Jack said. 'What's your business here?' His voice was not at all welcoming.

Mother would be mortified, thought Rosie.

5

'Rivers, sir. Sergeant Rivers.'

Her father waited, but the sergeant's eyes were not on him. His eyes focused on the ceiling and doors and the old fireplace. He moved across the room and ran his hand along the stout blackened timber mantelpiece till his fingers found the marks he seemed to know were there.

Old Seán's eyes followed the soldier's movements. A spark of remembrance flickered across his face.

Rosie regarded the American with open curiosity, her mind flitting through the possibilities. Perhaps he was a long-lost cousin? Every Irish family has a cousin, lost or otherwise, in America. Could he be theirs? She discounted this as she watched him. There was something different about this man. Darker skin, yes, but different in other ways too. Hair so black it had a dark-blue sheen, like a crow's wing. His high cheekbones and dark eyes were exotic and compellingly beautiful, but not feminine. He wasn't quite as tall as her father, but his shoulders were broad, and his body had an essence of quiet strength. Of maleness. She looked at her father who seemed perplexed, then at the grinning Maguire, then the other faces. No one appeared to be any wiser than she.

'*Ahem*, Sergeant Rivers,' Father Geraghty said to the soldier, 'I think you might have some explaining to do.'

CHAPTER 2

Jack watched as Rivers lifted his kitbag from the floor and from it took a long slim package wrapped in a blue-and-red-beaded canvas. He placed it carefully on the kitchen table, paused as if to say something, but didn't. Slowly he unwrapped the parcel.

It was a carved pipe. Not a smoking pipe — a flute, made from what had once been a dark but now was a faded rosewood. The flute was decorated with delicate flowers and birds and other unusual symbols. The symbols were intertwined with familiar Celtic circles and crosses.

Rivers' black eyes roamed the faces of the onlookers.

Seán moved from his chair and put his hand out to touch the pipe, as though he couldn't believe he was seeing it. He took a step back and put his hand to his mouth then left the room faster than he'd moved in a long time.

The voice on the radio droned on, cabbage bubbled

in the pot, but the group listened to the sounds coming from Seán's room: drawers opening and closing and the squeaking of the heavy wardrobe door. Finally, he returned carrying a long, slim box.

'Open it, Rosie,' he said, passing the box to her.

She carefully removed the lid to reveal another pipe. The twin of the one already on the table.

Everyone crowded around to see the two pipes, one a bit more worn than the other, but unmistakably made by the same hand. Jack tried to remember where he'd seen those markings before. He couldn't quite bring it to mind. Same size, shape, and the carvings were identical.

Seán smiled broadly at Rivers. 'I never believed the stories. I never thought it could be true,' he said.

'It was. It is true,' said Rivers.

Jack's eye was drawn to the silent Maguire soaking up the scene before him. He breathed a curse, crossed to the porch and took down the postman's mackintosh.

'Well, thanks for dropping in, Michael. We won't delay you.' He shook raindrops from the coat.

'Ah, that's no trouble at all. Sure, I was—'

'The post must get through, that right, Michael?' Jack did not move from the porch.

'I'd best be on my way, too,' said the priest. 'I'll give you a lift, Michael. We can tie the bike onto the back of the car.'

Maguire gave in, not quite gracefully. He muttered his thanks to the priest as he put his arms through the coat Jack was still holding. It took only moments for the bicycle to be tied, a little precariously, to the boot of the priest's car.

Jack watched Maguire climb uneasily into the seat.

8

He almost felt sorry for him. No one liked to be at the mercy of Father Geraghty's driving.

He closed the door and turned to see the little group examining the flutes. By now he knew where he'd seen the carvings before. He saw Rosie's face brighten as she realised the same thing.

'The mantelpiece, of course!' she said as she crossed to the fireplace just as Rivers had done and ran her hands across the blackened wood. The small flowers and Celtic crosses carved deep into it were just visible. There were other less decipherable symbols, but they had never given much thought to their origin. It hadn't been an enduring source of wonder or astonishment. Their home was full of things from past generations. The markings were just there, part of the fabric of the house.

'Rosie, put the food out,' said Jack and he indicated to Rivers to take a chair. 'There's things we have to get to the bottom of. First, how did you know about the markings in the mantelpiece?'

Rivers looked around the table. 'We know. I mean my people know of this house from the stories passed down.'

'What people? What stories?'

'The stories of Hatak Awaya.'

'Who?'

Rivers took the glass Rosie offered and sipped the water. 'You would know him as Matt O'Connell.'

'Matt O'Connell,' said Seán. 'There's a name I haven't heard spoken for many a year. My grandfather's brother, he was. Went to America. Do you remember me telling you that, Maureen?'

'I'm not Maureen, Grandad. I'm Rosie.'

Seán's eyes went to the ceiling as he searched for

memories. 'Went to America during the Great Famine.'

'During the Famine?' said Rivers. 'No. He was with my people before the Famine.'

'What "people" are you talking about?' Jack asked.

'I am of the Indian Choctaw Nation, Oklahoma. We don't have a written history of our ancestors. The stories are passed down, generation to generation. I can't say exactly what year it was. I just know it happened. The tribe helped him to help his people during the Famine.'

'A tribe of Indians helped Matt O'Connell's people? Seriously?' said Jack. 'How could they help, on the other side of the world. It was a hundred years ago. How would they even know that we needed help?'

'I don't know exactly. Parts of our history are not complete. Sometimes details were not passed on.' Rivers looked around the room. 'All I know is that he came here to help his people.'

'How can you be sure?' said Rosie.

'The markings in the mantelpiece.' Rivers moved to the fireplace and ran his fingers along the blackened timber. 'They are signs of the Choctaw. This is the Choctaw symbol for happiness. This is for love.' He moved to the far end of the mantelpiece. 'This is for peace. This is for friendship. The elders passed on the story of a house in a far-off land, near a religious place. In the centre of that house is a tree with the Choctaw signs of friendship between our two tribes.' He patted the sturdy timber.

'Dad, what religious place could that be?' asked Rosie.

'How would I know?' He regretted the sharpness when he saw her face fall. He wouldn't apologise, but he softened his tone. 'Well, it's probably the old abbey.' He turned to Rivers. 'This house was built from the stone of the ruined abbey. Half the walls of the county are built from bits of it.'

Jack produced a cigarette from his shirt pocket and struck a match sharply on the table. He lit his cigarette.

'But what are you doing here now?' he asked Rivers. 'You've hardly come all this way to show us a pipe!'

'What's your name, son?' Seán interrupted. 'I mean your first name?'

Rivers smiled at the old man. 'It's Redmond Rivers, sir, but everyone in the army just called me Rivers and I kinda like that now.'

'Rivers it is so,' said Seán.

Jack glared at Seán. 'I asked you a question, Rivers.'

'Well, sir, I came to Europe with the army—'

'I take it you were forced to join the army?' said Jack.

'No, many Choctaw and other American Indian tribes joined before we were drafted. Our country was under attack. How else would we respond?' He held Jack's eye and waited.

Jack shifted uneasily in his chair. 'Well, go on. I still don't know what you're doing here.'

'I kept the pipe with me. I hoped that I would get a chance to see Abbeyfield before I left Europe. My division returns stateside soon. We've come from Berlin and are waiting in Liverpool for our transit. I asked for permission to come here for a few days.'

'You've come hundreds of miles out of your way to see this farm?' said Jack. 'There must be something else. What are you really doing here? Is it something to do with Matt O'Connell?'

'It has everything to do with Matt O'Connell,' said

Rivers. 'Before Matt O'Connell travelled here from the territory now called Oklahoma, he was given a medallion. It was made from silver by the hands of our people. It bore the symbol of an arrow within a circle on one side and some other markings on the other.' He paused as though waiting for a sign of recognition. Nobody spoke. 'When he returned, he no longer had it.'

'You've come all this way to look for a medallion?' said Jack. 'Seriously? You expect me to believe that?'

'It's important to my people that I bring it back to them.'

'And you think it's here? A hundred years later?'

'Matt O'Connell said he left it here. In fact, he intended to come back and get it when he could. That was after our elders explained its significance to him on his return to Oklahoma. But he didn't manage to get back here.'

'And did he not say exactly where he had left it?' Jack asked, exasperated. 'Did he leave it with someone?'

'Well, that information was passed down by word of mouth and probably became confused as time went on. Some of our elders say he left it with a woman here at Abbeyfield. I was hoping that was true — that it might have been passed down in the family as an heirloom.'

'That didn't happen,' said Jack abruptly, sitting back and staring at Rivers challengingly. 'No one here has it.'

Rivers looked at Seán questioningly.

'No, son,' said the old man regretfully, 'I never heard anything like that. Never a word. And I think I would know if it was true.'

Rivers sighed. 'I suppose you would. Well, other elders say that he hid it somewhere here — though why he would do that I don't know. But I promised my people I would look for it. And I hoped you could help.'

'We have to help him!' said Seán. 'I remember my grandmother said that the Indians saved a lot of people from starvation. We owe them.'

'We are not in debt to the Indians,' said Jack.

'We owe them a debt of gratitude!' Seán thumped his stick on the floor.

'He's right, Dad. We have to help,' said Rosie.

Jack got to his feet and walked to the window. 'Have you not noticed the crops starting to rot in the field?' His voice was rising. 'Are we not in enough trouble without going off on a treasure hunt? I have more important things on my mind without this. I don't have the time.' He turned to Rivers. 'Come back in a few months. If we're still here, you can search all you like then.'

'I have only a week's special leave before I rejoin my regiment and go back to America. I doubt that I can return,' said Rivers. 'At least not for a very long time. I must find it while I am here, even if I search alone. I promised my family that I would try.'

'Impossible,' said Jack. 'Where would you start? We've lived here a long time. The attic is full of God knows what. It could be anywhere. There's old outhouses. He could have dug a hole and buried it somewhere on the farm. You'd have a better chance of finding leprechaun's gold!'

'Maybe easier than that — some of our elders say Matt O'Connell marked the spot where he left it.'

'Didn't you just say he gave it to a woman?' said Jack sharply.

'No, I said accounts differ. *Some* say he marked the spot — with that same symbol — an arrow with a circle.' He looked around at their blank faces. 'You've never seen anything like that around the farm?'

'No, we have not,' said Jack. 'Look, Rivers — I can't abandon everything to help a stranger find a lost trinket. I've too much at stake.'

'I understand. I realise you have more immediate problems,' said Rivers. 'But would you give me permission to search your land? I will try not to disrupt your lives here.' He stood up and looked around for his kitbag.

'Oh, sit down,' said Jack. 'Search all you want, for what good it'll do. If there ever was anything lost or hidden on the farm, it would have been found before now.' He glanced toward the steady rain. 'Stay if you want. You can sleep over the dairy.'

'Thank you,' said Rivers. 'I've been travelling since yesterday. I am very tired.'

'Dad!' said Rosie. 'It's not even been swept out and it's probably damp.' She moved closer to her father. 'Connie won't be here until next week, and the spare room just needs to be tidied up a bit.'

Jack hesitated for a moment. 'All right, Rivers. Sleep in the spare room. Rosie, show him where it is.'

Rosie led Rivers through the door to the front hall and up the stairs. The square landing had four bedrooms and a bathroom leading off it.

She fetched clean bedlinen and took Rivers into the spare bedroom. There was a serviceable bed, covered with mending and sewing waiting for attention. She put the bedlinen on a chair then gathered up the piles of sewing.

'I'll make up the bed for you,' she said.

'No need, I'm used to looking after myself. But thank you, Rosie. Goodnight.'

'It's only six o'clock — will you not come back down and talk for a while? I'm sure my grandfather would love to hear more stories about Matt.'

'Tomorrow, Rosie, I will enjoy talking with your grandfather tomorrow. I'm sorry, I've been travelling since yesterday. I need to sleep now.'

'Oh, yes. Of course. I'm sorry. Goodnight.'

Blushing, she went down the stairs, out into the damp evening air and walked along the hedgerow toward the haybarn. At least they'd managed to get the hay cut and baled and it filled the high wooden barn.

She barely noticed her surroundings or heard the bird's evensong as she thought of the events of the day. Rivers, the pipes, the way her father had managed to frogmarch Maguire out of the house.

No letter again, she thought. The disappointment had been delayed, but now she felt the weight of it. 'Tommy,' she whispered to the dropping sun, 'where are you? Why haven't you written?' She knew it must be difficult for him and she tried not to get her hopes up, but she couldn't quite manage to get 'hope' under control. She said his name again aloud. No one else ever spoke his name and she liked to say it, even though she was the only one to hear it. It kept him close to her.

That night sleep wouldn't come to her. The rain splattered against the window and she thought of Tommy again. There'd been a time when his name was all she said, when he was all she talked of.

It was 1939 when the world held the smell of excitement

and change. She was seventeen years old. After months of pleading, she was finally allowed to go to Dublin to the commercial college that her sister had attended — and had done so well at. Connie, of course, did well at everything.

Rosie had nodded enthusiastically as her father made it crystal clear that Connie was to keep an eye on her sister, and he would check up on her attendance at classes. But it didn't take long before the drudgery of learning a new skill took its toll on Rosie's enthusiasm for Rathmines Secretarial School.

I really will try to get there on time today, she'd said to herself that morning with the absolute best of intentions, though she'd spent at least fifteen minutes pinning up her long fair hair. Out she went into the brisk morning air and took a deep breath before starting off. *Best foot forward.*

Every morning she set off with just enough time for the journey, but something would always distract her. A lost dog one morning. An attempt at a short cut another day. Stick to the route, she told herself. On this day, a chilly January morning, it was the red shoes of a woman just in front of her. Red shoes, a black coat and, most astonishing, a red-silk bandana around her head. Such an outfit would cause a scandal in Knockanree. A woman with bright-red shoes would be castigated from the altar. It must be a film star, she thought. I bet it is. I must see her face. The red-shoed woman moved faster than Rosie would have thought possible in high heels. Rosie broke into a sort of half-walk half-trot. She was almost abreast of the red shoes when the woman suddenly stopped. Rosie carried on, gave a sidelong glance, but never saw the woman's face. She felt someone pull her arm sharply and was roughly dragged backwards. She lost her footing and landed on her backside on the footpath. A horse and cart had swerved to avoid her, the cart losing a good deal of its load.

The man who had rescued her tipped his hat and scurried off, muttering about the foolishness of today's youth.

The young driver of the cart jumped down, ashen-faced, but it wasn't to her side he ran. His immediate concern was for the horse. He ran his hands over the horse's haunches, legs and back.

'There, there, Freddy. It's okay. You're all right.'

Rosie smiled at the young man, whose red hair gleamed in the morning sun.

When he was certain Freddy was in no actual danger, he turned to Rosie but didn't return her smile.

'What did you think you were doing, stepping out like that?' he said. 'You nearly frightened Freddy half to death.' He began to pick up the scattered apples, carrots, turnips, and other assorted vegetables that lay across the road and footpath and put them back into their crates.

Rosie, red-faced, started to do the same, glancing at him every now and then. His red hair certainly matches his temper, she thought. Some passers-by stopped to help. She smiled at them, but then saw what they were really up to.

'*Put those back!*' she shouted at two women who were slipping carrots and onions into their pockets.

She shooed a group of hunkered children who were stuffing fruit into their jerseys. They ignored her. It was only when she threw Brussels sprouts at them that they ran off laughing, apples escaping from their jumpers

'Hey, what do you think you're doing with the sprouts?' said the cart-owner as he stopped her arm in mid-air.

'Sorry.' She looked up into his brown eyes. Even with a frown he was so attractive. 'I'm usually a better shot than that — though with snowballs, not sprouts. When it snows, I mean. I don't really ever throw sprouts, not usually, but . . .'

His frown deepened.

'Sorry.' She decided silence was the best option.

She helped him collect the last of the fruit and vegetables. He grumbled his thanks as he climbed back onto the cart.

She went to the horse's head and began to feed him one of the carrots. 'It's the least I could do, Freddy,' she said as she patted his face. 'I'm most awfully sorry. *Oh, Freddy! Can you ever forgive me?*' She placed the back of her hand across her forehead, like a heroine from the old silent films, and blinked her eyelashes furiously at the horse.

The driver laughed out loud. 'Can one offer madam a lift?' he said. 'Where are you going anyway in such a rush?' He held out his hand.

'Rathmines Secretarial College,' she said.

She took his hand and clambered up beside him.

'Tommy Farrell,' he said, her hand still firmly in his grasp.

'Rosaleen O'Connell,' she said. 'My friends call me Rosie.'

'Rosie it is so.' He tapped Freddy gently with the stick. 'Get up there, Freddy, we can't have Miss O'Connell late for class, now can we?

18

CHAPTER 3

Indian Territory

February 1847

The cabin door squeaked in the darkness as Matt stepped out onto the wooden stoop. He listened for a moment. Silence. Gently he pulled the door closed behind him. The aroma of coffee drifted in the air as he faced the rising sun. He sipped the hot drink and watched light creep onto the waters of the Arkansas River. Birds began to call. He closed his eyes and whistled softly in reply. He could almost believe he stood in the lane leading to Abbeyfield, except that when he opened his eyes the sun had begun to reveal the breadth of the sky, the width of the sparkling river, the expanse of the land beyond.

He knew the Indians were in the barn, their presence not given away by any sound they made but merely a shift in the stillness of the morning air. No matter how long he lived in Indian Territory, Matt knew he could never move, or even just stand, as quietly as the Choctaw.

He left his tin mug on the rocking chair, pulled on his

beaver-skin hat and ambled across to the small barn. He was a tall, loose-limbed man who seldom hurried. At thirty-eight he no longer considered himself young — his years of travelling and working in the sun showed on his face — but he smiled easily these days and the years did not weigh heavily on him. During the winter months he'd let his brown hair grow without interference from a barber and it now hung about his shoulders.

'Morning, lads.' Matt greeted the two with a smile, which they didn't return.

The Choctaws concentrated on the task in hand.

'Good morning, Hatak Awaya,' said Awachima.

His son, Loma, nodded and continued to tighten the ropes around the mules' girth.

They had called Matt this name after he'd taken a bride, Awachima's niece, the year before. *Hatak Awaya* meant 'married man'. Matt liked that he had another name. He fancied it made him sound more mysterious than plain old Matt O'Connell. He wasn't quite sure if he'd ended up with a wife by design or by chance, but there she was, asleep under the wolfskins, in his bed.

Matt saddled Surefoot and the three men set out for Fort Smith. Awachima and Loma told him the news of the tribe: births and deaths, plans for planting crops in the spring, movements of the wild herds, sightings of wolves in the north, settlers passing through their land. They rode for almost two hours before they were in sight of the fort.

Buildings made from sweet-smelling, newly hewn wood seemed to have multiplied each time Matt came to trade. Apart from the river traffic, it was a stop-off point for the Butterfield stage from Memphis. It was also a starting point for settlers heading west. It thrived on the hope of a new life, of possibilities.

Albert de Boer, known to all as Abe, was sweeping his front stoop underneath the General Store & Trading Post sign.

'Fine to see you, Matt. You got through the winter good?' The Dutchman smiled and held the door open.

'Not bad at all, Abe,' said Matt as they carried in the furs.

Matt knew there were plenty of merchants who would jump at the chance of the fine beaver and wolfskins that they brought, but he liked the Dutchman. He was fair, both to him and his Choctaw friends. That couldn't be said of all the traders in the fort. When Matt had first arrived in Fort Smith, he'd seen how the Indians were treated. The traders offered them one axe-head per pelt. It was only when Matt stepped in and offered to negotiate for them that the Choctaw began to receive a fair trade for their work. When Abe opened a trading post, Matt and the Choctaw gave him their business. During the fall, when the corn was ripe, they traded any extra crops that the tribe did not need. The Choctaw had for many years sustained themselves from the land and in turn had enriched and tended the earth.

When business was done, the Dutchman poured sarsaparillas for all of them. His smile widened to include Awachima and Loma, who didn't return the smile but accepted the sweet drinks.

Matt left the Indians to finish their drinks and crossed the muddy street to the post office. A long queue, mainly soldiers, snaked out of the wooden room. Matt noticed

21

immediately that the usual banter and jostling was absent today. He recognised many of the faces of the men waiting, most of them Irish. He knew a few to speak to. He stood behind Mullins who wore the sky-blue braid of an infantryman.

'Pay day?' asked Matt.

''Tis,' said Mullins, turning to face him. 'You've heard?'

'I've just come in. Heard what?'

'Things is bad at home.'

Matt shrugged his shoulders. 'Things are always bad at home. Sure, isn't that why we're all over here?'

'No. Really bad. It was even in the last lot of newspapers that came in.'

Matt's voice dropped to a whisper. 'A rebellion?'

'No, nothing like that. Not this time.' Mullins turned over the coins in his hand. 'It's the potatoes. The potatoes have failed.'

'I wouldn't worry. There'll always be a few spots where they won't thrive.'

'That's the thing.' The line inched along. Mullins took another step. '*All* the potatoes have failed. The newspaper said that there's hardly a field not infected. That's the very words it used. The sergeant read it out to us. It's the worst yet. The worst ever.'

'The newspapers probably don't have the whole story. It can't be as bad as that.'

'It was there in black and white, I'm telling you. The sergeant said it.' Mullins turned away from Matt and counted the coins in his hand again.

The postmaster handed Matt a letter. Even though he was sure Mullins, or his sergeant, had exaggerated, he was anxious for news of home and pulled it open as he went outside. He looked for the date. It had taken been written four months before: October 1846.

Dear Matthew,

I hope this letter finds you well and safe. Thank you for your kindness in sending money. Without it we, and many of our neighbours, would have starved.

The situation here in Knockanree has gone from bad to worse. The potato crop has failed. When we dug up the first lot, we had no cause for concern – the potatoes were a good size. Over the next few days, they started to rot. We tried to rescue what was left in the fields by digging them up as quickly as we could, but it was no use. They rotted to a stinking mess. We are hearing now that the same plague is everywhere, not just here in Kildare. It has spread across the whole of Ireland.

Our oat and wheat crop was small but healthy. The price of the seeds had gone up so much we could only sow half of what we would normally. We sold that and paid some of the rent, but now we are behind. I'd hoped to make some money from the public works, but I hear they are closing down.

Some of the neighbours decided to sow the seed potatoes quickly. If the second crop fails, they won't have anything to plant. I don't know what we can do. We are in a desperate situation. If you have anything at all to spare, please send it. Please God we can all survive this.

God bless and keep you safe.
Your brother,
Lorcan

Matt stood frozen on the wooden sidewalk. He barely noticed the people brushing past him. He had never felt the breadth of distance between here and home so keenly. He searched his pockets. Not much in cash — he'd traded for supplies — but he still had a few dollars. He returned to the post office and rejoined the queue.

The postmaster seemed unsurprised to see him again so quickly.

'How much do you want to send?'

'I have five dollars. What will that get them at home?'

'One pound.'

'That will have to do.'

Matt counted the money onto the counter just as Mullins had done earlier. The postmaster scooped it into a drawer. Matt scribbled a note while the postmaster completed the transaction and gave him a receipt. The money order and letter were added to the pile.

Matt looked at the large sack of letters lying on the floor. It's nothing short of a miracle if they all get to where they're going, he thought. There must be a fortune in those envelopes. *Please God, let the money get through to them.*

He could do no more, at least not today.

The three men began their homeward journey. As they rode, Matt talked about Knockanree, his brother and sister-in-law, Lorcan and Annie, in Abbeyfield, the neighbours, the town. He had often spoken about his homeland as though it were a paradise in another world. The smell of the land, the greenness of the fields, how sweet the air was to breathe. Now he spoke of the realities of his home. A people no longer the masters of their fate.

'They eat potatoes mostly,' said Matt. 'The potato is to

an Irishman what the buffalo is to the plains tribes.' He held up his hand. 'I know, I know, they don't have to hunt it or kill it. What I mean is that Irish people depend on the crop of potatoes to survive in the same way that some hunt the buffalo and in the way that you rely on your corn and maize and wheat. The difference is that the land you grow your crops on is yours. The land my people grow on was ours in the past, but we were invaded, our lands were the spoils of war, distributed among our enemies. They allow us to grow other crops, but we must use those to pay for the use of the land. The potato is what we grow for ourselves to eat, to keep our families alive.'

Loma and Awachima listened in silence. The Choctaw had been farmers for thousands of years; they understood what it meant when the crops failed. They knew the hardship it brought.

Darkness surrounded the cabin as they ate their evening meal. Matt told Mina the news from his family. She put her arms around his shoulders and held him to her. She shivered though the evening was not cold. Awachima watched Matt count the savings he kept in a tobacco tin. He counted the money more than once, as if that might increase its worth. Then he poured moonshine into tin mugs and raised a salute to Lorcan and Annie.

'Pray to God to keep them and the children safe!'

No sleep came to Matt that night. Hour by hour he watched the moon creep across the star-filled sky. He stared at the moon as though he might somehow connect with Lorcan through it. 'Keep a watch over them in Knockanree,' he whispered to the moon.

The moon returned his gaze and promised nothing.

25

CHAPTER 4

Knockanree

1946

The grey dawn crept into the yard as Rosie leant her bicycle against the side of the house. She lifted the latch to let herself in, paused and listened to the sound of the house. Except for the large clock ticking in the hall, it was quiet.

Dad will be in the milking shed for another hour, she thought. Grandad is probably still asleep. With a bit of luck, I'll have a whole hour of doing absolutely nothing —

'Good morning, Rosie. You've been out early.'

'Dear God, you frightened the life out of me. Anyway, it's not that early.'

Rivers took the empty egg basket from her and set it on the table as the hall clock's muted chimes struck seven.

Rosie struggled out of her raincoat and felt compelled to fill the silence between them.

'I sell eggs to some of the housewives in the town.' She pulled her long fair hair into a rough ponytail. 'I like to get it done early before . . . well, it's just easier.' Stop talking, Rosie, you'll say too much, she thought. She also sold butter to the housewives. It was still rationed and illegal to sell, but the demand was there and where was the harm? It wasn't as if they didn't need the money. Everyone thought the O'Connells were rolling in it. If only they knew, she thought.

She busily tied an apron around herself. 'Did you sleep all right?' He barely had time to nod before she rattled on. 'Now what do Americans eat for breakfast?' She rubbed her hands together. 'In the films they always eat pancakes, don't they? It just doesn't seem quite right here, does it? Do you? Want pancakes, I mean?' She stared into the pot of porridge she'd left steeping overnight as though it was the most interesting cereal in the world.

'I will eat whatever you usually have,' he said. 'I can help cook.'

'You can cook? I don't believe it. I'm sorry. I don't mean that I really don't believe it. Porridge it is, so!' Her voice sounded loud in her ears. She took an unsteady breath and tried to calm herself. 'Thank you. Help would be very much appreciated.' She handed him a wooden spoon and pointed at the pot. 'Stir.'

'Porridge?' Rivers looked inside. 'Oatmeal.' A smile softened his features.

Such a simple thing, a warm, genuine smile. It lifted her heart and she found herself smiling back at him.

Rosie wasn't used to sharing her workspace, and Rivers seemed to fill every inch of it. She edged around him as though the room had shrunk, and she felt awkward brushing past him — he smelled of soap — to put the kettle on the range, then stretch her arm by him to pick up the large spoon she'd left down.

27

I can't think of a single word to say, let alone something witty, she thought.

It was only when he sat at the table that she began to feel at ease. She turned to ask if the porridge was all right and caught him staring at her. He didn't look away when she met his eyes.

'I have some fresh eggs if you'd like some.' She felt the familiar warmth rise from her neck to her face and hoped he'd think it was from the heat of the range.

'Fresh eggs,' said Rivers. 'I haven't had fresh eggs for a very long time.'

'Why ever not?' She put the frying pan on the range and added some dripping.

'I don't think there are many chickens left in Europe,' said River. 'Certainly not enough to give everybody fresh eggs.'

She busied herself with the cooking, conscious of his eyes on her, cracking a couple of eggs into the frying pan and adding a thick slice of bread. She couldn't think of anything to say and wished he would speak again — but he remained silent.

She flipped the eggs and fried bread onto a plate and set it in front of him, together with a knife and fork.

'Thank you. That looks great. We've been — I mean the soldiers — have been living on rations, and C-ration food isn't exactly home cooking.' He began to eat.

'I'm sure.'

'Certainly nothing like this. It's good.'

'Jesus, it must have been worse than we thought if you think Rosie's cooking is good,' said Old Seán as he shuffled into the kitchen.

Rosie made a pretend swipe with the tea towel at her

grandfather. 'You can make your own breakfast if you're going to complain about my cooking!'

'You made eggs for him? Are you not going to sell them?'

'Grandad, why are you not dressed?' said Rosie. 'Go and put your clothes on.'

'I can't find any,' said Seán. He tried to sit at the table, but Rosie was already pulling him away.

'C'mon, Grandad, you know you can't sit in your pyjamas all day. I'll help you.'

'Then will you do me some eggs, like you did for the Indian man?'

'Clothes first, eggs second.'

'You're very good, Maureen.'

'I'm not Maureen, Grandad. I'm Rosie.' She led him back towards his bedroom, returning moments later, one slipper in her hand. 'I can't find his other one.'

Rivers bent and fetched the missing item from under the table. 'Who is Maureen?'

'My mother. He gets a bit confused sometimes. I can't blame him. I take after her.'

'Take after her?'

'I look a lot like her — when she was younger, I mean. She died almost three years ago.'

'I'm sorry, Rosie.'

Their fingers brushed as he handed her the slipper. She felt herself blush again as the back door opened and a cool breeze came in with her father.

'What's going on here?'

Rosie wished the ground would open up and swallow her. 'Nothing, Dad. Rivers found Grandad's slipper, that's all.'

Her father shook his head. 'If it's not his slippers it's his pipe.'

Jack helped himself to a bowl of porridge, sat down and began to eat hurriedly.

He paused, poured himself some tea and then turned to Rivers.

'I thought you had more important things to look for. Shouldn't you be in the attic or somewhere like that? I told you we haven't time to help, and we've no time to stand around chatting either. You couldn't have picked a worse time.'

'I didn't pick the time,' said Rivers. 'Maybe there's a reason why I am here now.'

'What do you mean?'

'Sometimes things happen for a reason, don't they?'

Jack continued to eat his porridge.

'I hoped you might show me the land, Mr O'Connell. If you have time,' said Rivers.

'What for?'

'I told you last night. We've heard much about Abbeyfield. I would like to walk through it with you.'

Jack drank slowly from his cup and watched Rivers over its rim.

'All right, if you want. We can go now while the rain has eased. But there's not much to see. You're going to need boots.

'Are you coming, Rosie?' said Rivers.

'She's busy,' said Jack quickly. 'Rosie, Connie is coming on Saturday. You'll need to get the bedroom ready.'

'Saturday? They weren't supposed to come until next week. Why are they coming early?'

'I asked her to. Is that a good enough reason for you?'

He threw back the rest of his tea and stood up. 'What size boot do you take, Rivers?' He went to the back porch and began to search through a pile of wellington boots and rain jackets.

Rosie looked away, ashamed that her father would snap at her in front of Rivers. 'I am. Busy, I mean. Sorry, Rivers, no, I can't come.'

'Thank you for the eggs. They were the best eggs I've eaten in years.'

'You told me they were the only eggs you'd eaten in years.'

'Well, that's true too,' he said as he followed Jack out to the back porch.

It was as though he hadn't noticed the sharpness of her father's tongue, or at least pretended he hadn't. She was grateful for the small consideration.

Jack paused to bless himself with the holy water from the small font nailed to the wall by the door. Rivers followed and dipped his fingers in the font, crossed himself as he'd seen Jack do. He didn't quite get the sequence right. He looked back at Rosie, eyebrows raised. She shook her head and smiled at him.

From the window Rosie watched the two men walk away towards the fields.

I can't remember the last time someone thanked me for cooking a meal, well, not since Mam was alive, she thought. She couldn't hear their conversation, but her father was pointing at the dairy and the haybarn and sheds, and Rivers inclined his head toward him and nodded as they walked away.

She turned from the window. Pull yourself together, for heaven's sake. She rubbed the fingers that still tingled a little from River's touch. Ridiculous, she thought. It's Tommy that I love, even with all his faults, and failings, and yes, even the lies. I've always been sure of it. Though maybe if Connie hadn't been so dead set against us, I wouldn't have been so adamant that he was the one for me. I'll never forget the look on Connie's face.

Rosie smiled to herself.

She'd come home from the secretarial school and had begun to tell Agnes, their flatmate, all about her adventure that morning.

'And his family own a fruit and vegetable shop and he does deliveries to all the big hotels and the best restaurants — he says he's practically running it all now with his father not being as young as he used to be and …' She paused as she heard the key in the hall door. 'The horse's name is Freddy, and he, I mean Tommy, did I tell you that's his name? Well, Tommy looks after Freddy as well, even though he has three sisters who do nothing. He always makes sure that Freddy has enough to eat and brushes him every single day.'

Connie came in from the hallway.

'Hi, Connie, you'd better sit down.' Agnes nodded towards Rosie. 'She's met someone.'

'Really? Who'd you meet, Rosie?' Connie tugged at her gloves, finger by finger, before carefully removing them.

'Don't start her off again,' said Agnes. 'Apparently he's a dreamy fruit-and-veg man with a cart and a horse. And what more could a girl want only a man with food and transport and plenty of shite for the garden?'

Rosie realised she'd been foolish to confide in Agnes,

obviously a girl with no romance in her soul. 'Well, he's lovely,' she said. 'And very kind. He said if I was at the bridge at eight in the morning, he'd take me to the college, even though it's a bit out of his way.'

'In the cart?' Connie shook her head.

Agnes looked from Connie to Rosie and picked up her purse. 'I'm going to the shop for … something … that I forget to get earlier,' and headed out the door.

'She didn't even take her jacket, and it's quite cool outside.' Connie looked out the window as Agnes disappeared down the garden path. 'So, what's all this about meeting a boy?'

'I've been offered a lift to the college by a lovely … person. He has a horse and cart. He delivers vegetables to—'

'Well, that's just completely out of the question,' said Connie. 'What would Mam and Dad say if you were seen riding around in a strange man's wagon at all hours of the day and night?'

'It's not all hours, it's eight o'clock in the morning for God's sake. Keep your hair on. Anyway, I've already said yes and thanked him for being so nice. So, I'll be there.' She folded her arms. 'I'm not going to break my word.'

Connie bit her lip and didn't reply.

Rosie felt that she'd won a small, but important, victory over her sister and, a few minutes before eight o'clock the next morning, she was waiting at Baggot Street bridge, wrapped up against the January chill, not completely sure which direction Tommy would come from. It wasn't quite light enough to make out the different horses and carts. She hadn't noticed before just how many there were on the streets.

She caught sight of him. He waved and urged a reluctant Freddy into a trot for the last few yards before he reached her. His warm smile lit up his face as he bent toward her, took her hand and pulled her up beside him.

'Good morning, Miss Rosie,' he said.

She noticed how white his teeth were.

Must be all the apples, she thought. Off they went, along the canal, chatting easily.

Tommy told her he was on his way to the Shelbourne Hotel.

'Isn't that the other way?' Rosie twisted in her seat.

'Plenty of time.'

He smiled at her, and she found herself drawn into his deep brown eyes.

He spoke about the hotel and the famous people who stayed there, how he would greet the doorman who'd tip his top hat and reply 'Good morning, Tommy' to him.

'How does he know your name?' said Rosie, wide-eyed.

'Oh, everybody knows everybody here. That's enough about me. I don't know the first thing about you. Tell me all about yourself, Rosie.'

'Well, I'm going to be an actress, or maybe a singer. I haven't really decided yet.'

'How do you get to be an actress or a singer?'

'I'll have to go for auditions, I suppose. Or maybe I'll be discovered by someone. I'm not really sure yet. But in Dublin there must be loads of opportunities for being discovered.'

'Oh, tons,' said Tommy. 'Where have you come from, to be discovered?'

'Knockanree.'

Tommy shook his head.

'It's in Kildare,' said Rosie. 'The most boring town in Kildare, probably in all of Ireland.'

'It can't be that bad. Are you farming people?'

'Yes, Abbeyfield farm. Fields and fields of wheat and oats and cows and sheep.'

'Sounds amazing.'

'It's certainly *not* amazing. The nearest picture house is four miles away.'

When they reached the secretarial college, he said 'Well, see you tomorrow morning, right?' before jumping down and hurrying around to help her. He put his hands on her waist and lifted her to the ground.

Rosie blushed and backed away from him, straight into Freddy's haunches. She stumbled and almost fell to her knees. Tommy caught her.

'I'd better see you to the door,' he said, but she steadied herself and told him there was no need.

On her way past Freddy she stopped to hug his neck and whispered, 'Sorry, Freddy,' before limping off across the road.

Rosie was mortified and her face blazed as she berated herself. He must think I'm a complete fool. Falling all over the place. I bet he won't be there tomorrow morning.

But he was.

The smell of damp earth mingled with turf smoke as Jack and Rivers walked down the lane, past the gorse decorated with heavy, dewy webs. As they reached the edge of the first field, Rivers asked questions about the fields and what buildings would have been there a hundred years ago. Jack pointed back to the house and the dairy and some of the stone outhouses. It hadn't changed much over the years, even with the extra land. Jack told him about the two recent storms, one shortly after the other, the ground holding the rain and the wind beating down the stalks. They leaned on the gate.

Rivers whistled when he saw the crops.

'Even if we got the reaper and thrasher into the field, it would sink under its own weight,' Jack told him. 'With the oats lying down like that, it's just not possible. We need a good bit of sunshine and a fair breeze to give us any hope. To tell you the truth, if we don't make a start on it next week, it's not going to happen. It's just not possible. And then on top of everything, the fucking labourers pick this time to go on strike. It makes my blood boil to listen to that feckin' Colin Lawlor moaning about a few measly pounds and there's people around here who will lose everything.'

'You will lose all the harvest?' Rivers asked.

Jack took off his cap. 'Yes, unless there's a drastic turn-around in the weather. I might have to plough the crop back into the land and take the loss. We may be able to get by on the bit we get for the potato crop. I always would have a few potatoes and a few beef cattle with the dairy cows and there's always the hens. We won't starve, I suppose we'll get through. I can't say the same for some of the neighbours — the Flynns, the Cullens — I don't know. But, by God, Colin Lawlor will never work anywhere around here again. It was him started them all, getting everyone worked up about their wages. I pay them fair and square the going rate. They're never feckin' happy. They should be glad to have a job instead of making trouble for everyone.'

'Colin Lawlor didn't make the storm,' said Rivers as he went past Jack into the field and pulled the top off a stalk. He rubbed it between his palms and blew away the chaff. 'I have to tell you, Mr O'Connell, that even in this state it's the best crop I've seen in years. You should see the farms in Europe. The fields, the crops, vines, people – anything in the path of war was trampled underfoot, broken to pieces. Finding food to feed the people is a struggle. Every country is trying to get itself back to the basics of their pre-war existence. Getting enough food is the biggest problem.'

Drops began to plop into puddles and they moved to shelter in one of the outbuildings. The tang of damp straw and manure hit the back of their throats.

Jack was talking again about Colin Lawlor as Rivers wandered further into the shed. The noise of the deluge dancing on the tin roof drowned out the sound of Jack's voice. Deeper into the building the rain and sunlight fell through rusted slits in the roof. Rivers muttered. He'd stumbled over something hard — an old bicycle wheel.

'I'd forgotten about that old junk,' said Jack. He looked at the broken buckets, oil cans and assorted pieces of rusty metal. 'I should sell it for scrap.'

Rivers found more pieces of scrap hanging from a rope along the walls of the shed, he pulled them down with a crash.

Jack drew nearer as Rivers divided the metal into piles.

'They're not in great shape, but I reckon, with a bit of cleaning and sharpening, you could make a start,' said Rivers.

'A start?' Then it dawned on Jack and he laughed out loud. 'What kind of an eejit are yeh?'

'There's nothing wrong with these.' A flash of annoyance passed across Rivers' face.

'You're not serious?' said Jack. He picked up a rusty scythe covered in pigeon droppings. 'Have you any idea how long it would take me to do even one acre using that?' He threw it back into the pile.

Rivers picked it up and swung it over his head. 'I'll help,' he said. 'I've used these before, a long time ago.'

Jack looked at the other man, unsure if he was serious. He shook his head. 'It would take an army, even if we had the men. If the weather doesn't pick up, it — it just won't work. There's too much against us. Sure, it would take a day to do one acre, if the oats were standing tall, but look at them.' He pointed toward the sodden fields. 'Not only an army – we'd need a miracle.'

Rivers swung a scythe backwards and forwards, reaping imaginary corn.

'It won't work,' said Jack. 'It just won't.'

Rivers gathered up the best of the rusty scythes and walked past Jack.

Jack trailed behind him and muttered under his breath. 'All right, all right, try if you must. You're as stubborn—'

'As a mule — I know,' finished Rivers.

For the rest of the morning they worked in the field with the scythes, rubber boots barely keeping the water out. Their feet sank into the ground, rain trickled down the back of their necks. In some parts of the field, the water came up over their ankles. Jack said the only way was to work as a pair. One tried to straighten an armful of sodden stalks, the other tried to cut them. It was laborious, backbreaking and painfully slow. After half a day's work they had little to show for it. The saturated crops they'd managed to cut were too wet to stand into stooks, so they loaded them onto a cart and brought them to the barn to dry out. By the end of it they were beyond exhaustion, every muscle in their arms and backs aching. Their feet and legs were cold and wet, and they squelched as they crossed the yard back to the house. The soldier rubbed the raised welts on his hands that were used to other work. They didn't need to speak. They both knew it was impossible. Not with the numbers they had, the time they had and especially not with nature against them.

CHAPTER 5

Dublin

1946

Connie O'Connell sat upright in her bed and began her morning routine. She carefully removed curlers from her short brown hair and placed them, one by one, in the drawer of her bedside locker. The clothes she'd ironed the previous evening — white shirt and black skirt — hung on the back of the door. She took them and tiptoed past the sleeping child to the cold bathroom. She washed and dressed quickly, all the while listening for Pádraig's gentle snores. Finally, she put on her glasses, gave herself the once-over in the mirror — tall, thin, neat as a pin — and went to the kitchen.

Agnes was already there, eating a bowlful of porridge. She nodded toward the pot. 'I've just turned it off.'

Connie helped herself and sat down.

'What's on the agenda for today, Connie?'

'Well, I have to pick up something from work first, then the Natural History Museum, then the National

Gallery and, if we've time, the Book of Kells.'

'Jesus, Connie, he's only six. Would you not take him to the pictures or something?'

Connie bit her tongue. Agnes had always been what the nuns would have called a 'flibbertigibbet' and had no clue about opening a child's mind to the world of science and art.

'Maybe at the weekend.' She planted her palms on the table. 'I'll do the front room when I get home. That rug could do with a good cleaning. If you check the rota, I think you'll find that it's your turn to put the bin out.'

'I'll put it out in a minute,' said Agnes, who had turned her attention to her red nail varnish and the sparkle of her engagement ring. 'I really don't know how we'd manage without that rota.'

Connie wasn't quite sure if there was a note of sarcasm in her flatmate's voice. She had a growing suspicion that, given the choice, Agnes would prefer not to have a rota at all. Then where would they be?

They heard Pádraig's footsteps padding along the hallway and his sleepy little head appeared round the door.

He came in and Connie restrained herself from hugging him — he'd made it perfectly clear that he was far too grown up for that. She ruffled his hair instead.

'Porridge?'

He nodded and yawned at the same time.

The phone began to ring in the hall outside and Connie went to answer it. By the time she returned, Agnes had drizzled a honey face onto the porridge and Pádraig was laughing into the bowl.

'We might have to cut your holiday short, Pádraig.

41

Looks like we're needed at home. Now eat up. I'm going to take you in to the newspaper office.'

'Will Fletch be there?' Pádraig stirred the honey face and looked up at his aunt.

Connie consulted her watch. Nine o'clock. 'Too early for Fletch, I'm afraid.'

Connie's was the smallest desk in the farthest corner of the noisy reporters' room. Its only saving grace was the small window behind her chair. The window had been painted shut years ago — trapping aromas that would be better out than in — but at least it allowed some natural light. She popped Pádraig onto her seat and told him to wait quietly while she went through her alphabetised files in the cabinet.

Fletcher came into the room, a head and shoulders above everyone else, and zigzagged his way through the crowded desks. Pádraig jumped from the chair and ran to meet him. The tall man scooped him up and swung him around.

'Hey, Paddy!' said Fletcher.

'*Pádraig, it's Pádraig!*' shouted the boy, dizzy from spinning at this great height.

'Put him down, Fletch. He's not long over his breakfast,' said Connie.

'Is that right, Pádraig?' He landed the unsteady boy. 'Too early for this, so.' He pulled a lollipop from his trench-coat pocket and handed it to him.

Connie rolled her eyes. 'Pádraig, come back here and sit down in my chair. You can have that if you promise to be good.'

He nodded enthusiastically and took the lollipop,

along with the crayons and paper she offered, back to the desk.

'Really, Fletch, he won't have a tooth in his head if you keep giving him that sort of stuff.'

'I have to spoil him when I can. I don't see him often enough,' said Fletcher.

'Can I talk to you for a minute?' Connie beckoned him over to a quieter part of the office. 'I had a call from my dad this morning. He wants me to go home on Saturday. It was a bad line. I couldn't make out all he was saying.'

'Your dad rang! Wonders will never cease. He actually used the telephone? Have Martians landed in Knockanree? Oh, come on, Connie, it's probably something to do with the harvest.'

'Maybe. I don't know. Well, that might be part of it.' She shook her head. 'This is stupid, but I could have sworn he said an Indian man was there. But that can't be right. An Indian man in Knockanree? Anyhow, he thinks there's going to be trouble.'

'Seriously, had he been drinking? An Indian? Surely not?'

'Maybe I misheard. But I'm more concerned with what kind of trouble. You might be right — it might be something to do with the harvest. You know how he gets at this time of year.'

'I know how he gets. Is there anything I can do?'

'Maybe. Thanks. I'll give you a ring when I know more.'

'There could be a story in it, Connie.'

'I doubt it. Nothing ever happens in Knockanree. Nothing worth writing about anyway.'

'Take your notepad just in case.' He put his hand on

his heart. 'I'll wait by my phone every evening.'

'Well, if it keeps you out of the pub that has to be a good thing.'

'Connie, you know reporters must drink. It goes with the job. I think it might even be in my contract.'

'Well, it certainly isn't in mine.'

'More's the pity.'

Fletcher sat down at his desk and winked at Pádraig. 'What are you doing there, Paddy?'

Pádraig held up a drawing of a stringy man with a hat, long coat and two odd socks. 'It's you!' A huge sticky smile spread across his face.

'With odd socks? Never!'

'Always,' said Connie.

'Well, that just proves I need a wife. Marry me, Connie.'

Neither she nor anyone else in the room reacted. Fletcher proposed at least once a day to whomever was around. It was almost his catchphrase.

'Some day I'm going to accept your proposal,' said Connie. 'Then what will you do?'

'I don't know.' He shrugged. 'But at least I'd have matching socks.'

Mr Carolan came into the reporters' room and frowned towards them.

'Fletch, shouldn't you be writing something? What are you doing here, Connie? I thought you were on holiday.'

'Connie might be on to a story, Mr Carolan. Could be big. I'm going to tag along with her to see how it goes.'

'No chance,' said the editor. 'You're on the Nuremberg trials till they finish.' He looked at Connie over the rim of his glasses. 'If you have a story, you'll have to pass it on to one of the reporters. You're not experienced enough. Writing about fashion shows and baking isn't exactly journalism, you know.'

Connie tapped a pencil against her knuckles. 'I didn't say there was a story. I'm going to visit my family, that's all. But if there is a story in Knockanree, then wouldn't I be best placed to tell it?'

'Until I hear otherwise,' said Mr Carolan quietly, 'I am still the editor of this newspaper. And if I say you're not ready, then you're not ready. Is that understood?'

'Yes, I'm sorry, Mr Carolan.' She bent her head like a penitent, but her mind screamed: *How can I ever be ready when you won't give me the chance?*

Mr Carolan seemed satisfied and softened a little. 'Well, all right, Fletcher — if there is a story, you look, but make sure you get the trial updates done first. Keep me posted.'

'They're on the closing statements. Shouldn't be long now, sir. I'll check out Connie's story as soon as possible.' Fletcher smiled brightly at Connie.

She waited for Mr Carolan to leave before she kicked Fletcher in the shin.

CHAPTER 6

Indian Territory

March 1847

Matt paced the length of the stoop. They were usually here before sun-up. His eyes strained toward the horizon. He'd not seen Awachima or Loma for a month, but they always came after a full moon.

He saw riders' dust, but from more than two horses. They're not coming alone, he thought. He glanced instinctively at his rifle by the door.

'*We've got company!*' he shouted to Mina.

He was right. As they drew nearer, he recognised the chief and the elders.

What did I do? I must have offended them somehow, he thought.

It happened from time to time that there would be a misunderstanding. Usually Awachima would mention it to him and it would be sorted with a small peace offering. He could think of nothing, no reason for the Indians to take offence. That worried him even more.

'*Bring out the good rugs!*' Matt called to his wife.

The elders and braves approached the cabin on horseback and waited until Matt gestured to them to sit on the rugs. Beads or eagles' feathers dangled from their necks and intertwined with their long black hair. Their green or turquoise-coloured shirts were worn over trousers made of fine buckskin. Some wore thick silver bands on their arms and gorgets around their necks. Matt understood that they were dressed for a solemn occasion.

His eyes sought Mina. Her face gave nothing away, but her fingers were on the silver medallion she wore around her neck. The medallion bore the Choctaw symbol for protection.

The elders arranged themselves into a circle around the warmth of the earth oven and indicated that Matt should sit beside the chief. They sat erect, proud and silent. The rest of the party formed an outer circle. When the circle was complete, the chief raised his head and everyone fell silent.

'We have learned about the suffering of your people, the hunger and the taking of your land,' the chief said. 'We share your sadness. We know your loss.'

Matt wasn't sure if he should say anything. His mother's voice came into his head: *Say nothing till you know more.* He said nothing but nodded in acknowledgement of the chief's words.

The chief leaned toward him. 'These are for you . . . to save your people.' He handed Matt a pouch made of buckskin.

Matt looked at the pouch, not quite sure that he'd understood correctly. His wife prodded him sharply.

'You're giving this to me?' He rubbed his back.

47

'To you for your people,' said the chief.

Matt looked around, uncertainty on his face. Again, he sought Mina's eyes. She nodded. He loosened the strings of the pouch and emptied the contents. Seventeen Gold Eagle coins fell into a small pile on the rug.

Matt looked from the coins to the chief, astonished.

'This is a lot of money. Are you sure that you want—'

'We know what hardship and hunger is. We know how it feels to lose your birthright. You must take this as a gift and use it to help your people.'

Matt bit his bottom lip and nodded. He didn't trust his voice for a few moments.

'Thank you.' His voice was soft.

Mina came to his side and addressed the chief and the elders.

'You will eat with us.'

She had baked Choctaw bread in the earth oven. She shared it among the elders and braves along with lamb's-quarter leaves and ragweed seeds. As often happened with gatherings the talk turned to the past. To the life they knew in the rich lands east of the Mississippi. They talked of the forests and the rivers that were once theirs to roam and fish in. Of a time before the treaties began to take parcels of what had been theirs. The shadow that came from the east and that could not be fought. They spoke of the different trails to the new land that some had taken. Matt knew the stories from Mina, though she'd been a child when the final blow was dealt. When the treaty of Dancing Rabbit Creek ceded the Choctaw land to the US Government. There was no real choice — to refuse would have caused war and the Choctaw were not a warring nation. They could only survive if they accepted the terms and agreed to move hundreds of miles to this place, where, it was promised, their way of life would be protected.

As they spoke Matt watched Mina. He knew this talk would upset her. She'd told him in the past about her journey here. What she remembered most was the snow, her cold wet feet, a large blue steamboat, the water rushing past. She'd been too young to remember her parents dying. She knew Awachima took her from their graveside, but only because he'd told her. She couldn't pull apart the memories from the nightmares. It was all black water and white snow. And cold.

When the chiefs and the others were gone Matt sat with Mina on the stoop.

'I can't believe it, really. It's a lot of money,' he said. 'How will they manage. Jesus, the tribe will go hungry because of this, won't they?'

'They might. It will depend on the harvest,' said Mina. She sat with her hands in her lap, her head bent.

'All that talk of the land east of the Mississippi, has it upset you? It must bring back some very bad memories.'

'Not whole memories — pieces of pictures — the noise of the steamboat that frightened me. Perhaps it was a blessing that I was too young to know what was going on, or to remember all of it.'

He put his arms around her and pulled her body close to his. 'The gift will save many lives, but do you understand what it means?'

'It means you can send the money to your brother and he can buy food.' She smiled up at him.

'I don't think I can send that much money.'

'What do you mean?' Her eyes narrowed.

'I mean I'll need to take the money to them. Not send it.'

She pulled away from him. 'You can send it the way you did before.'

'I don't know if I could trust anyone with that much. I hand over the money to the postmaster and he gives me a receipt right enough — but it's only a slip of paper with the amount of money that's sent written on it. What if it didn't get there? What if someone got their hands on it and got the money somehow?' He shook his head. 'No, the only way that I can be sure is for me to take it.'

He waited for her to speak. No words came.

'There's something else.' He stood and looked toward the river. 'I can't explain, but I feel the need to see them. To see my home place.' He turned and looked at her but could not read her face. 'It will be a long, dangerous journey, too dangerous to take you. I'm sorry. I have to go to my home.'

'I thought this was your home.' She stood and went inside the cabin.

He called her name. She did not come back, nor did he follow her inside.

Through the window he watched her sweep the floor with short, sharp strokes. She had a temper all right and he knew he'd have to bear the brunt of it. I have no choice, he thought. I can't take her with me. I can't tell her that to travel with an Indian woman would attract attention, probably trouble.

His thoughts turned to the journey and the weight of the money in the pouch in his hand. He could go soon. He'd already trapped some beaver and was planning to sell the pelts to Abe. Or maybe he should hold on to them until he got to New York. The pelts would bring a better price there as they were much in demand. He knew from Abe that there was good money to be made in trading furs. Abe sold them on to another trader and eventually they ended up as fancy hats in New York. It would all take time, and money, to get there. He'd need to gather more beaver pelts.

He knew ships didn't cross the ocean in the winter months. The harbours would start to open soon, if they weren't already. All depends on the weather, he thought. The sooner I go the better, but there's no point in going empty-handed. The gold the Indians had given him was for famine relief, not for his own family. He needed to make enough money to help his brother.

It will take two or three days to get to Memphis, and another week or so to Chicago, and from there it's the best part of a thousand miles to New York, he thought. Then there's the sea voyage. The whole journey will take months. That might be too long for them to survive — they're already in trouble. Please God the money I've sent already will last long enough to feed them. *Please, God, keep them safe until I get there.*

A few days later Awachima and Matt were fishing from the rocks that jutted into the water. They often fished together. Awachima had shown Matt the art of ice-fishing in the winter months and spearfishing in the summer. The Choctaw women fished using lines, like Matt did today, and it had taken him some time to convince Awachima that line-fishing was not only for women. The morning sky was clear blue but the sun had not yet begun to heat the earth. They sat on the smooth rocks with blankets over their shoulders and waited for a bass or catfish to take the bait.

Matt spoke of the gift. 'The money your people gave was very generous. Thank you.'

'It will help.'

'Yes, it will. Very much.' There was something about sitting side by side with Awachima, facing the sparkling water, that made it easier for Matt to talk. 'Mina told me what she remembers about the journey from your old land to here. It was before I came to America, and I've only heard a little about that time.'

For a few moments Matt thought Awachima wasn't going to speak.

Then he said, 'We have many stories of that time. I know what I saw and heard.' He stared into the water rushing past. 'The soldiers should not have told us to go in winter. We should have waited until spring, but they told us it would not be a hard journey. They told us they would provide food and blankets and tents to shelter us along the way. They were so sure in the words they spoke that we believed what they said. They told us these were the words of Andrew Jackson. We had fought beside him. He knew our people. We trusted his words. When they came to speak to us, they said we had a choice. The agents said we could go with them part of the way on river boats and walk the rest of the way. Or we could go alone and make our own way to meet with the others at Point Chicot. The starting place was Vicksburg on the Mississippi. My brother and his family, including Mina, went on one of the river boats. They travelled down the Mississippi, then turned up the Red River to where it meets the Ouachita River. Just past a bend on the Ouachita there are cliffs, with a small town at their feet called Ecore a Fabri. That was as far as the river boats could go. They were to march to Point Chicot from there.'

'So why did you not go with your brother?'

'We had horses and oxen to take to the new land. We knew we would have to take them along the trail. I travelled with about three hundred others and the animals. We crossed the river at Vicksburg. We were supposed to get provisions on the other side. They told us to go to Lake Providence, that there would be food and shelter for us and our animals.' Awachima looked to the sky and breathed deeply. 'One blanket and a little cornmeal. That was all they had for us. It had been snowing already, but then the storm started.'

'Only one blanket each?' Matt asked, incredulous.

'No — not one blanket for each person. They gave us one blanket for each family. They said the money to buy the food had not come, that the boats had cost much more than they had thought, that the merchants were charging two dollars for a bushel of corn instead of fifty cents.' He sighed deeply. "There was nowhere for us to shelter, so we took our animals onward. The sleet and snow cut into our faces. We were blind. The sky was hidden from us. We did not know the land — we became lost in a swamp — we could not find our way out. We were six days and nights without food or shelter. Our dead animals stood like rocks in the frozen snow. The old and sick began to die. We had given up when we heard the calls of our brothers. They had come searching for us. When we did not arrive at the place where the cliffs are, our brothers had pleaded with the agent and the captain of the boat to come back down the river to look for us. My brother and the agent called Cross and Captain Shirley found us. They led us out of the swamp and put us on the boat. We would have died in the swamp, though many died after we were brought out. It was not a good place. The boat brought us to the cliffs, where our people waited. They had refused to leave there until we were found. While they waited, the sick among them became worse and twenty-two people died in that place. Mina's mother died soon after. It did not feel right to leave them in the strange land, but we could not take them with us. We had still to face many days of walking, we were weak and slow, and the winter was harsh. We had no protection from the cold, and not enough food. My brother and many others died before we reached the fort.'

Awachima pulled his fishing line from the water. 'We still mourn the loss of them and one day we will reclaim them. I have marked the place in my memory.'

Later, Matt watched Mina sleeping. He put his arms around her sleeping body and gently pulled her closer to him.

CHAPTER 7

Knockanree

1946

The farmers leaned over the wireless in the kitchen of Abbeyfield farmhouse and listened to the weather report. It was inconclusive — there might or might not be rain over the next couple of days. The men swore loudly at the wireless and asked each other for the hundredth time what were they going to do. Rosie's opinion was not invited, and she would never interrupt the men to venture a view on farming matters, or any other matters. She concentrated on making the tea ration stretch to another pot, kept her movements small and slight and tried to fade into the wallpaper. She knew that none of the men would engage her in conversation, not in her father's kitchen. Though, when she passed by some of them in the town, she was aware of the leering, the whispered dirty words and the cold stares of their wives. In her father's house she was politely ignored.

She heard the back door open again but paid no

attention — there'd been people coming and going all morning. She listened instead for the sound of footfall in the room above. Have I missed him? Perhaps he's gone out looking already.

Then she heard a familiar voice.

'Can we talk, boss?' Colin Lawlor stepped into the centre of the room.

Rosie glanced quickly around. Everything about his appearance looked frayed and shabby. For the love of God, what is he doing? she thought. He must know he can't win this battle. If he'd waited until Dad was alone, there could have been some hope for him. But to approach him in front of the other farmers . . . it's like that kamikaze pilot in the newsreel.

Jack turned to face the labourer. 'What do you want? I've talked till I'm blue in the face. You want more. I can't give you any more.'

'We're not being unreasonable.' Lawlor twisted his cap in his hands and looked around the room. 'We earn two pound, ten shillings a week working in all weathers. It's been the same money for years. We could get more than double that if we worked in a factory.'

'Well, fuck off to the factory, then,' said Jack.

The other farmers murmured agreement.

Rosie wanted to intervene, to save Colin from mortification. She blushed for him but found she couldn't move from the sink.

'I've worked the land beside you.' Colin looked into their faces. 'Beside all of you, for ten years. I have nothing to show for it. I can't even put enough money together to buy a decent pair of shoes. Even so, it breaks my heart to see the crops rot in the fields.'

'If the weather doesn't break soon there'll be no harvest no matter what you do, or don't do,' said Jack.

'You won't be able to get the crops in without the labourers, even if the weather picks up,' said Lawlor.

'Ask for help,' said Rivers from the doorway.

Rosie, and everyone else, turned toward the voice.

'Who's he?' asked Gerry Flynn, staring at Rivers.

'Ask who? I told you I'd rather—' began Jack.

'Ask the people,' Rivers said.

'What people. Who is he?' said Flynn again. 'What's he talking about, Jack?'

'This is Rivers. He's a . . . friend of the family. Visiting . . . American,' said Jack.

'Explain what you mean, son,' said Seán from his chair. 'Who are you talking about?'

'Everyone. The people who will eat the bread. The people in the towns and cities.'

'The people who will eat the bread? Are you mad?' Jack turned to Old Seán. 'He's mad. Ask the jackeens? Not worth a damn, any of them. Sure, they wouldn't even know where to start.'

'You can't bring in outside labourers,' said Colin Lawlor. 'We won't stand for that.'

'It's nothing to do with you,' said Jack. 'We can get whoever we like. You can't stop us.'

'Don't do it, Jack,' warned Lawlor. 'There'll be trouble if you do.'

'Threatening me, are you?' said Jack, 'Get out of this house before I give you a kick up the arse.'

Colin Lawlor hesitated for a moment. He looked at the grim faces of the farmers, swore under his breath and glared at Rivers as he pushed past him.

ANGIE ROWE

Rosie watched him cross the yard. She'd known him forever. He'd eaten at their kitchen table almost every day. Until the strike. She couldn't speak up for him in front of the farmers. Not that anyone would listen, she thought.

The farmers ignored his departure and settled themselves around the table to carry on their conversation.

Rosie put a loaf into the egg basket and walked toward the door. She took a breath, ready to answer any enquiry as to where she might be going. Not as much as a glance in her direction.

As she left, she heard her father's commanding voice: 'They won't come. Why would they? Why? You're like drowning men clutching at straws. You saw how long it took to clear even a corner of a field. The whole thing is impossible.'

Rosie called Colin's name and he stopped and waited for her. She could see the sullen set of his shoulders and the scowl on his face as she neared him. He'd put his cap back on his head, but it failed to contain his black curly hair. She'd always thought his face a pleasant one, but when his temper flashed through his blue eyes, as it did now, she grew a little afraid of him.

'You wouldn't look at me in the house, as though I didn't exist. You didn't even offer me a cup of tea!' He spat the words. 'It was hard enough to stand in front of the farmers, all of them with their own land, all of them looking down on me.'

'I'm sorry. But you know what he's like. You've really riled him.'

She saw his mouth twitch as though he might smile.

'Well, that's something, I suppose. It's not everyone

58

would stand up to your father. Maybe that's something to be proud of in itself.'

He waited, as though for confirmation of his bravery.

She looked toward his family's cottage half a dozen fields away. 'Is your mother in?'

'Where else would she be?'

She tried to hand him the basket. 'Would you take this . . . for her.'

His hands stayed firmly in his pockets.

She left it at his feet.

'Why don't you come up to the house?' he said.

'You know I can't.' She glanced back toward her house. 'He'd have a fit.'

'Eaten bread is soon forgotten, isn't that what they say? He had no problem asking my mother to sit with his missus when she was bad.'

'That's different, Colin, and you know it. Your mother was a great help to us when Mam was ill, and after she died . . .' Rosie looked away.

'I'm sorry, Rosie. I shouldn't have brought that up. Your mother was a fine woman and Mam was honoured to be asked to help. Really she was.' He picked up the basket, looked away and back at her again. 'Mam says the whole village is asking about yer man that Father Geraghty brought. He's only here a couple of days and he's telling your dad to bring in scabs to do our jobs. Who the hell is he?'

'It's complicated. I'll tell you another time. I have to get back before they miss me.'

She looked toward his family's cottage. Turf smoke puffed from the chimney to join the grey clouds.

He followed her gaze. 'They think the world of you,

and of your dad. They won't hear a bad word said about him. They just say "Jack O'Connell will see us right". But he's changed, hasn't he?'

'He was never an easy man, Colin. You know that.'

'Indeed, I do. Though I think he got worse after you came back.'

She hadn't expected this. Not from him. She was always alert in the village for a stray enquiry. An innocent-sounding remark masked by a thin smile. A wedge to open the door to her story. A story she would not, could not, tell. Only the well-worn version of the truth — or the half-truth that she and her mother had concocted.

'There's no hurry bringing back the basket. Your mother might drop it in the next time she's passing.'

Rosie turned and walked back the way she came. She could feel his eyes on her as she tried to walk nonchalantly back through the sticky mud to the safety of her father's house.

Safety, is that the best I can hope for now? She stopped at the well and leaned over to look down into the blackness, into her past. When I was with Tommy, she thought, we were on the top of the world. I believed we'd be together for the rest of our lives. Happiness was so simple in those days, a walk around Stephen's Green, window-shopping in Grafton Street. The very odd time we had money for the pictures. The excitement of it. Swept into a world of cowboys, or an impossible romance set to music. No matter what, there was always the certainty of a happy ending and we were young enough to bring that certainty out into the real world. How foolish we were, so wrapped up in each other. I never dreamt that something happening hundreds of miles away would put a stop to everything. Then reality started to force its way into our world. Once England and Germany went to war it all changed. The only thing that anyone, including Tommy, talked of was the war.

I didn't want to listen to it. 'We're neutral, it has nothing to do with us.'

But he wasn't looking at me anymore, his eyes were on the sky.

CHAPTER 8

Rosie lit the oil lamp and hummed along to the melody coming from the wireless. Her father and grandfather, along with the neighbouring farmers, had disappeared off to Foley's pub. She savoured the freedom of being alone in the house.

The sun had begun to sink beyond the trees in the distance, hidden by pink-tinged clouds of red feathers. '*Red sky at night*,' she said aloud.

The heavy smell of damp earth hung in the air giving the evening a stillness that carried the sound of the horse and cart long before it turned into the yard. In the twilight she watched Rivers uncouple Monty from the wagon, saw him gently remove the harness and run his hands the length of the horse's back. Monty's ears moved as though listening to a soothing voice as he was led into the stable. She was at the sink when Rivers came into the warmth of the kitchen.

'Looks like I'll be staying a few more days after all, if that's OK?' he said. 'I have permission from the captain.' He took a plate to dry.

'Really? Well, I'm sure Dad would be glad of any help you can give.' She searched the soapy water for elusive teaspoons.

'I'm not really sure there's much I can do, but I'll try to find a way to help.'

They continued to wash and dry in silence.

He helped her put the delftware back in the dresser and then watched her lean across the table and wipe away crumbs.

Their eyes met in the silence and they both smiled.

'Rosie,' he said. 'How come you're here? How come you're not living in Dublin?'

'It's a long story,' she replied.

'I've got time,' he said and sat at the table.

She hesitated for a moment, then sat opposite him. She folded and refolded the tea towel, then she saw the expression on his face change. She knew he'd noticed the ring.

'I didn't realise you were married.' He sat back slightly into the wooden chair.

'Yes, I'm married,' she said, not meeting his eyes. 'I have a son.'

'A son. He isn't here?'

'He'll be back tomorrow. He's with my sister for a few days.'

Rivers remained silent and Rosie watched his face for the usual signs when people became aware that she had a son, but no husband in sight. The usual signs weren't there. She could see only concern in his eyes. The familiar flushing of her cheeks and neck began and she wanted to move but something kept her fixed in the chair.

'I'm sorry. I didn't mean to upset you,' he said. He started to rise.

'No, no, it's all right. Sit down, please.' She took a deep breath. 'It's just that around here I can't talk about . . . him. About my husband.'

'Why not?'

Rosie glanced toward the closed door. 'He's in the army.'

He shrugged his shoulders.

Even though she knew no one else was in the house, years of restraint whenever she spoke of Tommy made her lower her voice.

'The British army.'

'And that's a problem?'

'People round here, well, in most places in Ireland, look on that as almost treason. If they knew my husband fought for the British, my life wouldn't be worth living.'

He leaned forward, bringing his face closer to hers. 'Rosie, you should be proud of him, your son too, not whispering his name as though he were a criminal. As a man he should be able to fight under his own flag, Ireland's flag. That's where the shame lies. It is not his fault that his country stood by while Europe fought.'

'You don't understand,' she began.

'There is nothing to understand. Your husband put his life on the line even though his leaders would have the men stay away and be onlookers.'

He looked as though he wanted to say more. Instead he asked the very question she'd been asking herself for more than a year.

'Shouldn't he be back by now?'

Rosie took a deep breath. 'The last I heard he was in a prisoner-of-war camp. That was in 1940. There's been no word from him. I think that he might not . . .' She twisted the cloth in her hands.

He stilled her hands with his. 'You have to hope for the best. Don't give up, not yet. Europe is still in chaos — there are millions of people on the roads trying to get back to their lives. You could hear from him any time.'

He breathed hope into her heart, but his next words brought another fear.

'You must understand,' he went on, 'people come back to their old lives, but they are different. War changes anyone who's been through it, and not always for the better.'

Rosie raised her eyebrows. 'But he wasn't really in any of the fighting.'

'Even so,' he said. 'If he was in a prisoner-of-war camp, he *was* fighting — just a different kind of fight. Fighting for survival. He could come back a very different person from the one you remember.'

Rosie's bottom lip quivered. Fear joined with despair and tightened her heart. A tear escaped her lashes and slid down her cheek. She saw the pity in his eyes and watched as he stood and came to her side. She rose to meet him and welcomed his arms around her. He held her close to his body and let her cry. She did not want to break the embrace, to lose the comfort of his strength, but she knew she must step away from him now. Before it was too late.

She took a deep breath and he released her from his arms, but not from his eyes. She walked away, pulling air

ANGIE ROWE

into her lungs. The urge to tell him everything was almost
overwhelming.

'I've things to do in the dairy,' she said and went
through the door without looking back.

She lit a lamp in the chilly room, looked at the churn
without enthusiasm, but preferred to stay there until her
feelings and her thoughts settled.

When she'd left here years ago she'd never, for one
moment, thought that she'd be back in the dairy of
Abbeyfield Farm. She was sure something wonderful
waited in her future. She and Tommy were inseparable.

Tommy was up front about not having much money,
'It'll be different when I take over the shop,' he'd say.

She dropped hints about meeting his parents, but
Tommy always had an excuse as to why it didn't suit.
Looking back, she realised she'd accepted everything he
told her without question.

Tommy talked of nothing but the war. Then he told
her his plan.

'I don't think so, Tommy, what if you get hurt?' She
pulled at the stray blades of grass beside her. 'I just
couldn't bear it.'

'That's not going to happen, Rosie.' He put his arm
around her shoulders. 'I'll be very careful. Even if I'm
only there for a few months —'

'Months?'

'The pay is really good,' he said. 'And food and the
uniform and boots are included. A year at most and
we'd have a good start — it's the only way.'

'You'll take over the shop soon, you said you would.
There's no need to go away. You said your father wants
to retire. We can wait, can't we?'

Rosie turned her head toward him and caught the look on his face.

'I think you *want* to go to the war. I can see it in your eyes.'

'No, Jesus, no, it's the money,' he repeated. 'But, well, apart from that . . . I've been listening to the wireless and reading the papers. I think,' he looked around, 'the English are right.'

'Tommy! What are you saying? Mr de Valera is keeping us out of it for a reason.'

'Well, I won't tell him if you don't.'

'This is nothing to joke about,' said Rosie, springing to her feet. 'I don't see why you have to join up. What did your parents say?'

'It's not their decision. I'd make a lot more money there than I would staying here. And it's the right thing to do. When I come back we'll have enough for a little house, like we talked about.'

Rosie wasn't happy about it, but he was determined to go and so sure that he'd be back 'before you even miss me'.

He pulled her close to him and she wrapped her arms tightly around him. Already the thought of his going made her feel sick to her stomach.

A few weeks later he was gone. She received the letter that included a photo of him in his British army greatcoat. He looked so young and handsome. That was the one and only letter. Rosie was uneasy, already beginning to think that she might be pregnant. They hadn't meant for anything to happen, but his imminent departure gave an urgency to every moment they spent together, especially when they were alone in the flat, which wasn't often thanks to Connnie. But apparently just once was enough.

She wrote daily.

No reply came.

There was only one option left to her and she took it.

Babies were sleeping in prams outside open front doors as noisy children played on the shiny cobbles. Most of the children were involved in trying to make a cart out of an old set of pram wheels and a wooden crate which looked like it might have come from the fruit-and-vegetable shop she was now contemplating.

She could see the husband and wife through the open door, weighing and bagging and chatting to the customers. Tommy's dad was not unlike his son. His mother though looked formidable. A large woman with her dark hair bound up in a scarf. Her sleeves were rolled up above her elbows and the fat on her arms wobbled as she lifted a sack of cabbages onto the counter.

He must have told them about me, she thought. He must have.

She could wait no longer. Finding the shop had taken longer than she thought and now she really needed to find a toilet. She stepped inside.

Tommy's dad was serving an aged woman in a black coat. His mother was now counting apples into a large shopping bag held open by a woman who nodded as each apple dropped to the bottom. Rosie stood and listened while shoppers bemoaned the scarcity of tea and the shocking price of sugar in well-used phrases, each taking a turn to add to the stories of how awful the shortages were. Always ending with a desultory comment about the government who 'don't lift a finger to help us'.

The customers put their change into their purses and moved on toward the fishmonger's. It was Friday so no meat today.

Rosie waited quietly until Tommy's mother was free.

'Hello. Sorry, Mrs Farrell . . .' Rosie had rehearsed this so many times, but still couldn't get the words out. 'I was wondering if you'd heard anything from Tommy?'

'Tommy? She looked around to make sure the shop was empty. 'Why do you ask? Who are you?'

'Rosie.'

She looked from one to the other. They obviously had no idea who she was.

'I'm a . . . friend . . . of Tommy's,' she said.

'Is that so?' said the woman, arms crossed as she took in the girl's good leather shoes and wool coat.

'Has he not told you about me?' She felt dizzy.

'Not a word.' The woman did not move from her side of the counter. 'Why do you want to know anyhow?'

'I've written, but I've not heard back. I'm getting worried.'

'Was it you who put the idea in his head to join the army?' Tommy's mother drew her very black eyebrows together.

'Of course not, Mrs Farrell. I tried to talk him out of it. I'm worried but I can only imagine how worried you must be about your son.'

'Son!' she said. 'Not bloody likely. He's no son of mine.'

Rosie looked at Mr Farrell.

'Nor mine,' he said. 'Tommy is my brother's son. He's our nephew.'

The room began to spin. Rosie put her hand out to hold the counter.

Mr Farrell went to her side. 'There now, what's he been telling you? You've had a bit of a shock. Make her a cup of tea, Chrissie. The poor girl is as white as a ghost.'

Mrs Farrell hesitated but went into their kitchen at the back of the shop and soon the comforting sound of teamaking was heard.

When Rosie felt a little steadier, she asked to use the toilet and Mr Farrell pointed outside. While she was out there she saw Freddy alone in his little stable. Her heart ached to touch him and she couldn't resist going to hug his neck and whisper that she missed him too.

When she came back Mrs Farrell made her sit down and put a cup of tea into her hand, all the time watching her.

'He's lived with us since he was five or so,' she said. 'We put a roof over his head after his mother died and his father went to England. Of course, there were promises of sending us over the money for his keep. That came to nothing. Never saw a penny from him.' She sniffed. 'The boy works for his keep, though he's the laziest—'

'That's enough, Chrissie,' said Mr Farrell.

'So you haven't heard anything from him?' Rosie's eyes were almost overflowing.

'Not exactly,' replied Mrs Farrell. 'But I have heard news *of* him.'

She opened a drawer behind the counter and produced a folded telegram. She glanced toward the shop door as she handed it over.

'Feckin' eejit got captured,' she said.

Rosie took the official page and read the words **'REGRET TO INFORM YOU . . . CAPTURED . . . DUNKIRK . . . BELIEVED TO BE PRISONER OF WAR . . .'**

'Oh my God! Do you think he's all right?'

'Well, at least he's out of harm's way,' said Mr Farrell. 'That's something, isn't it? No one will be shooting at him. He's on the side-line now.'

'Yes, I suppose that is something. Do you think they'll send him home soon?'

'I wouldn't think so. I suppose they keep them locked up until the final whistle blows.'

Mr Farrell looked over at his wife as the pause lengthened. She remained silent, her eyes on the girl.

'Well, as long as he's safe, that's the main thing,' Rosie said, filling in the silence. 'Could I give you this?' She handed Mr Farrell a piece of paper with her address carefully written in large print. 'In case there's any more news.'

The shop door rattled, and Mr Farrell went to see to the customer.

Mrs Farrell leaned in toward the girl and whispered.

'I know what you're after. Well, you can forget all about it.'

'I'm not after anything,' said Rosie.

'Tommy is our flesh and blood. You have no claim on him — or his belongings.'

'I don't know what you mean.'

'Don't think you can sit there in your fine wool coat and leather shoes and think that you can get your hands on his wages. It's up to you to sort yourself out.'

'I–I don't—'

'Don't give me that. You're up the spout. It's as plain as the nose on your face. Let me tell you that anything Tommy is due from the army will come to us. We're his next of kin if he's dead.'

'Dead?'

71

'He might be. So if you're in trouble, don't think of coming here expecting a handout.'

Rosie stood up to go. The word '*dead*' stamped on her brain.

Mr Farrell turned and nodded and smiled as he watched his wife help the girl into her coat and button it up.

Only Rosie could see the disgust in Chrissy Farrell's eyes.

'And don't ever come back here,' said the woman in a low voice.

As Rosie turned to walk away the last insult landed. 'You slut!'

CHAPTER 9

Indian Territory

April 1847

Matt watched the sunrise from the jetty as though he'd never seen it before. He wanted to memorise the exact sequence: whereabouts the light first peeped over the ridge, the grey sky starting to pink, the yellow of the outcrop forming from the shadows, how long it took to see the breadth of the river. He'd become so used to the sound of the rushing water that it barely registered with him. Now he savoured every splash and gurgle.

He stood at the water's edge and looked back towards the house to see the orange glow of the lamp through the kitchen window. From out here it made the lopsided cabin look homely and comfortable.

Home. It had become home without him realising it. When he was travelling, before he settled here, home was Knockanree. When had that changed? He knew when though. He could hear Mina cooking breakfast, the smell of bacon and the sound of her special fried bread sizzling on the griddle. Usually she chattered non-stop while she fussed around the new stove he'd bought from Abe. This morning she was as quiet and cold as snow.

Neither of them ate much that last morning. He had gone over it time and again, trying to make her realise, to make her understand, why he had to go back.

'Am I not your family now?'

Her soft words cut right into him. She was his family now, his life, but he couldn't pretend that he was not needed elsewhere. Though they were four thousand miles away and it would be easy to stay here, he knew his family's hunger would gnaw away at his heart.

'I'll be back.' He looked into her eyes. 'You know I'll come back to you. No matter what happens, or how long it takes. I will never settle anywhere else. My heart is here. With you.'

They walked along the rickety jetty. The canoe in the river tugged at the rope like a puppy wanting to play. Awachima and Loma had come the evening before. They brought beaver skins stretched on circular frames made from the wood of the willow tree. Now they untied the skins and pushed them into a sack with the pelts that Matt had trapped.

'I can't take those from you,' said Matt. 'You've already given me so much.'

'Your people need help. Take them.' They took the heavy sack into the canoe with them and waited for him.

Mina slipped her hand into his. Emotions choked his throat. No words would come. At the last moment she took a doeskin pouch from around her neck and put it into his hand.

'Don't forget me, Matt O'Connell,' she said. 'This is to protect you. To bring you back to me.'

He stepped into the canoe and they manoeuvred it away from the overhanging boughs to the safety of the midstream. He called goodbye. The words were swallowed by the water. He waved his arm over his head, and she raised her arm in reply. He watched her until the river took him around the bend. Until he could see her no longer. He pulled open the leather strings of the pouch. Mina's silver medallion lay inside. He put it in his breast pocket and held it to his heart.

Matt dodged the wagons in Fort Smith to cross the street to Abe's trading post. It was crowded with men, women and children buying supplies for their passage west. There was a great deal of boisterous arguing over the cost of the flour, coffee and other necessities the travellers would need to continue on their journey.

Abe de Boer caught Matt's eye over the heads of his customers and motioned him to come to the end of the counter.

Abe handed him a pouch and lowered his voice. 'Here's the money I got for your last lot of furs.' He touched his finger to the side of his nose. 'And this is the name and address of the boarding house in New York. It's clean, and they are honest people.' He handed Matt the piece of paper. 'Don't lose that.'

Two men came to the end of the counter. 'We were here first. We want oatmeal and—'

'Yes, yes, in a moment, please give me a moment.' Abe rummaged among the papers under the counter. 'Where is it? Where is it?'

A woman with a crying toddler in her arms asked the cost of the lollipops in the big jars.

Abe breathed loudly. 'Take one, just take one.'

Every other child watched the crying toddler receive a lollipop and they immediately wailed in several different keys.

Abe emerged from under the counter waving a scrap of paper. 'This is the name of the ship and its captain. It will be in New York at the end of April or beginning of May. Depends on the weather, you know?' He shook a finger at the crying children. 'All right, all right! Take one each, but you must go outside to eat it.'

He held out the jar and the children instantly stopped wailing and each grabbed a lollipop.

Abe mopped his forehead then turned his attention back to Matt. 'The captain will send word to the boarding house.'

Matt took the piece of paper. He shook Abe warmly by the hand and tried to express his thanks, but Abe was intent on shooing the wayward children out of his shop onto the stoop.

Passengers for the stagecoach to Memphis were boarding and Matt carefully lifted the sack of pelts up to the helper on top and climbed inside. His last view, as the stage headed out of town, was of Abe de Boer bustling back into his store followed by a dozen lollipop-licking children.

CHAPTER 10

Matt looked around the stagecoach. Only three other passengers. One, a commercial traveller, a small balding man who clutched his sample bag. He didn't say what it contained. A regular on this route, he told them. He was given to calling out the names of features of the landscape as they passed. A soldier on leave from Fort Smith and his wife, travelling to visit her parents. The young officer was mindful of his wife, who held a handkerchief across her mouth. He fussed over her and constantly offered her water, a blanket, would she like the window open or closed?

Nobody paid much attention to Matt in his buckskin clothes, the best he owned. The material had stretched and worn itself into the shape of his body over the years. Perfect for the long journey ahead, he thought. Much more practical than the officer's uniform or the waistcoat and suit of the commercial traveller. As for the woman's outfit, he couldn't imagine his wife in such cumbersome clothes.

Matt took out the scraps of paper Abe had given him. He'd read and reread them a dozen times till he'd memorised the address in New York, the name of the ship, the captain. He refolded them and tucked them once again into his inside pocket. He was comforted by the touch of the doeskin pouch. If he could get there by the end of April, he could meet the captain of the *Agatha Maria* and he would be able to work his way across the Atlantic.

It was a dusty three-day journey, with two overnight stops, to Memphis. By the time they arrived in the city, every bone in Matt's lean body was shaken and sore. He planned to stay overnight there and take a steamboat and then canal boat to Chicago as soon as possible. But first he had another transaction to complete.

Matt regarded the three-storey house with interest. The open doorway stood between two large windows. He could see people were quietly going about their business. His mother had always praised the goodness of the Quakers. She had turned to them for help when she needed it and was never refused. He began to wonder if he should go inside.

A young woman came to the top of the steps.

'Sir,' she called, 'would you like to come in?'

You can't get a clearer sign than that, he thought. He smiled up at the girl in the doorway. 'Yes, thank you, I will come in.'

The girl tried to lead him toward a queue for soup.

'No, thank you. Can I speak to someone about a donation?' said Matt.

The young girl looked at him uncertainly. 'I'm not sure. Just wait a moment. I'll see what I can do.'

A few minutes later an older woman came quickly toward him, the girl behind, their full skirts swishing as they moved. Matt removed his hat.

'I'm sorry,' said the woman, 'we don't give donations of money but you are very welcome to some food.' She looked him up and down. 'We might have some clothes that you could use. Emily, see what you can find.' The woman took his arm and began to lead him toward the food. 'I'm Mrs Parker. Now, we have some nice soup and as much bread and cheese—'

'No, no, please, Mrs Parker, you don't understand. I want to *make* a donation — for the Irish famine.'

'Really?' Mrs Parker smiled at him. 'How exceedingly kind! Well, I'd better make a note of that, hadn't I? Come into the office.'

Inside she indicated a chair on one side of the desk, then sat opposite and took a ledger and a quill and ink from the desk drawer.

'Thank you kindly, ma'am,' Matt said, glad to sit down. All this city walking was taking its toll on his legs.

'It's good of you to spare something for those in need.' She waited patiently, pen in hand, while Matt fumbled with the strings of Abe's soft leather pouch.

A single gold coin tumbled out and rolled across the desk. She caught it and smiled broadly at Matt.

'Why, it's a Gold Eagle coin! How marvellous! Ten dollars is a remarkably generous donation. Thank you so much. The victims of the—'

Matt emptied the contents of the leather pouch noisily onto the desk in front of her. The Gold Eagle coins spread and gleamed in the afternoon sun.

'Seventeen eagles,' Matt said. 'That's one hundred and seventy dollars.'

'Goodness!' said Mrs Parker. 'Are you sure you can . . .? I mean, it's incredibly generous of you.'

'Oh, it's not from me,' he said. 'It's from the Indians.'

'I beg your pardon?' The pen in her hand hovered over the page. 'The Indians?' She looked over his shoulder as though some natives might suddenly appear in the doorway.

'Yes, ma'am. Could you write that it's from the Choctaw Indian Nation.'

'Of course,' she said and began writing. 'Could you spell that, please?' She nodded as he spelled out the name of the tribe. 'Thank you very much, sir, and please thank the, em . . . your friends.'

'Certainly will, ma'am.' He replaced his hat and stood to leave. 'How will you get the money to Ireland, if you don't mind me asking, ma'am?'

'We won't send the money. It will be added to all the other donations and we'll buy wheat and oats and corn here and ship it over. Our brother and sister Quakers in Ireland will distribute it to the needy. You can rest assured we will do our best to feed as many as possible.'

'I have no doubt of it, ma'am.' Matt put his hat on. 'Good day, ma'am.'

He left the Quaker house and whistled a tune as he went off down the street.

Matt left Memphis and journeyed by steamboat up the Mississippi. He arrived in Chicago just as the news that ports were beginning to reopen filtered in. The winter along the eastern seaboard had been even more severe than usual and the ice had lingered into April.

He intended to rest overnight in Chicago then figure out the best way to get to New York. Chicago was like Fort Smith multiplied by a thousand. A huge intersection of humanity crossed north and south, east and west. Train tracks driven into the ground were just starting to stitch the country together. Steam engines hissed and spat and pulled wagons with people, hurtling along faster than was right and proper, Matt thought.

Streets of haphazard buildings sprawled out in all directions, people living and working and dying and drunk and crying in every available space. It smelled of smoke and sweat, but the cold air coming from the lake freshened it every morning, and another furious day would begin. One, maybe two nights was all he could tolerate in a city that moved too fast for him.

As he walked, his eye was attracted by banners and posters asking for help for the victims of the famine in Ireland. He'd read accounts in the newspapers of fundraising to help the victims and each day he read of donations from all sorts of organisations as well as people on the street contributing to collections. Today's newspaper said that dozens of ships had left from ports along the east coast, laden with food destined for distribution in Ireland. His heart swelled at the goodness of the people of America. It gave him hope that everything would be all right.

Matt wiped the sides of his mouth, satisfied with the food he'd just eaten at the counter of a noisy saloon bar. It was early evening and men on their way home from work filled every table and chair. It was good to hear some Irish voices, louder as the night went on. The bar was bright and brash. A piano player plinked his way through some popular songs. Many 'ladies' sidled up to the male customers. At this time of the evening most men were more interested in the plates of stew and pints of beer. Once that immediate need was satisfied, the men's thoughts turned to other desires and found their arms around the waists of rouged women with untidy wigs. He didn't join in the spasmodic singing that broke out at random intervals but was happy to sip his beer and smile at the banter. He hoped that he might get to talk to someone who'd recently come over, but no one here seemed to be a new arrival.

A quiet man was sitting next to him at the crowded bar, his back turned to the revelry. Hunched over his pint, he made it clear he didn't want to talk. When the man looked up to catch the barman's eye, Matt nodded toward him.

'Thirsty work?' Matt asked over the noisy piano player and singers.

'No, not really, just want a drink.' He slurred his words slightly.

Obviously not his first drink of the day, Matt thought. The man had a soft Irish accent, but he didn't seem to fit in with the others. His clothes would have been smart had they been cleaned and pressed. He wore good leather shoes, not labourer's clogs like almost everyone else in the bar. Matt thought the few days' stubble on his unwashed face made him seem older than he probably was.

'Are yeh here long?' Matt asked.

The man turned a bleary eye to him and straightened

himself up a little. 'Sir, that depends entirely on your perspective of time and place. If you are asking how long I have been seated on this stool, in this establishment, then I have been here for a mere twinkling of an eye.'

'I see,' said Matt, not seeing at all.

'On the other hand,' the man took a deep breath, 'if you're asking how long I have been in this country, then I would have to say in reply, truthfully, that I have no idea.'

'Really?' Matt was sorry he'd ever spoken to him.

The man went back to staring at his half-empty glass of beer but, now that he was talking, there seemed to be no way of stemming the flow.

'The more perplexing question, of course, would be "Do I deserve to be here?", that's the thing.' It wasn't at all clear if the man was talking to Matt or himself. 'I have broken my oath already, you know. Not yet a year, and I've failed already.'

'Ah, I'm sure it's not as bad as you think. Maybe a good night's sleep will—'

'I left them there, all of them, even Benson.' His voice trembled, his dirty hand tightening around the glass.

'All? Who's Benson?'

'Dr Benson to you.' The man jerked up straight on the stool as though he'd been poked in the back, then raised his glass in mock toast: 'A fine and honourable man.' He slumped forward again. 'I walked out. No, not walked, I lie. *Ran* is the word, my good man — I ran as fast as my legs could carry me.' He moved two fingers across the bar, like little legs running, then hung his head and placed his elbows either side of his glass.

Matt decided this would be an opportune time to leave. He paid for his food and drink and said goodbye to the drunken man, who swung around, swaying slightly, but managed to keep his seat.

'Where are you going? I haven't finished telling you yet!'

'Maybe another time. I've a long way to go.' Matt put on his hat. 'I'm making my way back to Ireland. I have a boat to catch.'

The man reached across the space between them and grabbed Matt's collar, terror written across his face. '*Where? Not Quebec, don't go to Quebec. Don't . . . it's hell.*'

'I wasn't planning to—'

'That's where they are. That's where I left them.' He gripped Matt's collar tightly, his eyes wide. 'They're probably all dead now. I hope they're dead, for their sakes. The screams. Crying for water. Relentless.' He released Matt's collar and closed his eyes. 'The children . . . I couldn't do it any more. I couldn't look after them.'

Matt felt a cold hand on his heart. 'Who are they?' he asked, though he feared he knew the answer.

'The ships are queueing down the river. Fifty from Ireland waiting when I left. Full, all full of half-starved people with fever. Dysentery, typhus. How they even survived the journey I don't know. They're all on Grosse Isle. They can't get into Quebec. They're all outside on the island, dying, screaming for water.' He put his hands over his ears. 'I can still hear them.'

'But there must be people helping them?' Matt asked. 'There must be doctors tending to them.'

'The stench of them was worse than the noise.' The man wrinkled his nose. 'I know it wasn't their fault, but that stink . . . I still can't get rid of it. I can still smell them. Nowhere to put them, you understand? Tents, that's all, not even bedding.'

Matt stood beside the man and patted his shoulder. 'I'm sure you did everything you could.'

'I took the oath,' the man said. 'I'm a physician. God help me! Benson was doing everything he could, a few priests helping. Then the doctors started dying. I couldn't stay there. Dysentery. You understand? Rampant. Nothing could be done. Do you see? There are hundreds of them out there on the island. No one would come to help. Only the lowest of low came to rob the dead and the dying as they lay there.' The man put his head on the bar and began to cry without a sound.

Matt left the smoky bar and walked through the streets, glad to breathe deeply and feel the air on his face. He was in no rush to get back to the lodging house. He knew he would not sleep that night.

Later, as he lay in the bed and stared at the ceiling, he went over what the doctor had said. When he closed his eyes, he thought of the drunken man's story. He imagined the horror of the diseased ships clogging the ports, the husky cries for water, decaying bodies heaped on the shore.

Dear God, I pray my brother has not brought his family to that. Please stay in Knockanree, Lorcan. Please be there, or how will I ever find you?

85

CHAPTER 11

Dublin

1946

Connie wiped the seats with her handkerchief before she settled herself and her nephew into the train carriage. She handed him a new colouring book and crayons and he flicked through the pages until the train shuddered into life. With a clank, then a halting grinding noise, the train picked its way through a mangle of tracks out of the depot, picking up speed as it went. Garden sheds. Kitchen windows. Laundry lines. Then suddenly they were free of the city. Pádraig's book lay uncoloured as the clickity-clack motion of the train rocked his eyes closed. He leaned against his aunt's arm and drifted into sleep.

I used to love this trip home, Connie thought. These days I'm more like a buffer zone between Rosie and Dad. I hope they don't start complaining to me about each other, like the last time. If that happens, I think I'll try to find a reason to go back early. Mam always said they were too alike, each as stubborn as the other, and of course she was right.

I just don't have the knack of smoothing things over, the way you did, Mam. She took off her glasses, cleaned them with her handkerchief and dabbed her eyes. I miss you, Mam. I wish you were there. The house is so empty without you.

Pádraig half opened his eyes but surrendered again to the comfortable rocking and his aunt's arm around him. She ran her finger along his red cheek.

She remembered the day Rosie told her she was pregnant. She'd come home one evening to a distressed and tearful Rosie and the story had tumbled out. Rosie wanted to delay telling their parents, convinced that Tommy would be back soon. As the weeks went on and Rosie didn't visit home, their parents became suspicious and turned up at the flat without warning.

Connie still remembered the look on her father's face, the set of his jaw, when Rosie told them that she was going to have a baby.

There was absolute silence. Connie knew that wouldn't last for long.

When he spoke, her father's words were directed at her. They came out quietly, as though he was trying to control himself. 'Connie, what do you know about all this? You're supposed to be looking after her.'

She looked down, knew not to try to defend herself, and waited.

His voice grew louder, harsher. '*What the fuck's being going on here? You've been lying through your teeth, the pair of you!*' He spat out the words, cold grey eyes enraged. 'Now, we're not leaving here till we know the full story, and I mean the truth!' He banged the coffee table hard with the palm of his hand. 'For a start, has he asked you to marry him?'

'Oh yes, Tommy definitely wants to marry me.' Rosie had even smiled when she said that.

Her father shifted in his chair and let out a breath. 'Well, that's something. The sooner the better.'

'As soon as he gets back,' said Rosie.

'From where?' said her mother.

Connie exchanged glances with her sister. Rosie took a photo from the mantelpiece and handed it to her mother.

'This is Tommy,' she said.

Her father's eyes settled on the photograph.

'Is he wearing what I think he's wearing?' he asked.

Rosie nodded.

'An Irishman in that uniform. Shame on him, and on you for wanting to go with him. Where is he anyway?'

She told them that Tommy's aunt and uncle had a telegram to say he was missing since Dunkirk and was possibly a prisoner of war, but they didn't know where.

'Mighty handy, isn't it, a fucking prisoner of war?' said Jack. 'Sure, he could be anywhere. He might never be back. He could be dead.'

'Jack, for heaven's sake,' said her mother. 'Things are bad enough.'

'I don't think you realise how bad things really are!' said Jack. 'On the one hand,' he turned over his left palm, 'our daughter is going to have a fatherless child. A bastard. On the other hand,' he turned over his right palm, 'even if we could find this blackguard and she married him, we'd have a fucking British soldier in our family. There is no winning with this one, Maureen. Either way we're right in it, up to our oxters. Our daughter has made a mess of everything and she's going to drag us down with her. Jesus Christ, Rosie, you've been in Dublin only a year and look at the mess you're in.' He stood up. 'I can't even look at you. I'm going to the pub.' As he opened the door to leave, he stopped and turned. 'Make no mistake,' he pointed his finger at Rosie, 'you can't come to Knockanree while you're . . .' He pointed to her stomach. 'As soon as possible you make arrangements to have it adopted. There are places for that.' He lifted his hand as though he were stopping traffic. 'That's an end to it now.'

The door slammed loudly behind him and the three women flinched at the violence of the sound. They listened as his footsteps grew fainter.

'But I have to keep it, Mam. Tommy will be back soon and we'll get married. I can't tell him I gave our baby away.'

'What if he doesn't come back? How are you going to support yourself? I'll do what I can to help, but your father's right. You can't bring a child to Knockanree unless you have a husband. When this Tommy person comes back you must get married as soon as possible.'

'What if he doesn't come back soon?' Connie said.

'We'll speak to the nuns,' her mother said. 'They'll help us.'

They were nearly there. Connie became aware of the familiar scenery as it flew past the window. But it's not right. Where is everyone? Usually, at this time of year, the fields would be full of activity. Groups of men,

89

women and children all working together in the warm summer days, standing the oats or barley or wheat into stooks. Always an air of gaiety, with children and dogs chasing around the fields. There didn't seem to be any of that happening. The occasional forlorn group of people flashed past. There was no sign of a harvest of any sort — only field after field of desolated crops.

CHAPTER 12

Knockanree

1946

The train pulled in to Knockanree station and they stepped out of their compartment to hissing steam, noise, crates, and cases.

'*There's Mammy!*' shouted Pádraig and he ran the length of the platform into Rosie's arms. Hugs and kisses followed until Pádraig had to tell his mother she was holding him too tight and he wriggled free as Connie caught up.

'Wow, Connie, you're wearing trousers!' said Rosie. 'They really suit you, very smart.' She wrapped her cardigan tightly around her, hiding her old skirt and blouse.

They gathered up their belongings, all talking at the same time, and came out of the small station.

'I have new shoes.' Pádraig stopped and held his foot up for viewing.

'Connie, you shouldn't have!' said Rosie.

'And there's more stuff in that!' He pointed to the new suitcase.

'Really, Connie, we've spoken about this. I can provide his clothes.'

'It's fine, Rosie. It's just a few little things from his aunty.'

'That's not the point,' Rosie began, but Connie had started toward the horse and cart.

'Rosie, what's wrong? Why did Dad ask me to come up early? And what's all this about an Indian?'

She noticed the dark, attractive man who was heading towards them. A certain stillness came as though the breeze had suddenly fallen, as though everyone in the village held their breath as they watched. Connie knew that if she looked toward Maguire's shop a line of familiar faces would be turned eagerly toward them.

'Rosie, did you come into town on your own with . . . him? Is that one of Dad's shirts he's wearing?'

'Connie, this is Rivers. He's helping at the farm.'

'I'm pleased to meet you, Connie.'

They shook hands and Connie, unusually, found herself lost for words.

Rivers turned to Pádraig and held out his hand. 'You must be Pádraig. I've heard a lot about you.'

'Heard about me? From who?' asked Pádraig, solemnly shaking Rivers' hand.

'Monty, of course.'

'He can't talk.'

'Just because he never talked to you doesn't mean he can't talk. We've had long chats while you've been gone. Isn't that right, Monty?'

The horse ignored him.

The sisters laughed at Pádraig's wide-eyed expression as Rivers lifted him onto the cart.

'So, Mr Rivers, what brings you to Knockanree?' said Connie as the cart took off on the road to Abbeyfield.

'Maybe we should wait until we're home to talk about that,' said Rosie.

'OK.' Connie glanced at her sister. 'How's preparations for the harvest going?'

'According to Dad there isn't going to be a harvest.'

'The crops are all flattened — I saw it on the way here.'

'Yes. Ruined. Dad is up the walls,' said Rosie. 'On top of everything, Colin Lawlor – you remember him?'

'Yes, of course I remember him.'

'Well, he's organised all the land labourers and called a strike. They're looking for more money.'

'Do you know anything about this, Mr Rivers?'

'Sergeant Rivers,' he said. 'Nope. Nothing to do with me.'

'I'll have a word with Colin when I get home,' said Connie. 'He's worked for us for years. There must be a misunderstanding.'

'Why do you imagine that you can solve everything, Connie? Do you think we're eejits down here?'

'Of course not, Rosie,' said Connie in a calm voice. 'Just sometimes Dad can fly off the handle, can't he? Maybe a different approach would work. That's all.'

'Yeah, right, well, good luck with that. I'm sure everyone will be absolutely delighted to hear what you have to say.'

When Connie had settled in, the family gathered around the kitchen table and showed her the flutes. She picked them up and compared their markings to those in the mantelpiece as the others had done on the previous days.

'Fascinating!' she said as she sat down again. 'But, Rivers, tell me about this Matt O'Connell.'

Rivers began to tell Matt's story — how he had lived near the Chocktaw, how he had married into their tribe.

'We knew of Hatak Awaya's journey to this place. *Knockanree.*' His said the name carefully, as though it were sacred.

'*Cnoc an Rí* in Irish — "The Hill of the King",' said Seán from his chair by the fireplace. 'But I don't know what king or when.'

Rivers nodded, smiling. 'That is very fitting. In our stories Matt O'Connell was a great man indeed. So, when I came to Europe as a soldier, I hoped that I would be able to come here to his ancestral place, to find the medallion and take it back to my people. He said he left it here, Connie — that information has been passed down by word of mouth since his time.'

'A medallion?' said Connie. 'Why is it so important?'

'That's something that only a people who have lost everything can understand. It's a link to our past. We don't believe it's magical, nor is it worth a lot of money. But it holds information that we have been searching for.' He leaned his elbows on the table then raised his eyes to look at each one of the listeners. 'In the time before, the time when the Choctaw lived on the land east of the Mississippi, we were a prosperous tribe and the land was sacred to us. Our history began with the land. Every curve and hill held a story that was passed down through the generations. Long ago, we traded with the English and the French. One of the things we traded for was silver. We made it into necklaces or bracelets. Some we engraved with symbols for rivers or hills that were sacred to us and

94

handed down from mother to daughter. In our culture it was the women that held the things of value.'

'Quite right too,' said Connie.

Jack glared at her.

Rivers went on. 'As more and more settlers came, we were forced into treaties that took our land piece by piece until we had no choice but to leave it. Our tribe and other tribes were forced to move hundreds of miles — the Trail of Tears. Many died of exhaustion and starvation along the way.'

Connie took out her notebook and pencil. 'Is it OK if I make a few notes?'

Rivers nodded. 'Over the years we have tried to retrace the steps of the Trail of Tears, looking for the burial places of our people. It was said that the medallion shows a map that will lead us to one of those places.'

'A map is engraved onto the medallion? Extraordinary!' said Connie. 'This is a great story. We will help you look for the medallion.' She smiled and adjusted her glasses.

'Look, Connie,' said her father, 'there's nothing to prove that medallion was ever here.'

Rivers met Jack's gaze steadily. 'The medallion was brought here by Matt O'Connell, to this place. He left it here. I don't know for certain if it is still here. But I must search. You've dismissed the idea that he gave it to a woman here so—'

'A woman!' Connie's eyes narrowed. 'A woman. Would that have been Grandad's grandmother — Annie? In that case it would have been passed down, wouldn't it?'

'Connie, we already discussed all this with Rivers,' said Rosie, irritated that Connie was wading in as if she owned the whole thing now. 'We're agreed that didn't happen. Even Grandad has never heard of any such gift or any such heirloom. And he surely would have if it was passed on to his mother. *And* he would have seen it.'

'Still, it's possible.' Connie, true to form, was not to be deflected. 'Dad, did you ever see anything like that in Mam's jewellery box?'

Jack raised his shoulders. 'All her jewellery was divided between the two of you. I don't think there's anything left. The box is upstairs.'

Connie got quickly to her feet and was out the door and up the stairs before Rivers realised what she was doing.

'May I?'

'Go on,' said Jack.

Rivers hurried out, followed by an excited Pádraig.

Connie's mother's jewellery box lay under a fine coat of dust on the dressing table. She lifted the lid, almost expecting the silver piece to lie shining on the red velvet. The contents consisted of a few hairpins, odd buttons, a pair of shoelaces and a toy soldier belonging to Pádraig who grabbed it delightedly and disappeared down the stairs again.

'I'm sorry, Rivers,' said Connie. 'False alarm.'

They walked back together and into the living room.

'I told you it wasn't there,' said Rosie. 'It was the first place I looked.'

'You might have mentioned it,' said Connie.

Rosie shrugged.

'It might be hidden somewhere, though why he'd hide it or leave it in the first place I can't imagine.' Rivers took his seat again.

'Can you retrace the steps of the Trail of Tears?' asked Connie. 'Perhaps if you walked it, the burial grounds might be obvious.'

'For heaven's sake, Connie, I'm sure they've thought of that already,' said Rosie.

Rivers smiled. 'We have, but there was more than one route. Some went up the Mississippi through Memphis. Others went up the Red River, and some went by other routes that we do not know.'

'I'll help you,' said Connie. 'We'll all help. I'll make a list of the places it might be here, and we can go through it step by step. If it's here, we'll find it.'

She went to the table and picked up one of the pipes.

'So, Rivers, can you actually play anything on this, or is it purely decorative?'

Rivers took the flutes from her and handed one to Seán. 'There must be something we can play together,' he said. 'Not only were stories about Matt O'Connell passed down among my people — his music was too. Do you know this?'

The first few notes came from the flute and Seán nodded. 'I do, I do.'

They played an old tune that was vaguely familiar to Connie but she couldn't name.

Jack looked at them as they played. 'Amazing,' he said to Connie. 'He doesn't know what day of the week it is and yet he can play an oul' tune he hasn't heard in years. Would you credit that?'

Connie pretended she hadn't noticed the tear in her father's eye.

CHAPTER 13

New York

1847

Matt found the boarding house in Stone Street, New York. It was as comfortable, and Mrs Jansen as kindly, as Abe had promised. He was tired and was tempted to lie on the clean wide bed and let the soft breeze and sunshine wash over him. But what if the ship was already there, waiting? What if it was readying its sails as he stood here? Even though Mrs Jansen assured him there had been no message from the captain, he couldn't relax until he'd seen the docks for himself.

He slung his heavy sack of beaver pelts over his shoulder and found his way to the port. The list of ships due to arrive did not include the *Agatha Marie*. He was keen to continue his journey but now, facing the sea, fear began to curdle his stomach. He turned away from the smell of the water, oily thick and shiny with waste as it lapped the dock walls. He looked toward the streets he'd known years before when he'd first arrived in America.

New York had grown upwards and outwards and even inwards in the fifteen years since he'd passed through. Along Broadway and St Ann's the streets were wide and filled with promenading well-dressed citizens. He passed a long queue and had to lean back to see the top of the building they were waiting to enter. Barnum's American Museum: twenty-five cents to see all sorts of wonderous entertainments.

He continued down Broadway and stopped outside a shop window filled with a display of fur coats, hats and stoles draped across chairs. Bearskins were placed carefully across the width of the window. He felt their glass eyes watch him. Matt pushed open the door and a little bell tinkled over his head. Abe should get one of them, he thought. He moved toward the centre of the shop. Each step felt as though he walked on soft turf. The scent of flowers filled the air. Tall vases with long-stemmed lilies were placed on either end of a shining countertop, from behind which a dapper man peered at Matt. The man ran his eyes over Matt's clothes and shoes and the large sack. He came around the counter and pulled Matt by the sleeve back toward the door.

'Left, then left again down the laneway.'

Matt had no trouble finding the back entrance to the furriers and told the first person he saw that he had beaver pelts to sell. Moments later a man was beside him asking to see the quality of the furs.

Abe had been right to advise him to wait until he got to New York. Matt wasn't used to trading for money. The going rate for a beaver skin in the Indian Territory was one or two axe-heads. There was no talk of axe-heads here. The furrier offered him two hundred dollars

in gold coins. Matt put out his hand and they shook on
it.

On the way back to Mrs Jansen's, he wondered if
he'd been too hasty. Perhaps he could have bargained
for more. The shock of the offer had left him speechless.
He felt the weight of the money in his pocket. Twenty
Gold Eagle coins. A small fortune. He was already
thinking about how he would use it.

Every morning he went to the docks and checked the
board for any mention of the *Agatha Marie*, the ship
that would take him to Cork. He watched the business
of the docks unfold, unnoticed in the milling, noisy
crowds. When he tired of that, he set off, never sure
where he would end up, through the streets of the city.

As he passed through neighbourhoods, the accents
and languages changed. Some he recognised, some were
new to his ear, but the meaning could be deduced
regardless of the nationality of the mothers shouting to
the children in the noisy street below, or the groups of
elderly men engrossed in their card games, or the
peddlers trying to foist flowers, matches or apples on
him. The smell of food drifted from open windows and
changed from sweet to spicy to the familiar smell of
bread or boiling meat. Food stalls, clustered along the
streets, sold sizzling sausages or cheese or things he
didn't recognise — and wasn't tempted to try.

The dockland always drew him back. It was a rough
and ready place with cargo being hoisted aboard or
swung along gangplanks by robust lines of men. Matt
evaded ropes, boxes, horses and carts, files of dockers
toing and froing. The bustling workers shouted, called

and whistled signals to each other from the ships to the shore and paid him no heed. He stopped near the far end of the pier to watch a ship prepare to dock. As it came within range of the quayside, Matt's eyes widened as he saw the number of people on the deck.

That's not a cargo ship, he thought. That could be coming from Ireland. Matt made his way toward the landing spot. A growing group of barrel-chested men jostled for position around the gangplank. As he watched the first of the bedraggled immigrants disembark on unsteady legs, he noticed the surly expressions of the waiting men change to open and pleasant faces, greeting the new arrivals and reaching with helping hands to assist them the last few feet onto the new land. Something in the men's change of attitude gave him cause to remain in the shadows. Eventually the entire area was covered with groups of people looking bewildered and exhausted, milling around, unsure of their next step. More of these overly helpful men appeared as the ship disgorged its passengers onto American soil. It brought to Matt's mind a plague of locusts he'd once seen descending onto a field of corn.

A tug on his sleeve brought him back, and a young girl of about sixteen years asked him which was the way to go to the town. She pulled her thin shawl around her blazing red hair in the way of much older women. Three younger children, whom he took to be her siblings, clung to her skirts.

Before he could answer, a stocky black-haired youth with dancing blue eyes approached and pushed himself between them.

'I can help you find a place,' he said to her. 'Name's

Doherty, Shay Doherty. What's your name?'

'Katie McCauley,' said the girl. 'There's me father there.' She pointed to a man who looked more like he might be her grandfather, tired and weak, slouched against the wall. 'You'll have to talk to him.'

'I'd be only too delighted.' Doherty grinned broadly. 'Sure, I know how confusing this is for you, being from Erin meself not too long ago.' He moved away to talk to Katie's father.

'And are you here long, sir?' the girl asked Matt. 'Could you tell us a good lodging house that's not too dear? Me father's not well at all since we lost me mother. We had to let them put her into the sea. He's not over it yet. None of us are.' He watched her face struggle with the painful memory. 'But we're here now and we'll make the best of it, won't we?' She ran her fingers through the hair of her little sister who clung to her leg.

'I can show you where I'm lodging,' said Matt. 'There might be room. It's run by a Dutch couple—'

The young man was back and had pushed his elbow into Matt's side. 'On your way,' he growled. 'The girl doesn't need your help.'

Matt shook his head in amazement and the girl looked at both men, unsure what to do, but her father had already been persuaded. He tottered toward them.

'Katie, Shay here says his friend has a boarding house that we can stay in.' Her father patted the young man on the back.

'Father, this man knows somewhere too, and he'll bring us there now.' Katie looked into her father's eyes and clasped his arm.

'Where is this place?' Doherty asked in a hoarse voice.

'Stone Street,' said Matt.

The young man smiled again at the father and daughter. 'Sure, that place is a long walk from here and you're all exhausted. You know, there's no Irish staying in that neck of the woods. You're bound to find someone you know in my friend's house. All the Irish go there. Wouldn't go anywhere else, they all say. Not to mention the price. Sure, it's only sixpence for a good meal and a warm bed and your luggage will be stored for free. You won't get better than that. Fair and square.' He opened his arms wide, smiled and patted one of the younger children on the head.

'There we are now, Katie,' said her father. 'Didn't I tell you it would all work out, and this goodhearted young man has offered to buy me a drink to welcome us to America. Isn't that grand, now?'

Too good to be true, thought Matt.

Katie looked up at him and tucked her red hair behind her ears.

'Thanks all the same, sir,' she said and picked up her bag.

'Are you sure?' said Matt. 'It's really not as far as he's making out. I can take you . . .'

But by now Shay Doherty had taken the bag from her and offered to carry the father's bag too.

'That's very kind of you, sir.' Katie tilted her head and smiled up at Matt again. 'But me father knows best. Thanks all the same. We'll be all right now.'

He somehow doubted that.

She fell into step behind Doherty and her father and the children followed. In the short time they had stood there, many of the new immigrants had been approached either by friends or strangers and they'd all disappeared, quickly absorbed into the city.

Matt was uneasy about the exchange he'd witnessed. He reasoned that it could be a genuine way of getting customers for respectable boarding houses. But maybe not. He found himself walking in the same direction as the group, following at a distance. Their route took them through narrow foul-smelling streets. Matt's stomach churned as he recognised the stench of bone boiling. He followed the little group through filthy alleyways and they finally turned into a ramshackle wooden building, which looked as though it was supported by the two brick buildings on either side of it.

Matt walked past and could see that the ground floor was some sort of public house. He crossed the street and waited in the shadow of a doorway in case they reappeared. He told himself it was ridiculous to wait, that he had no real reason to suspect the family were in any danger. Yet he stayed and watched the door of the pub. People came and went about their business, not seeming to notice him. The heat of the day was fading. Lamplight began to glow in some of the windows of the surrounding buildings. There were fewer people about.

I should go on my way, he told himself.

But he couldn't bring himself to leave and, as he stood and watched, he knew why he still waited. It was the young girl, the way she'd pushed her hair behind her ears and smiled at him. It brought back a memory of a girl just like her. It was such a little gesture, but Katie had the same tilt to her head when she did it. But she's not the girl I once loved, or thought I loved, he reprimanded himself. He shook the memory from his head. I can't stand here any longer. I'll just go in and see if they got fixed up all right.

He crossed the road and went inside. It didn't look too bad, at first glance. Red coals filled the grate and threw shadows about the room. Black corners hid whispering men. Bottles of brandy and whiskey lined the shelves and reflected the glow from the fireplace. As his eyes adjusted, he saw posters of the patriots Wolfe Tone and Daniel O'Connell pasted onto the brown walls. Men puffed on corn-pipes as they played cards. The place was comforting in its familiarity.

A large unshaven man got up, tucked his hand of cards into his pocket, and lumbered toward him. Matt removed his hat and put it on the bar. He slipped his hand inside his jacket to his belt and briefly touched the reassuring handle of his knife. He nodded toward the gleaming bottles. The man poured him a glass of brandy.

'Anything else?' he asked. 'Are you looking for a bed?'

Matt threw some coins on the counter. 'I'm looking for a family. Just arrived today. A man and his four children.' He was aware of the silence of the card players.

'No one's come in today,' said the man.

'Are you sure? I was to meet them here.'

'Are you fuckin' deaf?'

The sound of men's voices drew Matt's eyes to a door at the rear of the room. A voice he recognised.

'Now that you're all sorted, we can have that drink I promised you.' Doherty came through the doorway, followed by Katie's father.

Doherty's eyes fixed on Matt and he went straight to him. 'What the fuck are you doing here? Did you follow us?' He threw a glance at the card players. 'He was touting down at the docks today.' His eyes blazed at Matt. 'Who do you think you are, coming in here. Who do you work for?'

'Where are the children?' asked Matt.

'Don't be worrying about them,' said Katie's father. 'They're fed and fit for nothing only bed. They're probably asleep by now. We're just going to have a drink, aren't we, Shay? Will you have one with us?'

'They're all safe?' asked Matt.

McCauley nodded. 'Of course. Of course. What'll you have? Shay's buying.'

'And Katie is with the young ones?'

'What's it to you?' said Doherty. 'Why all the questions? Who sent you? Was it Mulligan?'

'She's grand,' said Katie's father. 'Shay here knows a woman who's looking for help. He's going to take her there tomorrow. Isn't that right, Shay?'

'Certainly is. We'll soon have her bringing in a few dollars.'

Matt saw the smirk on the face of the barman who folded his meaty arms across his chest.

The room was silent and the hair on Matt's neck bristled. He slowly picked up his drink and took a small sip. Katie's father peered at the gleaming bottles.

Doherty's energy seemed barely in control as he met Matt's eyes.

Matt sipped again and thought about rattlesnakes. The bull rattlesnake was big and its rattle loud — but it wasn't deadly. The copperhead rattlesnake was smaller, wiry, fast — it could kill a man with a single bite. Matt looked at Doherty. Are you a bull or a copperhead? he thought. He drained his glass.

'Well, I'm glad you're all sorted. I'll come back another time for that drink.'

'Grand,' said McCauley. He drummed his fingers on the counter. 'What's in those bottles there, Shay?'

Doherty nodded to the barman. 'Pour Mr McCauley here a glass of whatever he'd like. I'll just make sure this man finds his way back. Many a person got lost on these streets. Treacherous they are.'

The card players were no longer at the table.

Matt grabbed his hat from the bar and moved quickly toward the door and out into the night.

A dull thud to the back of his neck and everything went black.

CHAPTER 14

Matt felt a soft breeze on his face. He forced his eyes open. The alleyway spun. The sour taste of grog came back up his throat. His head throbbed. It took him a moment to realise that someone — probably that bastard behind the bar — had a tight grip on his arms

'Who are you working for?' said a disembodied voice he didn't recognise.

'What? No one.'

Matt recognised Doherty's frame facing him There was three of them, maybe more. He knew by Doherty's stance that a punch was coming, knew he shouldn't tense up, but couldn't help it. The punches landed in his stomach. One, two, three, quick and sharp.

'Is it Mulligan you work for?'

Matt shook his head. 'I don't know what you're talking about.' He fixed his eyes on Doherty and waited. The next punches were harder. Deeper. The noise of splitting ribs cracked through the night. Matt groaned.

The voice asked him again. Matt didn't answer.

'Let me give it to him right this time.' Doherty's voice was high, excited. 'I'll knock it out of him.'

Matt watched him wind a cloth tightly, quickly, around his right hand. He knew what that meant.

'You'd better start talking,' the voice warned. 'Shay is only getting warmed up.'

The force of Doherty's fist flung Matt's skull backwards. Blood trickled into his eyes – he couldn't see Doherty anymore. His head spun with more blows to his face. Blood from his burst lip dribbled down his chin.

'I don't know — I don't know what you're talking about,' he tried to shout, but it came out in a hoarse whisper. He slumped forward and spewed red spittle.

The voice told Doherty to stop. He moved back slightly. Matt could smell the sweat of the younger man, could feel the heat from his pulsing body.

'This is no use. We'll be here all night,' said the voice. 'Take his eye out.'

'Which one?'

'He's only got two, just fucking pick one.'

Matt felt the cold blade lie against his cheek, felt its sharp point prick the skin beside his eye. He kept his head as still as he could.

'*Please, I don't know anything . . . I'd tell you . . . I don't know!*' His voice broke into a sob.

'Jesus, I hate it when they cry,' said the voice. 'I think he really doesn't know.' A cigarette tip glowed in the darkness. 'Shay, where was he trying to take the ones you brought in today?'

Doherty's eyes didn't leave Matt's face. 'Stone Street.'

'Stone Street? Jesus, Shay. Why would you think that Mulligan had anything to do with the Dutch?'

'What difference does it make? He's working for someone there.'

'We don't mess with the Dutch and they don't mess with us. Anyway, I don't think he's a tout — look at the state of him. Not exactly an advertisement for the land of milk and honey, is he? C'mon, I'm starving. Let him go. He's not one of Mulligans.'

They let Matt slump to the ground. He released a breath. Tears stung his eyes. He thought it was over.

'But he followed me here.' Doherty walked around Matt. 'We can't let him get away with it. We need to learn him a lesson.'

Doherty landed a kick into Matt's back. Pain shot up his spine.

'Leave it, Shay,' said the older voice, coming back toward him.

Matt felt a man kneel beside him — not Doherty, he smelled different to Doherty. Tobacco and something else, something Matt recognised but couldn't name. Apples mixed with . . . what was that?

The man breathed a whisper into Matt's bloodied ear. 'If I ever see you round here again, I won't be so kindly. I'll put an end to you. Do you get me?'

Matt nodded. He did not doubt those words, not for a second. He lay on his side as the men walked away. Watched Doherty follow slowly after them, saw him glance back, his face lit by the silver moon, the bloodlust in his eyes. He knew Doherty wasn't finished with him.

I have to move. Little by little he got to his knees. I don't think I can stand, he thought. Breathe, just breathe.

He was on all fours. Each breath brought sharp pain. Blood dripped from his face into the mud.

Whistling. Someone was whistling a tune in the misty evening. It was getting closer. Matt peered through the bloodied hair covering his eyes. *Jesus Christ, save me*, he prayed.

Doherty was carrying something. A long stick? No, not a stick, it looked heavier than that.

Matt knelt, bent over double and clutched his stomach. Doherty walked a little quicker, slapping the heavy bar into his fleshy palm. He stood tall over Matt and laughed down at him.

'See? This is what you get for messing with Shay Doherty. I'd piss on you, though I smell you've already pissed yourself.'

Matt kept his arms about him, as though he was protecting his stomach. I might get one chance, he thought. He twisted his head to look up at Doherty.

Doherty raised the iron bar high over his head. Before he could bring it down Matt pulled his knife from its sheath and thrust it into Doherty's side. He pushed it in, twisted it with all the force left in his body, with all the venom in his heart.

Doherty's eyes grew huge with shock. He stared at the knife sticking out of his side. His mouth formed a scream, but no sound came. He started to topple forward, Matt scrambled out of the way, got to his feet and left the laneway as fast as his legs would allow. Glad of the darkness now, he listened for footsteps chasing behind. Doherty might have made it back to the bar, he thought. They'll come looking for me.

He drenched his face in a horse trough, listened for

shouting voices, running footsteps. He started northward, toward the boarding house. His heart thumped in his chest. Keep to the shadows, he told himself. Put one foot in front of the other, that's all you have to do. Keep moving.

There was a carriage waiting outside Mrs Jansen's house. Matt had to think for a few minutes. Did I tell him the name of the boarding house? Did I tell Katie? He crept up to the window. He could see Mrs Jansen sitting on her chair. A tall man with gold braid on his shoulders stood with his back to the window.

A policeman? The uniformed man turned toward the window. Matt stumbled back down the steps. He heard the door open. He turned to run.

'*Matt, Matt!*' called Mrs Jansen from the doorway. '*Come back!* Oh my God! What happened to you? Captain Bakker has been waiting for you.'

Matt stumbled back to the steps. 'Captain?'

'*Captain Bakker!*' she called into the house.

The uniformed man appeared.

'Help me get him inside!' said Mrs Jansen.

'We have no time,' said Captain Bakker. 'Driver, go with Mrs. Jansen and get his things.'

The driver followed Mrs. Jansen into the house.

'Matt!' said the captain. 'Can you hear me? Do you understand? We must go now or we'll miss the tide. Are you fit enough to travel?'

Matt's eyes rolled in his head. 'Yes.' He swallowed. 'My bag!'

'They are bringing your bag. Come now, there's a good man — let's get you into the carriage.'

As the captain settled Matt in the carriage, the driver returned with the bag, Mrs Jansen in his wake.

'I think this is everything he had,' she said breathlessly.

'Thank you, madam.'

The driver whipped the horses and the carriage took off at speed.

'*Goodbye!*' Mrs Jansen called after them into the darkness. '*God speed!*'

CHAPTER 15

Knockanree

1946

The next morning Rosie made breakfast for everyone. She began to fry bacon and fetched eggs to scramble while they ate their porridge.

Connie was asking her father about the harvest.

'Do you know what the worst of it is?' He gripped his mug in his hands. 'It's that there's nothing I can do — that anyone can do. It makes my head ache, the worry of it. There's just not enough time.'

Connie looked at her father's face. When did those lines, those bags under his eyes get there? she wondered. I suppose I haven't looked at him, really looked at him, since . . . since an awfully long time. He looks old.

'Is there no hope, Dad? What's the forecast saying?'

'They say it'll get a little better in a couple of days. But there's not enough time, not enough manpower.'

'Rivers has an idea,' said Rosie unexpectedly. 'Haven't you, Rivers?'

Rivers shrugged. 'I don't think Jack is interested.'

'Any idea is worth listening to. What have we got to lose?' said Connie. 'C'mon, spit it out.' She picked up her notebook again.

Rivers remained silent.

'Rivers thinks we could get people from the town to come down and help with the harvest,' said Rosie.

Connie laughed out loud. 'You don't mean Maguire and the oul' fellas sitting in Foley's?'

Rosie turned away and beat the eggs for scrambling more fiercely than usual.

'Maybe I can explain,' said Rivers. 'Rosie, do you remember when you asked about the food in the tins, the soldiers' rations?'

Rosie nodded slightly and turned back to face them.

Connie watched her sister's face — she'd seen that look before. An uneasy thought crept into her mind but she dismissed it. Rivers was talking and she forced herself to concentrate on what he was saying.

'Part of my job in the army was logistics. That meant getting the fuel, the food, the ammunition, everything from one place to another. The front line was always shifting but everything had to be put into place to support the troops. Thousands of men had to be moved, fed, sheltered. The Germans spread their supply chain too thin, couldn't get the fuel to their tanks. That was one of the reasons they lost the war.'

'All right, I can see how important that would be, but I still don't understand the connection between the war and the harvest,' said Connie.

'It's about moving the men, the workforce, to where they're needed and looking after them once they get there.'

'So what you're saying is that we need to move the people in the cities to the farms.' Connie nodded. 'Yes, I see, but how would we even go about it?'

'Are you all mad in the head?' said her father. 'Nobody's going to up sticks and come running down here to help us.'

'The government don't seem to want to call the army out,' said Connie. 'What choice do we have? We need to get our own army together.'

'So, what do you suggest? Maybe I could go down to Foley's and ring everyone in Dublin one by one to tell them it's raining.'

'Stop that, Dad,' said Rosie. 'Rivers here is trying to put forward ideas, and you're doing nothing but pulling them down — at least have the decency to give it some consideration.'

Connie saw the expression on Rosie's face and thought she might have gone too far, but to her surprise her father looked abashed.

'I'm sorry, Rivers,' said Jack. 'I don't mean to be ungrateful, but I just don't see how it would work.'

'We need to make a plan,' said Connie, her face alight with enthusiasm. She loved to make plans.

'Before you get carried away,' said Rivers. 'What exactly is it that you're going to plan for? Are you talking about getting people to help you and your neighbours here, or are you thinking of the country as a whole?'

'The country as a whole? I hadn't thought of that.' Connie perched on the edge of a chair. 'But we should, shouldn't we? If it's as bad everywhere else as it is here, then why not? Of course, we'll have to get the government involved.'

'Ah, now, hold on,' said Jack.

'Aren't you getting ahead of yourself?' said Rosie as she placed a platter of bacon on the table. 'I thought you were going to try to reason with Colin Lawlor.'

Connie paused. That would probably be the best course, to try to mend fences with the land labourers. But she could just imagine the excitement of planning to overcome a national disaster. She could almost see herself presenting the story to her editor and saying, '*Here, Mr Carolan, now tell me I'm not ready!*' She pushed her glasses up the bridge of her nose and said, 'I'm sure Dad has listened to everything Colin had to say. Didn't you, Dad?'

'Of course I did.' He shifted in his chair. 'Couldn't reason with him at all.'

'For a start,' said Connie, on her feet again, 'we should let the people in the cities know the state the crops are in and that there won't be enough food to go around in the winter.'

'Wait,' said Rivers. 'Everyone needs to have their say. 'Rosie, what do you think?'

Rosie paused as she served the scrambled eggs and turned to her father. She spoke in a soft voice. 'Dad, if you do nothing, you're as much as saying that the land labourers have won. I know it's about the weather and the state of the crops, but they'll still say that they won, that there was no harvest because of their strike. Right or wrong they'll claim a victory over you.'

Connie looked at Rosie. What's got into her? she thought. I haven't heard her give an opinion on anything for years. Where's this coming from? She caught Rosie's glance toward Rivers and his answering nod. Could there be something between them? Surely not. Not under her father's roof. Rosie wouldn't dare.

'It's up to you, Jack,' said Rivers. 'If you're not behind it, there's no point taking it further.'

'Rosie's right,' said her father. 'It would come between me and my sleep to let that Colin Lawlor think he'd got the better of me. We'll do it. But we only know about our own area. We're not in a position to make a plan for the country. Stick to what we know, and if others want to follow, then that's their business.'

'Makes sense,' said Rivers. 'Let's get started. Tell me about the roads. What condition are they in? There's the train too. That can be used.'

Populations, organisations, communications. Old Seán and Jack had never before realised how little they knew about the world outside of Knockanree. They scratched their heads and tried to provide answers. Rivers made notes of the information they gave him and drew up a list. Connie's knowledge of government departments and national organisations helped form the plan and the soldier's logistical experience moving large bodies of men, equipment, supplies made them think that this could work. The list of what needed to be done grew.

Connie left the table and pulled on her coat.

'Where are you going?' said Rosie. 'You haven't finished your breakfast. Are you going to see Colin Lawlor after all?'

'Nope. I'm going to phone Fletcher. We're going to need his help more than Colin Lawlor's.'

Fletcher put the phone down, and tried to make sense of the conversation, if he could call it a conversation. The usually contained Connie had talked in snatches about a famine and what seemed to be a treasure hunt. Fletcher tapped his pencil against the table and cast his eyes over his scribbled notes. She wants me to get her in to see the Minister of Agriculture. What on earth is she up to?

He knew Connie had good instincts, better than some of the hacks on the paper. Even so, a famine? He finished his coffee and lit another cigarette.

What the hell, he thought, as he dialled his editor's number. If Connie O'Connell says there's going to be a famine, who the hell am I to argue with her?

The next day he was able to tell Connie they had an appointment to see the minister on Wednesday, two days away.

'I'll meet you at the station,' he said.

'Great,' she said. 'But I'm not coming alone.'

CHAPTER 16

Knockanree

1946

Pádraig held the bucket handle across his arm like a shopping bag, and his short legs struggled to keep up with his mother. Cows occasionally lifted their heads to regard the approaching humans. Rosie ambled amongst the small herd, carrying the milking stool from cow to cow as people had done here 'since there were cows', she told him.

'How long is that, Mam?' said Pádraig.

'Since cows were invented. Since God made them and put them here.'

She carried on with the milking, glad of the warmth of the sun on her skin, lost in her own thoughts.

They'd all left on the early train. All except her and Pádraig and Grandad. She'd overheard her father ask Rivers to go with them to Dublin and he'd agreed. If Rivers wondered why Connie and her father couldn't convey the bones of the plan to the minister, he didn't say so.

She knew the real reason. Dad would never leave her alone overnight in the house with a young man. No matter who. Once bitten and all that. If the neighbours got wind of it, the tiny bit of respectability she'd managed to claw back would be wiped out. She could see his thinking. If I leave myself open to gossip, even the few housewives who bought the eggs and butter would close their door in my face, she thought.

She'd smiled and cooked their breakfast. Waved them off, hid her feelings, as she usually did. So now it's just me and the very old and the very young, she thought.

Pádraig pulled open the gate for his mother and swung it closed when she stepped through. It was a little soggy underfoot, but the meadow was on a slope and was one of the best-drained areas of the farm. It still had a wildness to it, contained by a small stone higgledy-piggledy wall that circled behind a cluster of ancient trees and reappeared on the other side. Unexpected plants, white and purple, were dotted among the gorse. Blackberry bushes and pink tea roses weaved in and out along the broken wall. 'The kind of place where fairies would be,' she told Pádraig, and she pointed out the bell-shaped flowers that her mother had told her the fairies liked to live near.

She put the stool in place and warned Pádraig, not for the first time, not to walk behind the cows.

'They could give you a mighty kick and knock you across the hedge.' She leaned her cheek against the side of the cow as she sang the soft milking melody that calmed the cows.

Pádraig busied himself with digging holes to look for what he called 'Rivers' treasure'. He disappeared under the trailing branches of a nearby oak tree.

'What's this, Mam?' he called.

'What?'

'It's a cross in the tree!"

'That's Éamonn's cross. It's to remember someone who died in the famine — a little boy it was. That's probably why the shrine to the Blessed Virgin is in the wall there.' Rosie pointed to a recess in the ivy-covered wall where a small, rather worn statue stood, arms outstretched, almost hidden by dead foliage and rotten leaves.

Pádraig came running out, alarmed.

'Is he buried under the tree, Mam?'

'He might be, love. I don't know.'

'Did he not have a guardian angel, like I do?'

'Well, maybe it was just his time to go.'

'Oh. I see.'

Rosie paused in her milking. 'Pádraig? Have you told anyone about your guardian angel? I told you it was a secret.'

'I didn't mean to, but teacher said we all have guardian angels but we can't see them. I told her I had a picture of mine.'

'What did she say?' Rosie turned to face her son.

'She showed me a picture of her angel in her prayer book. It had a shiny circle over its head and it had big wings. It didn't look like the one of my guardian angel.'

'But you know that's your father in the photograph.' She tried to keep her voice light.

'You said he'd be watching over me. Isn't that what the angel does?

'Well, yes, but—'

'Hello, Rosie.' Colin Lawlor's low voice startled her.

'Jesus! Colin! I nearly knocked the milk over.'

'You're easily frightened. How are you, anyway? You never seem to have any time to talk these days. Whenever I see you, you're always in a fierce hurry.'

'Well, a farm doesn't run itself, and Dad is gone to Dublin, so I'm up to my eyes.'

'Why is he gone to Dublin? Did he take the American with him?'

Rosie bit her lip. She'd said too much already but couldn't think how to dodge the question. 'Yes, they're both gone.' She turned to look for her son. 'C'mon, Pádraig, we have eggs to collect.'

'Will you be singing at the wedding next month? They've asked me to bring the fiddle. We should do a few tunes together. We haven't done that in a while.'

'No, we haven't,' she agreed. She lifted the milk bucket and turned away from him. She wouldn't tell him she hadn't been invited. 'I can't think that far ahead. Pádraig, hurry up, bring the stool!' she called.

Pádraig lifted the milking-stool to his head, the legs of it sticking out.

'*I'm a bull, Mam!*' he shouted as he charged off down the uneven pathway.

'I'll carry that for you,' said Colin, taking the bucket from her. 'You've no man around to look after you, have you?'

The question went unanswered, but Rosie let him take the bucket.

'We've known each other a long time, haven't we, Rosie?'

She nodded and looked further down the pathway to where Pádraig charged the gatepost, still clutching his 'horns'.

'I remember you as a young girl before you went to Dublin. You had a smile that would melt the hardest heart. I'd say you still have that smile, Rosie. Though I never see it these days.'

'Not much to smile about here.' Where is he going with this? she thought.

'Yes, it must be difficult with a child to raise on your own.'

'But I'm not on my own.'

'Well —' he stopped walking and turned to look at her, '— I don't see a husband around. All I see is a young woman, a fine young woman at that, with a son.' He looked towards the child. 'You don't have many . . . options.'

'What exactly are you trying to say, Colin?'

'Pádraig is a good kid. I wouldn't mind stepping in and taking care of you and the boy.'

'He has a father already.'

Colin put down the milk bucket and looked at the sky as though the right words were written in the clouds.

'Rosie, you don't have to pretend with me. I'd be willing to take on the both of you.'

'The both of us. Why on earth?'

'To give the boy a father, a name. It's not fitting that Jack O'Connell's grandson doesn't have a name of his own.'

'His name is Pádraig Farrell and I'm Mrs. Farrell, in case you've forgotten.' She poked his chest. 'My son's father will be home soon. So just back off. I don't need saving by you.'

She called to Pádraig to wait and picked up the milking pail.

'Maguire says he's never delivered a letter to you by

that name. Where is this mystery man? Does he even exist?'

'*Pádraig! I told you to wait!*' She walked as fast as she could, the milk slopped dangerously near the rim.

'*You know where I am!*' Colin called after her. '*I don't think you'll be going anywhere soon, Rosie O'Connell!*'

CHAPTER 17

Knockanree

1847

Matt remembered the shop in Knockanree as being a much humbler enterprise. It seemed to have expanded and grown and eaten into whatever space had been on either side of it. The sign over the door now said **T. Maguire and Sons**. Matt looked at the small display of goods in the window: kitchenware, a rug, a couple of wooden stools that looked vaguely familiar. Nothing edible was on view. He became aware of his own reflection in the glass, his tired eyes, sunken cheeks. He smoothed his beard and noticed the grey patches. They must have arrived during the sea journey. He remembered little of it. The first few weeks he could do nothing but rest and let his wounds be tended to.

When he finally made his way to the deck to see Captain Bakker he tried to apologise. "I'm supposed to be working my way, sir. Not creating an inconvenience for you to tend to. I'll be fine in a few days, then you can set me to work, I promise."

He was as good as his word. His physical wounds healed but he could not find sleep. The face of the young man he'd stabbed, those wide blue eyes, came to stare at him by night.

When Matt finally opened the door to the shop, he breathed in the smell of food. It made his mouth water. His eyes travelled around the wealth of flour and oatmeal and cornmeal lined up in sacks along the floor. Butter and eggs filled the shelves; cured shanks and flitches of meat, chickens and rabbits swung from hooks. Turnips — past their best — languished in a corner. A short, rotund man stood behind the counter, his dusky green jacket not quite closing across his middle.

'It's a fine store you have here, sir,' said Matt

'Thank you, Mister . . . ?'

'O'Connell, Matthew O'Connell.'

'I thought there was a look of the O'Connells about you.'

Matt realised the man had been watching him through the window. 'Are you T. Maguire?' Matt pointed upward, as though the sign hung over them.

'Toddy Maguire at your service, and this is my eldest, Brian. What can I do for you today?'

'I remember this place as Sweeney's.'

'The parents of my good wife, Maud,' said Toddy.

Matt remembered Maud as a plump girl with golden curls. A girl who brought the art of pouting to new heights. There was nothing her parents would, or could, refuse her. Matt felt a wave of sympathy for Toddy Maguire.

'I need some supplies,' said Matt. 'Flour, oatmeal, butter, eggs, a side of bacon, a couple of chickens.'

Brian ran around collecting the items. He carefully weighed the flour and oatmeal on the scales.

'Six pence a pound for the oatmeal. A shilling a pound for the flour,' said Toddy.

Matt raised his eyebrows. The prices were ridiculously high, but he had no other option.

Toddy took the pencil from behind his ear, licked the lead and, with a smiling face, wrote the cost of each item on the corner of the wrapping paper. He began to tally it up.

'Have any of my family been in lately?' asked Matt.

'Not since they left Abbeyfield.' Toddy didn't lift his eyes from the paper.

Matt's heart sank. 'They left? Where are they now?'

Toddy slowly rechecked the calculation. 'Well, I don't know where they are. So many people on the move these days. They might have gone to America, or Canada.'

'They wouldn't do that,' said Matt.

Toddy shrugged.

Matt paid the bill with some of the banknotes he'd exchanged for the gold coins and bade the shopkeeper and his son a good day.

Just as he got to the door he turned and asked, 'Does Foley still rent out horses and carts?'

'Yes. Absolutely, he does. Tell him I sent you.'

Matt thought Toddy's smile seemed a little strained. I suppose I'd be a little strained too if I were married to Maud Sweeney, he thought. He tipped his hat and left.

He carried his purchases across the road to Foley's Inn, a sturdy two-storey establishment that appeared at odds with the desolation of the town. Matt went past the inn and into the stables. He looked at the horses on offer; most of them had seen better days. Joe Foley came out to the yard and Matt could see the puzzled look on his face.

'I know you, don't I?' asked Joe.

'You do indeed, Joe, though its over fifteen years since you've seen me.'

'Matt O'Connell. Jesus Christ, is it you under that beard? What are you thinking of, coming back here, when everyone else in the country is going in the opposite direction?'

'Needs must, Joe. Have you any idea where Lorcan might be?'

Joe scratched his head. 'Well, you can see how things are. We can't keep track of everyone.' He turned toward the stables. 'Are you looking for a horse?'

Matt picked a small wagon and the best horse he could find. Joe hitched it up for him.

'You seem to be doing all right,' said Matt.

'Not too bad.' Joe handed him the reins. 'You know how it is. There's always them that'll find a copper for a pint.'

'Joe, where do people go when they're evicted? Where might Lorcan and Annie be?'

Joe adjusted the harness. 'The workhouse in Kildare is where most seem to head for. That's the nearest.'

'It's twenty miles, for God's sake.' Matt fought to control his temper. 'Was there nothing you could do—'

'Look, you've no idea what it's been like. If you give to one, there's a crowd around your door in minutes with their hands out.' Joe sighed and rubbed his eyes. 'Maybe a month since I saw them. I think it was them.' He looked at the ground. 'They were in the small meadow near the farm. I didn't stop. I knew they shouldn't be there. I turned a blind eye.'

Matt looked back towards the shop and again at Foley's Inn. A blind eye, he thought. Mighty handy to have a blind eye when it suits.

Matt urged the horse toward the road to Abbeyfield.

A month without a roof over their heads, maybe even without a bite to eat, he thought. Please God let them still be there. Let them still be alive.

He wished he could take his time, savour the sight of the prickly yellow furze bordering the road ahead for miles, enjoy the soft wind on his tanned skin, appreciate the call of the corncrake in the air. He could see fields of green and gold waving in the soft breeze. All through the country crops seemed to be growing well. There was no shortage of food, just the potato.

He came around the bend in the bohereen and heard the squeak of the open gate before he saw it. It was the only sound breaking the silence. The absence of noise from the house, the sheds, the dairy, was eerie. The birds he'd often heard echoes of in Indian Territory seemed to have stopped chirping and were waiting, twisting their heads to watch him. No children's voices, no dogs barking, no cows, or horses in the sheds. He closed the gate behind him — some habits die hard. Even after fifteen years, the house he thought he would never see again except in his dreams regarded him dispassionately. The boarded-up doorway and windows looked like heavy scars on its face. He wrenched the boards from the kitchen door and, though he knew they were not inside, he couldn't help calling '*Lorcan? Annie?*' when he stepped across the threshold. He went from room to room. There was less furniture than he remembered. The heavy kitchen table still stood in the centre of the room. The cold grate was without a pot. He turned to look through a crack in the boarded-up window, hoping the family would suddenly appear at the bottom of the lane. In his heart he knew they would not.

Matt sat on the floor of the kitchen, his face in his hands, his stomach churning. Are they all dead? Why did I not come back sooner? Though he reproached himself, he knew he could not have travelled back any faster than he had, but the germ of guilt seeded in his brain.

He heard the thud of a horse's hooves coming up the laneway and they sparked a wave of hope in his breast. *They're back! They're here after all!* He flung the door open and rushed out.

The well-dressed rider pulled up the reins and looked down at him with suspicion.

'What's your business here?' The man confronted him with the voice of authority.

'I could ask you the same question,' replied Matt. 'This is the farm of my brother, Lorcan O'Connell.'

'I think you'll find that this is the land of Lord Marlinton. I am Carbury, His Lordship's agent. The tenant on this property, you say, is your brother. I have no doubt of that. There is certainly a family resemblance. He and his family were evicted more than two weeks ago.'

'Mother of God, you evicted them? We've worked this land for a hundred years.' Matt tried to keep his voice steady. 'The lease on this land is for another dozen years or so.'

'True enough, but only if the rent is paid in May and in November. I received no rent in November of last year. The tenant promised to pay the whole amount in May this year but failed to do so. His Lordship was left with was no option but to remove him and his family from the property. They were given every opportunity to pay. Lord Marlinton had no alternative but to resort to eviction — he has been more than patient.'

'Where are they now? Where did they go?'

'How would I know?' Carbury seemed genuinely surprised at the question. 'Possibly the workhouse. Now, leave this property immediately. New tenants are interested in this house.'

'No, please don't do that. How much is owed in rent?'

'Are you suggesting that you can afford to pay the back rent?' Carbury's interest appeared be piqued. 'Well, perhaps it could be arranged, I suppose. I expect His Lordship would also want some assurance that the rent due in November will be paid in advance.'

Blood-sucking louse, thought Matt. He smiled up at the agent. 'Of course. I would hate His Lordship to be out of pocket. How much is due?'

'From memory, the amount outstanding is in the region of ten pounds. I would have to consult the ledgers for the exact figure.'

Matt took banknotes from his bag.

'Here, I can pay the outstanding rent on behalf of my brother. Take it.'

Carbury hesitated, his eyes on the banknotes. 'I will accept the back rent from you, but the lease has been revoked and I can't be certain that His Lordship will agree to another long lease. This money will, however, secure the tenancy for the time being. Come to my office for the receipt. I will consult with His Lordship on a new lease. Good day to you.' He turned his horse and started back toward the gate. He stopped and turned back to Matt. 'What if your brother isn't . . . in a position to return to Abbeyfield?'

'I'll find him.'

Carbury shrugged and continued on his way.

Matt watched the agent disappear down the lane. I'd forgotten how quickly news travels in Knockanree, he thought. Nevertheless, whoever had told Carbury that he was here had done him a good turn, however unintentional that may have been. He was relieved to get the house secured, but the whereabouts of his brother and family was uppermost in his mind. So, the nearest workhouse was in Kildare town, some twenty miles away. He prayed he would find them there. He prayed that he might still be in time.

There was only an hour or so of daylight left. Should I leave now or wait till morning? He wouldn't be there before midnight, and who knew what dangers might be on the roads? He let the horse graze for a while on the pasture before leading him to the stable. The night was full of movement; a westerly wind held the promise of rain and ruffled the branches of the trees. He felt uneasy, as though a storm was coming, as though he was being watched. He put his hand to the sheath where his knife should have been. The memory of how he'd lost the knife made his stomach churn. He made a rough bed in the stable with the horse. If things are as bad as Foley said, no animal is safe, he thought. He looked into the brown eyes of the scraggy horse. 'We'll just have to look out for each other,' he said to him. The barn door rattled in the wind. Matt thought he wouldn't sleep, but somehow the night passed without him opening his eyes again until long past dawn.

CHAPTER 18

Dublin

1946

Connie adjusted her glasses as she looked around the comfortable waiting room in the Ministry of Agriculture. She approved of the heavy dark-green velvet curtains and the thick pale-green carpet, all appropriate for ministerial room. High-backed chairs were placed around occasional tables decorated with floral bouquets in crystal vases. She liked things to match, a sense of order.

'Do you think Rosie will be able to manage on her own?' said her father. He loosened his tie a little.

'She'll be fine. You have more important things to worry about, Dad. You have to talk on behalf of all the farmers in Ireland.'

'That doesn't exactly put me at ease, Connie. Why don't you do the talking. You're better at explaining things.'

'Nobody's better placed than you,' she said as she tightened his tie again and brushed a little dandruff from his shoulder.

He fastened, then unfastened the buttons on the suit he hadn't wanted to wear.

Mother would have killed me if I'd let him come in his old tweed jacket and baggy trousers, Connie thought. In a low voice she said, 'You could have left Rivers there to help her if you were so worried about her being on her own.'

'Yes, well, we don't need any more controversy where Rosie is concerned. Better on her own than . . .' He nodded toward Rivers who stood looking out the window.

Fletcher paced back and forth, papers in his hands. 'I'll begin,' he said. 'It's me he thinks he's meeting. I'll talk to Minister Ryan about the Copenhagen Conference. It's a bit of a hobby horse with him. Once he's in a good mood you can wade in, Jack, OK?'

Jack tugged at his collar again. 'I won't be able to get a word out with this feckin' shirt,' he said.

They were ushered into the office, a much larger version of the waiting room. Glass-fronted bookshelves lined an entire wall. The minister's polished oak desk was in front of a tall window. He came around and shook hands as his assistant introduced each member of the party. He welcomed them warmly and gestured towards the seats. If he thought it an odd group, he didn't show it.

'What can I do for you?' He opened the cigarette box on his desk and offered the contents around.

Jack took one and the minister handed him the lighter.

'It's about the conference in Copenhagen, Minister,' began Fletcher.

Connie stood. 'I'm sorry, Minister, it's not about that. I'm sure it's an important conference but we've come about the harvest.' From the corner of her eye she could see Fletcher glaring at her.

Minister Ryan held up his hand. 'Miss O'Connell, if you've come to ask if I can call out the defence forces to help bring in your harvest, then I have to tell you we are not in a position to do that at this point in time.'

'But why not?' said Connie. 'It's not just our farm, every farmer is in trouble.'

The minister sat behind his desk and rubbed his forehead. 'Perhaps we can release small numbers of men, here and there, if they want to. But the truth of it is there wouldn't be enough men to reach every corner of the country. In fact, nowhere near enough.' He turned to Fletcher. 'This is off the record.'

Fletcher returned his pen to his top pocket. Connie saw he was annoyed at being side-lined. She made a mental note to apologise to him later. After all, if it weren't for him, they'd never have got this far.

'You see,' the minister drew on his cigarette, 'during the Emergency many of our soldiers deserted to the British army. Our numbers were lower, are still lower, than they've ever been. I thought, well, we all assumed, that once the war was over the men would come flooding back.' His shook his head. 'It hasn't happened. We've lost a generation of young Irishmen. Lost to a war Ireland wasn't supposed to be involved in. Even those who survived injury and death made a home for themselves in England.'

'So, it's as bad as we thought,' said Jack. 'Minister, we're in real trouble. In our neck of the woods — Knockanree in Kildare — the land labourers have gone on strike. We have no help at all. Then Rivers here came up with an idea, and maybe you'll help us get it off the ground. There's no reason why it couldn't work for every farm.'

Jack looked around. Rivers was sitting quietly in a corner.

'Rivers, come over here and explain it to him.'

Rivers stood slowly and handed Connie the map he carried. 'You explain, Connie.'

Connie glanced up at him. 'Well, it was your idea, really.'

'For God's sake, will somebody tell me what's going on?' said the minister. He stubbed out his cigarette in the glass ashtray.

'Basically,' said Rivers, 'the plan is to use the same tactics as the army in times of war to bring essential supplies to the frontline. I've observed the success of this with the Red Ball Express truck convoys in Europe in 1944 and have some experience in this type of mass movement of men and machines. Sir, the idea is to relocate the workforce from the cities and large towns to where they're needed. We've drawn up how this will work in Kildare, but the system can be transferred and mapped to other counties. You can see in this map that we'll need transportation, accommodation and food distribution in place before we can begin. We use the existing organisations in each city or town. Garda stations, the town hall, wherever the workforce can register to help. We've listed these for Kildare but each county town will have its own centres and resources. We'll need drivers and trucks to take them to the farms. In some cases, they will stay there, or they can be returned to the towns, though it would be more practical if we can arrange food and lodging locally on the farms for the workforce.'

'And what workforce is this exactly?'

'Sir,' said Rivers, 'you will need to put a call-to-arms out to the citizens. They appear to be unaware of the danger of the harvest failing.'

'Go on the wireless and broadcast an appeal, is that it?'

'And the newspapers,' put in Connie.

'Yes,' said Rivers. 'But first we need to set up centres where people can report for duty. There's no point in alarming them without letting them know how they can help, and how important their help is to the success of the mission.'

The minister looked at the rough plans. 'Look, I think there's a chance it might work, but to put this plan into action we're going to need cooperation across various departments. That's going to take a bit of organising, but we can get voluntary organisations on board too.' He rolled up the map. 'I'll set up an emergency meeting with the Taoiseach and other ministers to get this plan into action. You can use the offices in Parnell Square as the central control office. I'll get Bates to set that up for you and assign some staff to assist.'

'Me, sir?' said Rivers.

'We need someone with your experience just to get the basics in place. I'd very much appreciate it. The importance of getting the crops in is enormous. We're not just talking about feeding our own nation here, we're committed to export to England and the rest of Europe. You've been there so you'll have seen the result of the severe rationing that's had to be put in place.'

'Yes, sir, I have. I'd be happy to help.' Then he added, 'For a while.'

'Just a couple of days, that's all I'm asking. I'd like you and Jack to attend some meetings with me.'

'I don't think there's anything I can do here,' said Jack.

'There is, Mr O'Connell. There's one thing in particular I have in mind that I would value your help with. I'll be in touch with you soon. Don't worry, I won't keep you too long from your farm. I can see you're anxious to get back.'

As they left the minister's office, Connie patted Rivers on the back. 'Don't worry, we haven't forgotten about the medallion. As soon as we get back to Knockanree we'll really get down to it. I promise.' She turned her head to smile at Rivers and caught the annoyance on Fletcher's face. He must be really annoyed at not getting to talk about Copenhagen, she thought.

Parnell Square in Dublin's City centre consisted of tall red-brick Georgian houses set around a small green park. The building that the minister had provided sat directly across from the entrance to the park. The paint was peeling a little from the door and the front steps could have done with a good scrub, but inside it was clean, and the proportions were grand, with impressive, bright rooms.

Connie hadn't been able to resist going along to see the premises.

Bates showed them a small flat at the top of the house, where they could stay.

'You know you can both stay with me,' said Connie, looking at the rather bare rooms. 'I'm sure Agnes won't mind.' She was quite sure that Agnes would mind very much, but she'd have to deal with it.

'Ah, no, love, this is grand. We prefer to be in the centre of it all, don't we, Rivers?'

Jack seemed unusually cheerful.

'Whatever you say, Mr O'Connell.'

'Call me Jack.'

'Whatever you say, Jack.'

Staff arrived with typewriters, stationary and everything else they needed. For the next few days Minister Ryan brought Jack and Rivers to meetings with government agencies. Long into the evenings they discussed ways to get enough food to feed the volunteers and fuel for transportation. They decided how all the agencies would link together and who would take charge of the overall operation.

Just as Jack began to think it was time to return to Knockanree, the minister phoned him.

'Jack, I want you to come with me to the radio station this evening. I want you to say a few words, explain about the crops and what's needed . . .'

The radio station was much smaller than Connie thought it would be. She watched the three men, newsreader, minister and farmer arrange themselves around the table in the dimmed light while she waited in the production manager's booth.

The production manager showed them which microphone to talk into and warned them not to get too close to it. 'It's important to speak in your normal voice,' he said in hushed tones. 'You don't need to shout or speak too loudly. Try not to rush. Take your time and talk as if the listener is just beside you.' He gave an encouraging smile and quietly closed the door as he went in to join Connie. They both looked through the large window.

Connie saw small beads of sweat form on her father's brow and began to feel nervous for him.

The broadcast began with the newsreader, then a voice inside their headphones said, 'And now we have a special message from the minister of agriculture, Minister Jim Ryan.'

Minister Ryan opened his folder and began to read the typed speech from his page. She wished she'd insisted on typing out her father's notes, but he'd shooed her away and said that he could manage with what he had. The dog-eared piece of paper shook slightly in his hand as he fumbled with his glasses. He didn't seem to be aware that the minister had stopped talking and Connie tried to tap on the glass, but the production manager raised his hand to prevent her.

'*Erm*,' Jack cleared his throat. The production manager grimaced, but Jack went on. 'Eh, yes, everything he said, I mean the minister said, is true.' He looked at the page, wiped his brow and put it down.

'Oh no,' said Connie. She got up from her chair, had her hand on the door handle when her father's voice stopped her in her tracks. She turned to watch him through the window.

'Look. Anyone who knows me, knows that I hate to make a speech. I'm the last person who'll ever ask for help, sometimes to my own detriment. My wife, God rest her, was always giving out to me about that.' He caught Connie's eye and she nodded encouragement. 'The situation we're in now, well, we're all in it. It's not just the farmers. This is going to affect everyone, whether you live in a city or in the country. Because no matter where you live, you have to eat.'

The minister nodded and Connie sat down. She started taking notes.

Her father went on. 'Usually at this time of year we're all busy, out in the field getting in the crops, the crops that will eventually end up on your table. Barley for the brewers, oats to feed ourselves, wheat that will make bread. It's all part of the cycle, we're all part of the cycle. We take it all for granted — until something goes wrong — and by God something has gone wrong this year. Drastically wrong. We're going to have to fight to put bread on the table. If you could see the state the fields are in now. The crops are lying down sodden. If we can't take them up soon, they'll start to rot. If that happens, I don't know how we'll feed ourselves. How we'll feed all of you listening. So, I have to ask you people listening to help. The only way to take up the crops is to lift and reap by hand. I'll tell you now it's hard work, backbreaking work, and there'll be no pay for it, but it's our only chance. We won't be able to save the harvest without your help, and that's the God's honest truth.'

Jack sat back from the microphone and mopped his brow. He looked exhausted. The newsreader took the cue and started to read the list of locations where people could register to help.

CHAPTER 19

Dublin

1946

Rivers slept soundly on a makeshift bed, but Jack couldn't settle at all after the broadcast. He hated sleeping away from the farm, but that night he couldn't have slept no matter where he laid his head. They had stayed up late in the empty building, talking into the night.

'What I don't understand,' said Jack, 'is why would you do it? Why would you join up when you didn't have to? I still can't get over it, an Indian joining the US army. It's like you joined the enemy.'

'No, Jack, not the enemy. America is my country, the country of my people.'

'From what you've told me already, it's not as if they treated you very well, is it?'

'It's not about that. We chose to go to war. We queued all night to sign up. If an enemy threatens us, we fight. We were part of a bigger cause. It called to something that is deep within us. It felt good to have the respect of other soldiers. The Choctaws are not afraid of battle, of killing an enemy. We were praised for our bravery many times. You can't live in the past, going over old wrongs. Sooner or later you must look forward, to the future. You cannot live in the past.'

'Some wrongs you can never get over,' said Jack. 'We had eight hundred years of wrongs.'

'I know that you were treated badly, had your lands taken,' said Rivers. 'Pushed out of your home. Our history is the same. But, at some time, you have to put it behind and look at what is right today.'

'Well, who's to say what's right and what's wrong?' Jack shook his head. 'We have to make up our own minds and, as far as I'm concerned, we were right not to get involved in that war. It was not of our making, none of our business.' He sat back and folded his arms.

'I met many Irishmen fighting in France and in Holland,' said Rivers. 'They wore British army uniforms. If the Irish ports had been open to the Allies it would have shortened the war, saved many lives, perhaps the lives of some of those men.'

'*At what cost?*' Jack shouted. 'We would have been bombed out of it and lives of innocent men, women and children lost! It would have been too high a price to pay. As for Irishmen joining the British army, they went for the money, nothing more. It's a spit in the eye for anyone who had to live through the Black and Tans. They turned their back on their heritage and forgot what we had to go through to get the bastards out of Ireland. An Irishman in a British uniform is an abomination. How can they live with themselves?'

They didn't talk for much longer. Each knew he

couldn't turn the other man's point of view.

When the sky began to lighten a little Jack was glad to rise and get dressed. He had decided during the sleepless night that he was going to catch the first train home. As he stood beside the gas ring in the kitchen, waiting for the kettle to boil, he went over the previous evening's events yet again in his head.

I'm mortified, he thought. Made an eejit of myself in front of the whole country.

But Rivers, even the minister, had said how well he'd sounded and that he'd got the message across.

'Well, I tried, Maureen,' he said aloud. 'That's all you can do, isn't it?'

Two floors below the front door opened and Jack went and leaned across the bannister to see who was coming in. A young clerk entered the hall and quietly closed the door behind him. He caught sight of Jack and waved up the staircase to him.

'I'm George, sir. Are you Mr O'Connell? I heard you last night. Everyone on the bus was talking about it this morning.'

Jack came down the stairs, cup of tea in hand.

The young man was taking paper and ink out of the desk drawers as he spoke. 'We definitely have a busy day ahead.'

'Good morning, George. I hope we'll get a few in during the day,' said Jack, encouraged by the young man's enthusiasm.

'What?' The clerk stopped what he was doing and looked at Jack. 'Have you not seen outside?'

He shook his head in reply.

George walked over to the tall window and unfolded the heavy wooden shutters.

Jack spluttered his tea, and George slapped him on his back.

'Are you all right?'

'There must be two hundred men out there,' said Jack.

'And it's not even eight o'clock,' said George. 'I told you it's going to be a busy day.'

Jack ran up the stairs calling for Rivers. The two men went to the window on the top floor and looked down on the crowd. One side of the square was completely full of men standing quietly, waiting for the door to open. Jack ran his hand through his hair.

'I never thought for a minute that we'd get that many. How are we going to sort them out? We'll never manage.' A note of panic had crept into his voice.

'It's all in hand, Jack, don't worry,' said Rivers as he patted Jack's shoulder. 'We have transport lined up. Everything is arranged. It's up to the ministers to manage all that. We need to get back to Knockanree to let everyone know that help is coming and they're going to need to show the volunteers how to use the equipment.'

'I don't believe it,' said Jack, unable to pull himself away from the window. 'I never thought we'd get so many.'

More clerks arrived, and soon the doors opened to the volunteers. They queued down the street and, when their turn came, gave their name and were assigned to a truck or a bus. If they were willing to spend a few days away, they were sent home to get some necessities. Men who were prepared to labour for the day were sent to farms on the outskirts of Dublin and surrounding counties. Arrangements were made to collect them in the evening.

Phones rang constantly in the office. Word was coming in from all over the country, in towns everywhere there were queues forming to go to save the harvest.

Their work here was done. Finally they could go home.

Jack couldn't keep the smile off his face at Rosie's reaction.

'Oh my God, Dad, it's you! On the front page. Who's that with you?'

'It's the Minister of Agriculture. Fletcher got the photographer to take the picture. See, it says the names underneath.' He rang his finger along the text as he read it out loud. '*Minister Jim Ryan with Jack O'Connell of Knockanree.* That was taken at our headquarters.'

'*Your* headquarters? You had headquarters?' Rosie looked again at the front page of the newspaper. 'You look really well in that, Dad.'

'Thank you, Rosie. I'll tell you all about it. Where's your grandfather? I want to show him.'

'In the barn counting the scythes.'

'Put the kettle on, I'll go and get him.'

How long has it been since he spoke to me like that — like he wants to talk to me, she thought.

'It's good to see you smiling,' said Rivers.

'I'm pleased that Dad is happy with how things went.'

'I was worried about you here on your own, with no one to protect you.'

'Protect me from what? What harm could come to me in my own home? Anyway, Grandad was here.'

'Of course, but he is elderly.' He looked toward the window. 'What about the men on strike? There could be some bad feeling.'

'You're not saying that you think the labourers could get violent?'

'Maybe.' he put his hands in his pockets and leaned against the door frame. 'They will see their livelihoods at risk.'

'I can't believe that you think they'd do us any actual harm.'

'Just be careful. Feelings will run high when the volunteers start arriving. I don't think your father has thought about the possibilities.'

'Probably not. He can be a bit of a bull in a china shop when it comes to other people's feelings, or even just seeing things from someone else's point of view.' She smiled at him. 'Thank you for your concern. It's good of you to worry about me . . . I mean about us.'

Rivers seemed about to reply but Jack ushered Seán into the room and sat him at the table with the newspaper open in front of him.

'If you don't mind,' said Rivers, 'I'll continue my search of your attic.'

Jack settled himself at the table and began to tell her and Seán all about the radio studio, and Parnell Square and the crowds of people. Rosie nodded as he spoke. It used to be like this all the time. Before. He used to chat without snapping at her, he used to smile and listen to her questions.

Seán wanted to know when the volunteers would be arriving.

'No idea. Just make sure we're ready no matter when they get here.'

'I'll clean out the room over the dairy and sort out bedding,' said Rosie. 'They'll all fit there. Dad, you'll need to send a couple of sheep to slaughter. We don't know how many we'll need to feed. It'll be mutton stew for the foreseeable. Is that OK?'

'You're right, Rosie.' Jack looked at his daughter. 'I hadn't thought. I'll sort that out tomorrow.'

'We'd better make sure we've got enough scythes,' said Sean. 'I'm going out to count them. I suppose there's not one of them who knows how to use them. I suppose I'll have to show all those young jackeens how it's done.'

'Yes, Dad,' said Jack. 'You go and count the scythes — I'm depending on you for that.'

'What about me, Grandad, what will I do?' asked Pádraig.

'We'll need you to keep an eye on the chickens, and to help with the milking.'

'*Aw*, I do that anyway,' he said. 'Can I drive the wagon with Rivers?'

'Rivers will be busy. Don't worry, there'll be plenty of work for everybody.'

CHAPTER 20

Knockanree

1847

A bell tolled in his sleep. The ship's bell, he thought, though he knew that wasn't right. Not a ship's bell, a church bell. His eyes opened and for a moment he couldn't remember where he was. The bell tolled steadily. 'Jesus Christ, it's the midday Angelus.' He cursed his tiredness, gathered up the food he'd bought the previous day and hid it in the house. He hitched the wagon and steered it out onto the road, thinking it would take about four hours to make the journey, but he hadn't reckoned on the numbers of people already on the road, all travelling toward Kildare.

In the summer shower of light rain he tried to make out the faces of the people in case he might find his family walking among them. Men, women and children moved in silence, or sat by the side of the road too exhausted or ill to take another step. He stopped at the first groups he came across and offered them a lift. Their gratitude was out of proportion to the small kindness. Matt thought that perhaps it had been a while since any small consideration was shown to them. He helped two women and some children into the cart. The men thanked him again and said they could walk. Matt did not insist — there was no point in hurting their pride — they had nothing else left to them.

As they drew nearer the town the crowds grew denser. There was aggravation, murmurs of dissatisfaction, in the long queues for soup. They waited. Bowls held tightly, necks strained to watch the large cauldron growing emptier. Angry words from people further down the queue. They shuffled forward, the fear of not getting to the top in time plain on their ravaged faces.

'That's changed,' said one of Matt's passengers. 'Twelve months ago, people wouldn't queue up for the food. They were too proud, said it was belittling them to hold out their bowls for soup. But now it's all there is. No point in biting off your nose to spite your face. Take the soup or starve. If it wasn't for the Quakers, we'd all be dead by now.'

'Is there no work for the men?' asked Matt.

'There used to be work on the roads, if yeh'd call it work, but they've even stopped that now. It was killing more than it was saving. Backbreaking, it was. All they paid was ten pence a day. What would that get a family? A couple of loaves of bread, gone in a minute. The men were on their knees, trying their best. Most of them half dead.' She wiped her dripping nose on her torn sleeve. 'Some of them died on the roads and they wouldn't even give the family the money they'd earned during the day. They knew in their hearts that families were depending on the few pence. How can they sleep at night, sir, I ask you? Our family might have been all right if it hadn't been for that bastard in England, Lord Gregory. Excuse my impertinence. We had just over an acre to work for ourselves, and we could grow enough on it to feed the family for the year. We were getting by, barely, but we would have just about managed. We maybe could have held on except that we couldn't afford seeds, so we didn't have a crop coming in.'

'But you'll be all right when this is over. You can go back and start again.' Matt was heartened by the thought that some people would come out the other end of this and get back to a normal life.

'You don't understand, sir, though it's not your fault. I can tell from your clothes and your hat that you're not from around here. They brought in a new law. That's what I mean about Lord Gregory. It was him that thought of it. Anyone holding more than a quarter of an acre had to give up their bit of land or they couldn't get into the poorhouse. As I say, we didn't have anything left to sow, so we'd no harvest coming in, but still we had to give up the acre and leave the house. They'll give you nothing until they're sure you can't go any lower. As if you'd go beggin' for a bowl of soup if you had any other choice.'

Matt didn't speak. The weight of the money belt, sweaty and itchy, under his shirt irritated him. The nearer they got to their destination, the quieter the women became. They drew their ragged shawls tighter around their thin shoulders, seeking protection and comfort in the poor frayed weave.

Crowds gathered at the closed entrance gate of a tall

building, its narrow windows high in the cold grey walls. He drew the horse to a halt and his passengers climbed down. As he helped the oldest woman, he quietly put some coins into her hand and closed her fingers over them. She lifted her rheumy eyes to him and whispered a blessing in his ear. Holding her fist closed, she followed her family and was absorbed into the pile of humankind. The disorganised assembly looked like flotsam and jetsam washed up after a shipwreck onto the shore of the workhouse — unable to move, the exertion of their journey written on their faces, wretched bodies barely covered by rags that were once clothes.

Matt's eyes searched the crowds. He was fearful that, even if they were there, he might not be able to recognise his family. The people all looked the same: pale taut skin stretched across bony features, too exhausted and bewildered to even shed a tear.

Treading carefully through the bodies, he approached the gate, and the crowd parted slowly to let him past.

'They're full,' a skeletal face told him. 'They'll be open in the morning when they've taken out their dead.' The man's lips were cracked and sore. 'By that time many here will be gone too.'

Looking around, Matt did not doubt that many of them would, indeed, be dead by nightfall. The dying lay in groups around the gate and in the ditches on the side of the road. He thought that some of them looked as though they had already breathed their last, but he shied away from looking too closely. From time to time women cried aloud when a battle to keep a swollen-bellied child from slipping away was lost to the pull of death. There were dead among the living, but the living — too weak to move the bodies

— could barely keep the ever-vigilant vermin at bay.

'It's not a bed I'm looking for,' he said.

He made his way to the iron gates that protected the front door to the workhouse and pulled hard on the rope that rang the bell so that it clanged loud and clear. He could hear the echo of the bell pervade the internal corridors. No sound of answering footsteps reached him so he continued ringing the bell until he heard the bolt slide and a tall man opened the door. He allowed only his bald round head to protrude to the outside. The crowd stirred as one, distracted from their fate by the bold actions of the stranger.

'Stop that. Get away, we're full. I'll call the soldiers if you ring that bell again.'

'Sir,' said Matt, 'I've come to take my family home. Let me in to find them, I beg you.'

The crowd moved closer to the gate. A glimmer of hope on their faces. Anyone with the strength to stand began to get to their feet. The shuffling ripple that spread through the onlookers seemed to alarm the master.

'Come back later.' He slammed the door.

Matt knocked loudly. '*Open this door or I will shoot my way in*,' he shouted, '*and I'll bring all these people in with me!*'

After a moment's pause, he heard the bolt slide back once again and he pushed his way into the large cool hallway.

'Where's the O'Connell family?' he asked the master.

'The board of directors will hear about this.' The man folded his arms.

Matt repeated his question more loudly and this time the master responded.

'Those that are well enough are working. The others are in the dormitories. The men are in the left side, the women are on the right.'

'Jesus Christ, they're not even together?'

'Of course not.' The master shook his head and tutted. 'I'll consult the records. When did they arrive?' He went through a doorway to a small office, opened a large bound book and began to turn the long pages of the register. He nodded in a self-satisfied way at the neatly written text.

Matt didn't have time for that.

'On the left, you said.' He took off in that direction, shouting his brother's name.

His footsteps echoed as he ran into the long, narrow dormitory filled on each side with men lying on beds of straw. The rays of the watery sun found their way through the small windows and gave him just enough light to make out the features of the men. He looked at each one and called Lorcan's name until he finally found him unmoving, huddled in a corner, his eyes closed. Matt stopped, afraid to move closer for fear of what he would find. He put his hand on his brother's arm, felt his bone through the flimsy cloth, but his skin was warm.

Lorcan opened his caked eyes and sought the face of the man kneeling beside him.

'Is it you? Am I dead?'

Matt swallowed hard, leaned forward, and scooped up his brother. He carried him easily.

'Where's Annie?' said Matt.

Lorcan didn't answer.

Matt carried his brother to the sparse hallway. There was nothing to lay him on, so he gently sat his wasted body against the wall, more slouching than sitting.

'I have sent Mrs Porter to fetch Mrs O'Connell and her daughter,' the master informed Matt. His body filled the doorway leading to the women's quarters.

Matt set off for the boys' quarters. He'd never met his nephews and had no idea what they looked like. He shouted, '*O'Connell? Is there any O'Connell here?*' Three young boys sat up and looked at the strange man. Matt scooped up the smallest and shouted to the others, '*C'mon, boys, your mother is waiting for you!*' They scrambled to their feet and moved quickly through the doorway.

Mrs Porter led Annie into the hallway as Matt and the children arrived. Annie looked as though she might be walking through a dream, not quite comprehending what was happening.

'Her baby was dead in her arms,' said Mrs Porter, and the master went briskly to the register to record this information. 'I'll go to fetch it now.'

Annie looked at the people in the hallway as though she could not quite recognise them, or perhaps thought that they might be ghosts of her family. Matt crossed the hall to her. He would not have recognised her in a roomful of women. She wore the rough uniform of the workhouse and her hair, once dark and lustrous, fell in wispy unkempt strands. As Matt approached, she raised her hands to her mouth, then covered her eyes.

'*No, no, it can't be you, not now! You're too late, why did you not come before?*' She took away her hands. Her eyes searched again for Matt. She dropped to her knees and pounded the floor with her fists. '*No, no, I am dreaming. How can you be so cruel?*'

Matt recoiled.

Two of Annie's sons went to her and put their arms around her. She embraced them as bitter tears fell from her eyes. Matt was distraught. He had come as quickly as he could, but he was not quick enough for Annie. What awful things had happened to her, to the family?

She saw Lorcan half-conscious lying against the wall and crawled across the floor to him. Matt bent to help her. She slapped his hands away.

The master looked at the scene of desolation and did not interfere. Annie called Lorcan's name and put her arms around him. Her puzzled eyes swept the hallway.

'Where's Éamonn?' she said.

'He's here.' Matt pointed to the boy by the door.

Annie looked from Matt to the boy. Slowly she got to her feet. 'That's not Éamonn,' she said. 'Tomás, where's your brother?'

'They took him yesterday,' the boy whispered.

The master returned to the register and ran his finger along the lines of neat script, 'Yes, I think I remember. Yes, here it is. Éamonn O'Connell, aged twelve years. Fever hospital, admitted yesterday.' He paused and assumed his official stance. 'I regret to inform you that he died this morning.'

His words hung in the air.

'No!' Annie put her hand to the wall to steady herself as the boys clung to her.

When Matt came to comfort her this time, she let him.

'I want to see him,' she said.

'Not possible,' replied the master. 'The hunger fever is so contagious that the victims must be interred

158

immediately. He would have been buried in the municipal grave a few hours ago.'

She swayed on her feet. Matthew put his arm around her waist to support her.

The boy who was not Éamonn stood quietly waiting, watching the family's grief unfold. After a few moments he pulled at Matt's sleeve. 'When is my mother coming?' he asked.

'What's your name?' asked Matt. 'Is it O'Connell?'

The boy shook his head.

'Why did you answer to O'Connell then?'

'You said my mother was waiting for me,' said the boy. 'Where is she?'

'I made a mistake,' said Matt.

The boy looked up at Matt, his lip trembling. Tears slid down his face.

Matt went to the master and asked if the boy's parents were in the workhouse with him.

He turned the pages with a slight twitch of annoyance. 'What's your name?'

'Billy Lawlor,' said the boy.

The master looked down the list. 'Yes. The boy's mother and father are here, for the moment.'

Matt took a half crown from his pocket and placed it in the hand of the master. 'Make sure the boy gets his full rations,' he said. 'I'll be back to check.'

Mrs Porter returned to the hall with a bundle wrapped in clean linen. She placed the body of the dead infant into its mother's arms.

'I thought you'd prefer to have the child buried in the church graveyard,' said Mrs Porter, not unkindly. 'Though you can leave her with us to be buried if you prefer.'

Annie pulled back the cloth covering Gráinne's frozen face. She breathed a soft prayer into the child's ear.

Matt put his arm gently around her shoulders to guide her towards the door. 'Come, Annie. Boys, help me with your father. We're going home.'

Matt picked Lorcan up and carried him outside. The crowd of people stood back to allow them through. He lifted the semi-conscious Lorcan into the back of the wagon, followed by Annie. Tomás and Seamus climbed up beside Matt. He guided the horse through the quiet, respectful crowd. Some crossed themselves and murmured unanswered prayers.

As the heavy door closed, Matt glimpsed the face of the boy in the hallway staring after them. The bolt slid into place and Matt pictured the boy being led back to the dormitory. He bit his lip, picked up the reins and began the long slow journey back to Knockanree.

CHAPTER 21

Knockanree

1946

Colin Lawlor watched the men jump down from the trucks and walk up the lane to the yard. He'd listened to the broadcast but thought that people would be foolish to do that work unless they had to. Like he had to.

A dozen noisy men joked and laughed as they looked at the unfamiliar surroundings. Old Seán led them towards the barn to collect the scythes and hooks as Colin stood hidden behind the gorse listening to them talk about how they'd enjoy being out in the air for the day.

'Jaysus!' said a young volunteer. 'I thought I was coming out to fresh air. What the hell is that smell?'

With shaking hands Colin lit a cigarette. They'll be wrecked in an hour, let alone a day, he thought. They've no idea what they're getting into. He left the farm and went in search of the other labourers. He found them in the back room of Foley's.

'We've got to put a stop to this,' he told them. 'The

farmers won't pay us anything at all if they can get the work done for nothing. We can't let this happen.'

The small group walked toward Abbeyfield. They stopped at the abbey ruins and climbed up through the crumbling walls. From there they could see the O'Connells' fields.

They sniggered at the early attempts of the volunteers to follow Jack and Old Seán's instructions. They laughed out loud as Jack tried to show them what to do. The volunteers seemed keen, but the land labourers knew that using the scythe was not as easy as it seemed.

'One of them's going to lose a leg if they keep up like that,' said Colin Lawlor. 'Jack O'Connell might be a big fella, but teaching isn't one of his skills.'

The labourers made bets on how long the volunteers would last.

But the volunteers had more staying power than they'd given them credit for. The chatter quietened and they were slow but careful in their attempts. They worked in pairs, one lifting the stalks and the other sweeping the scythe through them. At first, they were overcautious and cut the stalks too short, leaving long stubble in the field. As the day went on, they became more confident, sure of their movements. In the late afternoon Colin and farm labourers watched as unsteady stooks of corn and oats began to appear in the fields.

One by one the land labourers drifted back to Foley's.

Jack was aware that the labourers were watching the progress but chose to concentrate on the job in hand. It wasn't pretty, but progress was being made. He looked toward the sky. At least the weather was on their side, for the moment. That could all change with a shift in the wind.

At the end of the day the men came in from the fields and Rosie sat each man at the table and gave him a bowl of mutton stew. The men were tired but they had the satisfaction of a day's work behind them. The trucks came to take the day workers home and the other men went to the room over the dairy. Rosie had cleaned and aired the large room and put fresh bedding there for anyone who was going to stay a few days.

Everyone had had a long and tiring day and most took to their beds as soon as they had eaten.

Jack walked through his fields and could see fields in neighbouring farms showed signs of clearing. He reached the graveyard before the sun began to set and laid flowers from the small meadow on Maureen's grave.

'Do you know what, Maureen? It just might work. I'm beginning to think that it might just be all right.'

The next morning the land labourers waited at the bottom of the lane, silently noting the grey edge to the low clouds. Some of them shared a single cigarette with short angry drags. The sound of an approaching vehicle filled the air and drowned out the birdsong. The truck shuddered to a halt and the volunteers started to jump out, stretching their legs and rubbing their backs. The laneway was blocked by the land labourers.

'Remember, now, I'll do the talking,' Colin Lawlor said in a low voice to his group. Then he turned toward the newly arrived men and held up his arms.

'There's no work to be done here today, lads. You can take the truck back to wherever you've come from.'

'More than two hours we've been sitting in that,' answered one of the workers, pointing his thumb at the truck. 'Me arse is numb. I'm not getting back into it.' The young man started past Colin, who put his hand on his young man's shoulder.

'I don't think you heard me. *Get back on the fucking truck.*'

'*Or wha*'? *You gonna make me? Fucking culchie!*' The youth squared up to Colin.

From up the laneway came the sound of the O'Connells' door slamming and dogs barking.

Jack came around the corner with his shotgun bent over his arm.

'What's going on here? You causing more trouble, Lawlor?'

'*You can't do this! You're taking our livelihood away!*' shouted Colin. '*How are we to make a living if this lot are coming in here and doing our job for nothing?*'

The volunteers, who had started to walk toward the house, stopped and turned around.

'*Who do you think usually brings in the harvest?*' Colin called to them. '*Did ye think he does it on his own? No, it's the likes of me and them working like dogs for a few pence a week, that's who!*'

The men glanced at one another or stared at the ground.

'I didn't think we were scabs,' said one of the men. 'I didn't know there was a problem coming here.'

The other men shifted from one foot to the other, undecided about what to do.

One of the young volunteers stepped toward Jack. 'Mister, are they on strike?' he said.

'We are,' said Colin. 'We're only looking for a few extra shillings a week. We'd get twice as much in a factory.'

'I'm glad you think so,' said another volunteer. 'You might think there's loads of jobs in factories, but you go out looking and all of a sudden there's no jobs, and what there is won't pay the rent in Dublin.'

'Even so,' said Lawlor, 'if you come here and do our work, you're putting us out on the road.'

'Look,' said Jack, 'we've got to think about what's best for everyone. We don't have time for this. The crops are starting to go to seed, we've just got to get them in. If we don't, there won't be any jobs for anyone. There won't be any bread for anyone. We've got to get moving.'

'He's right, you know,' said the young volunteer. 'Jacob's laid off seventy yesterday, said there was no flour to make the biscuits. They said there'd be more jobs gone next week if they can't get any.'

'No, I'm not staying.' Another volunteer moved toward the truck. 'Me da would kill me if I crossed a picket line. I'm going back to ask to be sent somewhere there isn't a strike on.' Several men got back on the truck, but a few stayed. Along with the men who had stayed on from yesterday and were sleeping over the dairy, it would be enough to make some progress. Jack pointed toward the house and told them to get a cup of tea before they started.

Colin Lawlor and the other labourers seemed pleased they'd won a small victory, that they'd made an impression on the volunteers and that some of them, at least, had turned back. They drifted down the lane.

'We can make their life a little more unpleasant,' Colin said to the others. 'They'll be all gone back on the trucks by the time we've finished with them.'

Jack had followed them. 'Listen to me, lads. There's

no need for animosity. I'll pay any of you who will work alongside the volunteers.'

'What rate?' Colin asked.

'The usual rate.' Jack watched the reaction as the men weighed up the situation. One by one they turned, shoulders hunched, defeated. They walked back up the laneway to the house.

All except Colin Lawlor.

'It's a bad year, Colin,' said Jack. 'We can talk about it next year. Things might be better then. What about it?'

Colin Lawlor muttered a curse, turned back down the lane, and walked away, alone.

CHAPTER 22

Dublin

1946

Connie and Fletcher had reported on the first day of the volunteers' arrival at Parnell Square. Two days later they reported that the numbers had doubled.

Fletcher swept into the reporters' room, passed his desk, and went directly to Connie.

'Carolan wants to see us. It's about the volunteers' story.'

'Did you say "us"?'

'Told him there'd be no story if it hadn't been for you taking the bull by the horns, so to speak.'

'You said that? Really?'

'Really. Come on. Bring your notebook.'

She straightened her skirt and her glasses and followed Fletcher into Mr Carolan's office. It smelled of pipe tobacco, though the window was open, and a breeze gently lifted the net curtain behind him.

He pointed to the chairs and they sat.

'This story of yours has grown legs. It's been picked up by an English paper. We're going to run with it for a while. Tell me what you're thinking of for the next few days.'

He looked at Fletcher, who turned toward Connie and nodded.

'Yes, Mr Carolan.' She knew her voice sounded shaky. 'Well, I'd like to take a look at the big picture, Mr Carolan. If that's all right. Everyone is concerned about their own corner of the land but really the story is about all of Ireland working together, isn't it? I'd like to report on the whole effort and report how the harvest is going county by county and the tonnage of crops saved and show the size of the whole operation. I think that would be really impressive.'

'Really, Connie?' Mr Carolan looked toward the ceiling and Connie fought the instinct to follow his eyes. 'Well, I suppose there is a need to report the facts and figures and I'm sure you'll be good at that. Make sure you find out how many volunteers there are nationwide, too. If we're going to present a whole picture, we'll need to include all the statistics. I hear you've impressed Minister Ryan already – an extremely useful source to have.'

'Yes, sir. I'll make sure it's a very comprehensive piece.' Connie beamed at him.

'What about you, Fletch?' asked Mr Carolan.

'I'm thinking of a different angle. What if I go for a few days as a volunteer, to see what it's like for the ordinary guy from the city, take it down a level to the personal story. I think it's a good angle. It will complement Connie's piece. This will be about the actual people leaving their desks and shops and going out into the fields.'

Fletcher and Connie waited while Mr O'Carroll lit his pipe. He leaned back on his chair and stared at the ceiling again.

'OK, OK. Just one day, not two. Give me a thousand words and I'll see if we can use it. But you must work, mind, not just talk about other people working, and you can't let them know you're a reporter. When you get back, I'll check your palms for callouses.' He turned toward Connie. 'Make sure those figures are correct. Run everything by the Department. OK, go now. Get to work. We've deadlines to meet.'

Every day for the next week Connie faithfully reported the figures produced by the Department of Agriculture. She found it a very satisfying task when, day by day, she added tonnage and hundredweights of oats and barley, wheat and rye to the tallies. Acres cleared, silos filled. Each day the statistics appeared in a column in the newspaper and Connie cross-checked with all the departments involved and ensured that the printed figures were accurate and correct.

Toward the end of the second week, she walked through the city in the morning sunlight, from the newspaper office across town to Parnell Square. It was late morning but there was still a lot of activity in the harvest HQ. The large hall door was wedged open.

Connie popped in to see George and check the number of volunteers registered and asked about getting figures for the whole country.

'Sure, Miss O'Connell, I'll do that. Can you wait while I make a few phone calls, just to check today's numbers?'

'I'd be happy to. Is there anything I can do to help while I'm here?'

'The sandwich-makers are hard at it still. They're sending out lunchtime deliveries to North Dublin. They'd probably be delighted at an extra pair of hands.'

People came and went through the open door. All ages, shapes and sizes. Connie noticed an older woman leaning against the doorpost. She seemed out of place here, completely still among all the hustle and bustle. Connie went over to her.

'Are you all right? Would you like to sit down?'

'I'm fine, really. Well, maybe I'll just sit for a moment before I start home.'

Connie took her arm, led her to the bench in the hall, and went to get her a drink of water.

'So kind of you,' said the lady. She sipped the water slowly and took off her headscarf.

'Perhaps you should open your coat a little,' said Connie. The tweed coat was spotlessly clean, the cuffs and buttonholes well worn. It was far too heavy to wear on a day like this, she thought.

'Silly of me to walk all the way.' The lady smiled at Connie. 'I'd forgotten how far it is. But I wanted to bring something to donate.' From her pocket she took a small package, wrapped in greaseproof paper. 'It's not much, but I read about the Red Cross making the sandwiches and I thought, with the rationing, they would need all the butter they can get.' She put the package into Connie's hand.

'I'm sure they don't—' Connie saw the light in the tired woman's eyes flicker for a moment, '— don't ever have enough butter. They're always saying they use so

170

much every day, and you're right — it's so hard to get. They'll be delighted, I'm sure.'

The woman sighed and smiled. 'Yes, that's what I thought. I don't really need it. I'm on my own now. It's too much for one. Far better to give it to those that need it more. Isn't that right?'

The woman's eyes shone as she watched the activity. 'Reminds me of the suffragettes back in the day — I should say the Irish Women's Franchise League. Hannah was very particular about that. We ran the newspaper from a house just like this one.' She looked at Connie's hand. 'You should get that butter to wherever it's supposed to be, or it'll melt and ruin your lovely suit.'

'Absolutely right. I'll just run up with it now. Sorry, what's your name?'

'Doris.'

'And the Hannah that you mentioned?

'Hannah Sheehy Skeffington. You'll surely have heard of her? She was such an important figure in the suffrage and nationalist movement.'

Connie's heart leapt. 'Of course I've heard of her! Wait here, Doris. I'll be back in a moment. I'd really like to have a chat with you.'

'Don't worry, love. I'm not in a hurry, not at all.' Doris sipped her water and waited.

171

CHAPTER 23

Knockanree

1847

The clouds had a yellow hue about their edges as the sun descended into the night. From time to time, Matt turned to watch Lorcan, who drifted in and out of sleep without ever properly waking. They made slow progress, unwilling to rock the cart too much. Annie put her hand on his head, the children knew what that meant, and they watched her face anxiously until she said, 'He'll be all right.'

Matt took comfort from the certainty in her voice, though he suspected she was not as sure as she sounded.

It was the early hours of the morning by the time they turned up the laneway to Abbeyfield farmhouse. The clouds had cleared and the stars shimmered in the blackness. Matt opened the door as the children vied to be the first one back in their home. They went from room to room as though looking for their lost home, for the safety they had felt there in the past. The empty rooms did not welcome them in the way they remembered.

Annie placed Gráinne in a small woven basket, still in the clean linen that Mrs. Porter had wrapped her in. She looked around for candles but could find none.

'Annie,' said Matt in a soft voice, 'should we take the child to the church?'

'I can't let her go. Not just yet, not yet. Please.'

It almost broke his heart to watch her. She hung her shawl across the window as a poor curtain, and an apron over the mirror covering the glass in case the soul of the departed should get caught.

'In a few hours,' she said. 'Let her have a little time with us, in our home, before she must go. I know she must go in a little while. But not yet.'

Matt left her alone and went to see to the children. He sent them to fetch water from the well then produced the food he had bought from Maguire's shop and set about making a meal. When Annie returned to the kitchen, she stood and watched him carry out the domestic tasks. As she watched, something near normality returned to her features. The actions of pouring the water and lighting the fire seemed to soothe her. She called the boys and left the house with them for a few minutes. When she returned, they were carrying pots, pans, bowls, and other household things they had hidden from the evictors. She seemed pleased to lay them all out on the table.

Matt fried bacon and eggs on the skillet.

The aroma of cooking food filled the kitchen, and the children watched the skillet and jumped back when they got too close to the spitting bacon. Their eyes darted between Matt and the food. Lorcan slept fitfully in the

173

other room, half-waking, calling out for Annie. She knelt beside him and fed him mashed eggs and buttermilk, a little at a time, and he slept again.

Matt warned the boys not to eat too fast or they would get sick. They nodded their understanding, but once the first few mouthfuls slid down their throats a primal urge overtook them. They stood and gobbled up the food as fast as they could, almost choking from the bread stuffed into their hungry mouths. Hardly a word was spoken between them, their eyes watching each other's servings until both bowls were licked clean.

'That's enough for now,' said Annie.

Tomás and Seamus didn't argue. Their unusually full stomachs made them sleepy, but their eyes were too wild and alert to allow them lower their guard.

'Come in and say a prayer for your sister.'

There were no chairs. Annie sat on the floor, a son each side, her face composed, resigned. The boys lay down and slept beside her. Annie stared straight ahead and maintained her vigil.

Matt watched her from the other side of the room. He could not read her face, could not see her grief. He thought she would not allow herself the luxury of tears.

As the children slept, she rose and pulled back the corner of the shawl hanging in the window and looked out to the familiar scene — the yard, the closed gate, the laneway all revealed in the cool mist of a new day.

'What are you looking for?' Matt said.

'Everything looks the same,' she said. 'It looks as it has always looked. How can that be? The whole world has changed. Nothing can ever be the same again. I want the heavens to rage at what happened to us, to everyone.

But the sun will shine and the birds will sing. Already I hear them. I want to believe that time will stop, that it was all a terrible dream. My eldest son and my baby girl are gone forever. My heart goes on beating, but I wish it would stop.'

Matt went to embrace her, but she stiffened in his arms and turned away.

'We will take her to the church now,' she said.

Matt chose a spot under a yew tree in the corner of the cemetery and dug a neat grave as the priest spoke the ancient Latin words over the child. Annie's arms hung loosely by her sides as Matt put a makeshift cross on the little pile of disturbed earth. She raised her forlorn face to him. He put his arm around her shoulders and led her back to the cart.

'I'm sorry for what I said earlier when you came to find us,' Annie said. Her voice was raw. 'I was maddened by the grief and the hunger and the worry of the fever. Of course you came as soon as you could, I know that.' She patted his arm absently.

'I did come as soon as I could, really, Annie. I could not have got here any quicker than I did.'

'Of course. I know. It's not your fault that the children are dead.'

The words struck his heart. What if I'd gone yesterday, he thought. Though it would have been foolish to travel in the black night. He felt Annie believed exactly the opposite to the words she spoke, that she would never forgive him for not saving her children. In that moment he felt that he would never forgive himself.

CHAPTER 24

Knockanree

1946

Rosie cycled to town to buy the newspaper in Maguires'. The shop was divided into two sections: post office at one end and the shop counter at the other. The public phone, and it was indeed very public, was beside the post office. Shelves in the shop were piled high with assorted tins and boxes. A mound of potatoes lay loose in a corner, and other fruit and vegetables in open crates on the floor. The shop sold everything from bread soda to ribbons, shovels to sewing needles.

While Rosie waited, she watched old Mrs Maguire pick a few potatoes from the pile in the corner, cut slices of cheese and wrap them neatly in paper, then weigh a quarter pound of boiled sweets into a paper bag. There was no 'young' Mrs Maguire as her son, Michael the postman, had never married.

Occasionally she wiped her hands on the corner of her apron as she chatted to the customer about the volunteers. 'I hear they're a bit of a nuisance really. I'm told they haven't a clue,' she said as she counted out the change into Mrs Beattie's hand.

Rosie stood back and flicked through the pages of the newspaper, looking for Fletcher and Connie's articles. She was pleased with the morning's outing. She usually dreaded trips to the village but, as the volunteers seemed to be the centre of gossip these days, there'd been no awkward questions for her to dodge, no insinuations made.

When it was her turn, Rosie handed over the coins, managed to exchange the minimum amount of words required and was about to leave as Michael Maguire came back from his rounds.

'Ah, it's yourself, Mrs *Far-rell*.' He rolled her name around his tongue. 'How are things above at the farm? I can see from the road there's great activity in the fields. Wonderful, isn't it, eh?' He gave a thin smile.

'Yes, we're delighted, Mr Maguire.' She moved to go past him.

'I'll be up your way soon, with a letter.' He didn't move from the doorway.

She tilted her head to one side. She knew she'd just have to wait it out. 'Really?'

'Well, you know I'm on the school board?'

She could almost see his puny chest swell.

'One of the items for discussion is the regularising of our records. We've been going through the files and, you may not be aware, but the school should have a copy of each child's birth certificate. We noticed that we don't have a copy of Pádraig's.'

'Don't you already have his baptismal certificate?' Rosie tried to keep her voice even.

'Ah, yes. That is a point.'

'Well, a child has to be born to be baptised, so what difference can it make to your records?'

'You see, Rosie,' the tip of his tongue licked his top lip like a snake about to strike, 'it's a government matter. The Department of Education of course recognises the importance of the baptismal certificate, but we like to keep the school records as complete as possible and there would be more information on the birth certificate.'

Rosie became aware of the stillness in the shop. She felt the beady eyes of Mrs Maguire dancing in her head from behind the counter. The post office clock began to sound the hour.

'I see. Well, I must be going now.' Rosie's stomach turned over as she pushed past Maguire.

He followed her to the pavement. 'I'll collect it so, soon. Save you the journey in,' he said, as though he were doing her a great favour.

She walked on, hearing the shop bell tinkle as the door closed firmly behind her.

Rosie slowly cycled the four miles to Abbeyfield. She barely noticed the fields busy with men and women working, calling to each other. Her mind was focused on one thing and one thing only: Pádraig's birth certificate. In the section headed 'Mother's Status' the awful word *Spinster* was written. There was no father's name recorded.

Her mother believed her when she said Tommy would be back, that everything would be all right. She'd clung to the hope that somehow Rosie could come to Abbeyfield as Mrs Farrell, with Tommy and Pádraig, and if the dates were a little muddled, well, who would know? Her mother had stood in that very same shop and told everyone that she was married in England. Whether they believed her or not, Rosie didn't know, but no one had the guts to confront her parents. There had been whispering around the town, she knew by the attitude of some of them. The long cold stare, the 'Hello, I can't stop to talk,' unless there was no one around and then they'd have all the time in the world to bring the conversation around to her time away in England, and her husband and Pádraig.

If Maguire gets his hands on the birth certificate, then everyone will know, she thought. Not only about Pádraig, but they'll know that Mam went to her grave with a sin on her soul. A lie. They'll never forgive a barefaced lie. I'll have to leave. I can't stay here any longer.

Rosie steered the bicycle into the farmyard. The door to the henhouse had been left open. Grandad was getting worse. The hens had ventured out and were pecking around the doorway. Just like me, she thought. Even if I could get away, where would I go? Where else would I fit in? Where would we be safe?

She was glad the house was quiet, but there was work to be done, meals to make, mouths to feed. She put the newspaper aside and began preparing the food. I'll read the stories later, she thought. Maybe not Connie's, though. All those numbers give me a headache.

CHAPTER 25

Knockanree

Summer 1847

Although the wild dark look slowly left Annie's face, Matt would sometimes catch the desolation in her eyes as she began to tend to the routine tasks of her house. She scrubbed the slate floor, the hearth, the doors, until her hands were red-raw. It was as though she needed to wipe the horror from everything. Scald it out of their lives. But it could never be done, no matter how hot she made the water, no matter how hard she tried. She shrugged aside Matt's concern and bent her head to the task. Matt knew she had always been the cornerstone of the family, had always been strong. He had never before realised that there was a cost to that strength.

'Annie, come with me to the village. We have to get some more supplies. You know best what we need,' said Matt.

Annie looked down at her workhouse clothes.

'I don't want to go like this.'

'Where are your own clothes?'

She looked at him in disbelief.

'You really don't know anything, do you, nothing of what we went through to survive?' She leaned her hand on the mantlepiece. 'Maguire bought everything we had. I suppose if he hadn't bought it, we would have gone to the workhouse sooner. Maybe I should have been more grateful, like Lorcan was.' She pulled at some loose strands of hair and tucked them behind her ear. He'd seen her do that a thousand times or more. He didn't know why it brought a lump to his throat.

'I'll get the horse and cart.'

Matt held the door open for Annie. Despite her workhouse clothes she walked with her head held high into Maguires' shop.

Maguire came around the counter to greet her as though she were an old friend. 'Annie, how good it is to see you looking so well.' He let his eyes travel the length of her dress.

She swallowed and looked at Matt.

'Mr Maguire,' he began. 'I believe you have certain items belonging to the family. We would like to retrieve them.'

Maguire scratched his head.

'Haven't you left Abbeyfield? The dresser and the chairs are gone. I heard you'd left the farm and the house for good.'

'You heard wrong,' said Matt.

'Isn't there back rent to be paid?' said Maguire.

Annie looked up from the sacks of grain. 'Who told you about that?'

Maguire took a sudden fit of coughing and held up his hand as though he could no longer speak. His son, Brian, came running from the back of the shop with a glass of beer for his father.

They waited while he caught his breath.

Annie looked toward the back of the shop. 'I can see our kitchen stools there, we'll have them.'

'Yes, of course you can take them. Sixpence each.'

'You only gave me tuppence each for them.'

Toddy smiled at Annie in the way men sometimes smile at women or imbeciles.

Matt watched Annie's shoulders straighten. Oh Toddy, big mistake, he thought.

'Well, my dear,' Toddy produced his handkerchief and dabbed his brow, ''tis the principle of *laissez faire*, you see. It means "whatever the market will bear" and of course one must make a profit.'

'A profit,' she said. 'That is your first concern? That you turn a profit? You have not seen fit to ask after my husband or children, so worried are you for *your profit!*' She spat the words at him. 'Look at the price you are charging for oatmeal and cornmeal. Have you no shame? You know your neighbours cannot buy at these prices. For the love of God, man, people you have known for years are dying of hunger. What are you doing here surrounded by food with bars on your doors and windows?'

'I am sorry for your loss, but I have my own wife and family to support,' said Maguire coolly. 'Perhaps you're confusing me with the Quakers? They are the people handing out the free soup. Did you know I supply the meal for the stirabout to the Quakers and to the workhouse?'

Maguire rocked back on his heels and hooked his thumbs into his waistcoat pockets.

'At what cost?' she said.

'I've told you already. Whatever the market will pay.'

She shook her head and raised her hands as though giving up. But she wasn't finished yet. 'I will pray for you, Toddy Maguire. I will pray that you live to survive these times. I will pray that, when you are on your deathbed, you might still ask forgiveness for what you have done.'

Toddy returned her stare. 'I have nothing to ask forgiveness for, whatever you may think.'

She took a breath, as though a reply was on her lips, but Matt put a hand on her shoulder.

'Annie, take a look at some material. The boys and Lorcan need shirts, and you said something about a dress.'

Their eyes met, she sighed, and walked away.

'Toddy, you have some mighty fine hunting knives here,' said Matt. 'Could I look?'

Toddy's face brightened and he led Matt to the cabinet.

Annie's eyes followed the men for a moment before she turned to young Brian who stood motionless in the corner of the room, staring at her. She began to recite the items she'd come to buy.

Maguire showed Matt the knives and asked him if he intended to stay long in Abbeyfield.

'You seem to take a keen interest in our farm.'

'Well, it's a fine house,' said Maguire. 'I heard it was built from the stones of the old abbey by the same man that built the manor house. Is that right?'

Matt nodded. 'As far as I know.'

'And the land backs on to His Lordship's land, isn't that so?'

'It is.'

'And would you ever see His Lordship, I mean, when he's over from London? You can see the manor house from the top of Nine-Acre Field, can't you?'

Matt lifted one of the knives and tested its weight in his hand. 'We don't move in the same circles, but you are right, the manor house is easily in walking distance of Abbeyfield.'

'Well, that's if a family were walking but . . .' began Maguire.

Matt waited for the end of the sentence, but Maguire turned away and became interested in tidying tins of tobacco.

'I'll take this one. Add it to the bill,' said Matt. He put the knife in the sheath that had been empty too long.

Matt carried the supplies out to the wagon. So Carbury wasn't bluffing. Toddy and Maud have their eyes on Abbeyfield. Probably think they can get it for a song. I'm not about to let that happen.

Lorcan grew in strength every day. The children gladly carried out chores they had once complained of. None of them, apart from Annie, appeared to want to stray far from the farm. They clung to the house and would go no further than the well or to collect firewood.

As the days passed, Annie and Lorcan began to talk to Matt about what had happened. On a humid summer evening they sat outside in the yard, and the occasional chatter of the children reached them through the still air.

Annie spread a rug on the ground, and they sat and wondered at the size of the pink-tinged 'mackerel whale' clouds above them. The slowly falling sun warmed their faces.

Lorcan talked of when the potato crop first failed. 'Two years ago,' he said. '1845. Was it only two years ago? There was no warning. '45 had been a good year. The summer was long and everything seemed to flourish. We were sure we'd have a huge crop of potatoes to eat as well as the other crops to sell. We were on the pig's back. You should have seen the spuds when we dug up the first lot. Delighted we were with the size of them and they looked perfect. It was the next morning, when we went out to the barn that we saw they'd all turned black and soft. The smell of them was awful. It was the same story for everyone. We had money from the oat and wheat crops for the rent in November that year. We managed on what was left and the winter vegetables to get us through. We prayed the winter frosts would kill any plague in the ground and that '46 would be a better year. We were not too bad compared to most — we had seed potatoes but we held off sowing them. The neighbours used up their seed potatoes early in the spring. It wasn't good. When they lifted them, they rotted even faster than the year before. They lost everything. We tried to help them as much as we could. But we had very little. We don't even know where they are now. They could be dead for all we know.' His eyes sought Annie's. 'We just about managed to pay the May rent on what we had and what we got from the relief work. You should have seen the queues to get taken on. It was hard work and long days, building roads, breaking boulders. We knew it wasn't work that was necessary or worth the effort. Half the roads weren't even needed, they were going nowhere but that didn't matter. We didn't care. We thought it would only be for a few months and we'd make do on a little oatmeal every day and prayed the potatoes would be all right in September. When we lifted them and saw them turn black, we knew that we couldn't survive. It was a terrible time, Matt. That's when I wrote to you. I went up to Carbury and told him I was expecting money from America, I said I wouldn't have it in time for the November rent but everything would be paid as soon as I got it. That was the only reason he didn't put us out, the chance that money was coming.'

Lorcan's voice trembled, and Annie moved to sit beside him. She put her arm across his shoulders and took up the story, still watching his face.

'There was only one way to get any money and that was the relief work. Éamonn helped carry the buckets of stones, doing whatever he could to help.' Annie's lip quivered at the memory of brave Éamonn dragging the rocks, his small body not able for the backbreaking work but determined to help his father.

Lorcan nodded. 'They kept the relief work going through the winter. Matt, it was the worst winter we'd ever seen. The snow started in November, gales of snow and icy winds for months on end. But still we had to go every day to the relief work. Those were frightening times. I saw a terrible change in people. Where once there was a bond between tenants, now there were crowds of men every day desperate for work, all shoving and pushing to get picked. Who could blame them? I was one of them. We all knew that if we weren't picked our family wouldn't eat. They paid ten pence a day to a man and four pence to a woman or a child, not enough to feed a family, but anyone who could get it took it. No matter how hard we worked, that was all they would give, sometimes the paymaster wasn't there at the end of the day to pay the men. There was awful trouble over that. Riots sometimes. You'd be surprised how starving men can gather the strength to be violent when they're facing injustice. The paymasters were afraid sometimes to come to the works without police protection.' Lorcan shook his head at the memory.

Annie rested her hand on his shoulder. 'The two of them would come home worn down, frozen with the cold, backs nearly broken, sometimes empty-handed. There was many a day we didn't eat at all. We sold anything we could. Maguire in the town bought our chairs and clothes and rugs, but we kept the roof over our head. The winter dragged on. We were at our lowest when we got the money you sent. I can't tell you how much that meant to us — it saved our lives and many of our neighbours. We were able to buy enough food to keep us. We would have bought seeds, but the price had trebled. Any kind of food was scarce and the cost of oatmeal — well, you've seen for yourself the price of it. When the agent came in May for the rent, we didn't have it, or anything left to sell. No chance of getting it. He said he would be back with an eviction order and soldiers to enforce it. We begged him, on our knees, for more time, but he wouldn't even look at us. We told him that you were going to send more money, we showed him your letter. But he wouldn't listen.'

187

'They came one morning, before dawn,' said Lorcan. 'Carbury stood back and let the bailiffs do the dirty work. They forced their way in and dragged us out to the yard. Just over there they threw the few belongings we had after us. Carbury went through them to see if there was anything of value — there wasn't.'

Annie allowed herself a brief smile. 'I'd hidden those old pots and pans — not worth anything but I was afraid they'd take them. The soldiers stood by with their rifles and watched. When they were finished they put us out on the lane and closed the gate behind us. I heard one of the soldiers ask Carbury if they should set fire to the roof, but he said no to that. Thank God. They boarded up the door and the windows and warned us not to try to get back in or we'd be arrested for trespassing and taken to prison. All of us, even the children. They moved on to the farmers living in the small cottages further along. They were put out and the roofs pulled off them so no one could go back to live there. I think Carbury must have had plans for this place or else he would have pulled off the roof of this house too.'

'Did you go straight to the workhouse then?' asked Matt.

'We had to,' she said. 'We waited a day, just in case you came, or sent a letter, but in the end we had to. We joined the crowds and walked during the day, exhausted, and at night we slept in the fields, under bushes. We thanked God that it was a fine summer and thought that maybe we could survive outside. The Quakers, God bless them, had set up a good soup kitchen in the town. But we knew the weather could turn any time. We waited for days outside the workhouse gates. I'll never forget it. Every morning we watched while they carried out the bodies of the people who had died during the night and buried them in huge graves. It's not right, not Christian.' She blessed herself. 'The workhouse would take in a few from outside the gates every day. We got in about two weeks before you found us. I thought we were never going to get out, that we'd die in there. But what else could we do? We thought it was for the best. We got food, stirabout, but we couldn't even talk to each other at the table. The women and men and children were all fed at different times. Why would they do that? They were so intent on not letting men and women mix together. It was as if they went out of their way to break our hearts. If the fever didn't kill us, we'd surely have died of sadness, if such a thing is possible.'

Lorcan nodded and reached for Annie's hand. 'I can't believe I'll never see Éamonn and Gráinne again,' he murmured.

They were past tears. Others would think they were the lucky ones, they knew. That night other people slept in the beds they had vacated. People who would never come out of that place.

At least not alive.

CHAPTER 26

Knockanree

1946

Colin Lawlor crept along the prickly hedgerows as the sun finally sank into a blaze of pink clouds. He'd waited ages for the volunteers to go. They were always hanging on, talking in small groups, trying to outdo each other with stories of the reaping they'd done, followed by shouts of disbelief and good-natured laughs. What the hell did they have to laugh about?

In the fading light the line of stooks looked regimental. As he got closer, their unsteadiness was clear, and he tutted as he kicked some of the corn over. Amateurs, he thought. Any sort of a wind will take these. They haven't a clue.

He strode through bristles of shorn stalks sticking up unevenly from the ground and paused briefly as a laugh carried across the still air to him. Did they never shut up?

In the beginning the labourers had caused trouble in some areas around the country. The gardaí had been called to farms where there'd been scuffles between farm labourers and volunteers. It was short-lived; their hearts weren't in it. After a few days all — well, almost all — the land labourers had returned to work . . . at the old rate. As had happened here in Abbeyfield.

He would never have believed that so many would come out to help, but here was the proof of it. He'd read in the newspapers that the big factories had let their staff go to the fields — on full pay. Not only men, women too. He couldn't believe that businesses would do that. Even cinemas and dancehalls closed. Day after day they'd come in their thousands, across the whole country, and there wasn't a thing he could do to stop it. Week after week they came, football and hurling matches abandoned. They came on foot and in lorries. A bit awkward at first, till they got into the rhythm of the work. Even at weekends he'd seen truck after truck come with hundreds of volunteers and drop them at farms. Then they descended on the fields. He put his hand to one of the stooks. The corn was still a bit damp. It would start to bud if it didn't dry out soon.

He'd watched this field earlier. When the rain started, the volunteers didn't run for cover: they'd kept going. He knew what that felt like, to work with the rain running down the back of your neck as you bent over to tie up the bundles of corn or barley. They'd stayed on to get the field finished.

Even with the weather against them, it was plain to see it had worked. Some fields were too far gone. The ones that bordered the river were still half under water. But, he hated to admit it — the volunteers had won the battle.

He complained to anyone who would listen. To him

it was a personal insult. He had thought, hoped, that Jack O'Connell might admire him for making a stand, that he might earn some respect from the big man. That didn't happen. They grew further apart, and a bitterness had set in that couldn't be forgotten. The young man brooded over his loss.

'But I am in the right, we deserve more!' he said to his father. 'It's not fair.'

'Life's not fair — you should know that by now,' his father had said. 'You'll just have to swallow your pride and ask to be taken back.'

'Never, never in a million years. I'll go to one of the beet factories first. They're taking on, I heard. I'll never set foot on the O'Connell farm again.'

Connie sat at her corner desk, typing the paragraph of her daily report on the harvest. She'd spent most of yesterday evening working on bits and pieces, nothing completed, mostly half-written stories and ideas to take to Knockanree and finish if she got any time to herself. She was secretly pleased with the story she'd written about Rivers' quest to find the missing medallion. She'd described Rivers and his people, his time spent in the forces and how that had brought him to Knockanree, to the search.

Fletcher wandered in about noon, just as she was starting to tidy up.

'Here.' She handed him the Rivers story. 'What do you think?'

She studied his face while he read. She knew every twitch of his lips, every flicker of his eye. She knew that a frown wasn't necessarily a bad thing. The one thing she wasn't used to was this. He handed it back to her in silence.

'Well, what's wrong with it?'

'Nothing. Nothing at all.'

'I know that look — there's something wrong with it. Why won't you tell me?'

'It has everything you could want in a story, but I don't think it's suitable for the paper. For a start, it's way too long.'

She tapped her pencil while she waited. She knew him well enough to realise there was more to come. 'Spit it out, Fletcher.'

'It's him. Rivers. The way you describe him. Far too personal. It's even in the way you talk about him. Like he's some sort of romantic hero. You describe him there as "tall, dark and extremely handsome".'

'*Aw*, come on, Fletch, what's got into you? You know you have to lay it on a bit thick to hook the reader. What about the one you did last week — the girl from the Civil Service going to the harvest in make-up and high heels. You made her seem cute and funny instead of pure stupid.'

'I think you've fallen for Rivers. You've fallen and you won't admit it. Not the ice-cold, practical "I've no interest in marriage" Connie O'Connell.'

'That's ridiculous. Why would you say that?'

'I've proposed to you a thousand times.'

'You've proposed to Mrs Quinn in the canteen at least that many times,' she said. 'Not to mention Irene in the pub and practically every typist in the office. But I suppose you're right. I've no intention of marrying anyone, not for a long time.' She looked at the pages in her hand. Perhaps there was something in what he said.

She put the papers into her bag and struggled into her coat. Fletcher didn't move to help her.

'I'll take another look at it. Maybe I overdid it a bit,' she said.

'Couldn't hurt.' He started toward his desk.

'You're still coming on Saturday, aren't you, Fletch? We haven't had a harvest party in Abbeyfield since . . . for a few years.'

'Sure, I'll be there. I might invite Mrs Quinn,' he said with a lopsided grin.

'Well, her husband might object but bring whoever you like. I'm off. I've a train to catch.'

She flew out of the reporter's room without a backward glance.

CHAPTER 27

Knockanree

1946

Abbeyfield farmhouse sparkled in the morning sun. Every inch had been washed and tidied. The previous evening Connie and Rosie decided to risk putting the chairs out in the farmyard and had left the little Child of Prague statue outside the front door. 'For good weather,' they'd said to Rivers, who'd nodded as though he understood completely. Truth be told, neither sister understood the connection between the statue and good weather, but it was something their mother had always done, and it comforted them to carry on the tradition.

Jack and Rivers lingered over their breakfast. Rosie wished they'd hurry up so she could clear those dishes away. She was at the far end of the table kneading the next batch of brown bread. The of smell baking loaves filled the room.

'I never thought we'd do it — honest to God, I thought we'd lose everything,' said Jack.

Rosie could hear the emotion in her father's voice.

'When you look at it now to where it was a few weeks ago, well, it's unbelievable,' said Jack. 'Except for those few pockets down near the river, I think we did very well. You especially, Rivers. You've been a tremendous help to us.'

'Tremendous,' said Seán.

Rosie focused her eyes on the dough. The party was supposed to be just for the volunteers, but her father had invited everyone from the village, all the neighbours, without a thought for who was going to manage it all.

It had been her idea to have some sort of a celebration as a thank-you to the volunteers who had brought in the harvest. She knew it had been a poor harvest, but better than nothing. Her father had dithered, but Rivers said it would be a good thing to show appreciation to everyone who'd helped. Connie jumped in and said it would be a great thing to do. She began making lists straight away. Not that she was there to actually carry out the tasks on the lists, but at least she'd finally arrived. Though she seemed to spend most of her time working. Where was she now? The clickity-clack of the typewriter came from her room upstairs.

She'll be down in a minute saying she's exhausted, Rosie thought. How can she be so tired just from writing down a few words, for God's sake?

The kitchen had gone quiet, even Connie's tapping had stopped. Rosie lifted her head and glanced toward Rivers. Tomorrow he would be gone and would probably never come back. He hadn't found the medallion or the sign, though she'd helped him search every inch of the house and as much as they could outdoors. It seemed it just wasn't there.

There's something in his attitude, she thought. He's going to say something. I just know it. Does he want to stay, or at least return soon? She could barely imagine what life with Rivers would be like. But she knew what life without Rivers would hold.

Connie came downstairs to join the others.

'What will I start with, Rosie? I see you have the bread under control. I'll start washing glasses. I hope we have enough. I could ask Foley if he'll loan us some. What do you think?'

Rosie wasn't listening. There's only one thing for it, she thought. I'll have to tell him. I can't let him just walk out of my life and take with him the only bit of hope I have. I know he cares about me. I know he wants me. Tonight I'll tell him the truth about Tommy. That's the only thing that's holding him back, I'm sure of it. As soon as he realises there's no reason for him to deny his feelings, then everything will be all right.

Tonight, at the party, I'll tell him how I feel.

CHAPTER 28

Knockanree

1847

Mr Carbury let it be known that he had been instructed to convene a meeting of tenants on the next Sunday at noon. He sent messengers to all His Lordship's cottages and farms to say that it would be advantageous for people to attend. There was to be a 'special announcement'.

Long before the appointed time, people began to make their way across the old stone bridge to the field. Tall hedgerows blocked the view to the manor house, but it was a pleasant place to sit and wait on a summer's day. A wagon had been placed at the top of the field as a platform for Mr Carbury to address the crowds.

Lorcan and Annie sat with the boys near the reeds at the river's edge. They watched fish jump and snatch at the flies as the river drifted lazily by. Matt spotted Joe Foley talking to a group of farmers beside the wagon and wandered over to hear what was being said.

'I heard that His Lordship is going to let us off paying

the rents until we get back on our feet,' said one of the men.

'Why? Ask yourself. Why would he do that now when he's evicted so many already.'

'It's not that farfetched,' said Joe. 'It's been in the papers that some of them have written off the debts of their tenants, at least for a year.'

'I've read those lists,' said Matt. 'And do you know what struck me? It was that the lords that wrote off the debt were the very ones that are here on the land with us. The ones that see what's going on around them. The bastards in London couldn't care less. They treat their tenants as a something to be used, just there to work their land and line their pockets. That kind don't care about us. You can forget it.'

At the sight of Mr Carbury, some of the crowd shuffled to their feet. He was helped up to the wagon and seemed pleased to view the people from his elevated position. He raised his arms. Silence fell.

'I am speaking to you today on behalf of your landlord, Lord Marlinton. He is acutely aware of your circumstances and has proposed a most generous solution for you.'

The spirit of the crowd lifted. One man shouted, '*God Bless His Lordship!*'

'Indeed,' replied Mr Carbury. 'I am instructed by His Lordship to offer to any family —' he lifted his head and surveyed the crowd '— family, mind you, not individuals —' he filled his lungs with air again '— passage to British North America on the basis that His Lordship will pay the full travel expenses.'

The crowd began to murmur.

Carbury held up his hand for quiet. 'Also on the basis that the family will pull down their living accommodation, whatever that may be, before they leave.'

The crowd murmured again. Some were pleased with the offer, others muttered that they would never leave their homes.

'Why is he doing that?' whispered Matt to Lorcan. 'Why would he pay to be rid of tenants?'

Noise began to rise from the crowd. They turned to each other 'What does he mean? British North America? He'll pay for the whole lot of us. People began to get to their feet. They pushed nearer the wagon telling each other to be quiet so they could hear.

'There will be provisions on the ships for you, food and water during the crossing, and when you reach Quebec you will be given the sum of two pounds per adult, with the good wishes of Lord Marlinton, for your new life in Canada. If you are willing to enter into this commitment, you must come to see me today and arrangements will be made.'

Matt and Lorcan were standing near Joe Foley.

'Did you know about this, Joe?' asked Lorcan.

'Well, I thought something would happen, all right. You heard about the new law?'

The brothers shook their heads.

'They're going to empty the poorhouses, send everyone back to their landlords to feed them. Make the landlords pay. It's cheaper for Their Lordships to pay passage and get rid of their liabilities than it would be to support them, maybe for years.'

'But they don't know what's ahead of them,' Matt said.

'Know what?' said Lorcan, but Matt was gone.

'C'mon, Joe! After him!' said Lorcan. 'He never feckin' stops to think. He'll get us all into trouble.'

Matt waded through the crowds, unable to bear the look of relief on all their faces. He didn't want to hear hopeful words form on their lips. He was about to pull hope from their hearts, suffocate it, drag away any thought of a new life, hope of a way out, hope of survival. He climbed onto a cart and stood facing the excited crowd.

'*Wait!*' he shouted. '*I've come back from America and I've seen the people arrive from those ships. Many on the journey die from disease and hunger. Often there isn't enough food and water for everybody. Half the people on the ships don't make it to Quebec!*'

'Were you in Quebec?' shouted a man at the front of the crowd.

'No!' he shouted. '*I was warned not to go there. The ships coming in were full of Irish people like yourselves who hoped for a better life but never even made it ashore. These ships are full of disease. Everyone is crammed together, the sick and the healthy together, until there are no healthy.*'

The crowd looked around in confusion, everyone talking at once.

Mr Carbury held up his hand again for quiet. He produced a sheet of paper and waved it in the air. 'I have His Lordship's instructions here to commission a captain and a ship. Your safety will be ensured. You are not being forced to go. You have a choice to stay – if you can pay your rent, you are perfectly at liberty to remain. However, be aware, that the rent is due in November and then again in May. His Lordship will not tolerate non-payment and if you do not meet the terms of your lease, you will be evicted. Be assured if that happens there will be no help to emigrate.'

The murmuring began again.

'*Listen to me, listen! Don't do it!*' Matt called, but his voice was lost in the noise.

'You're wasting your breath, O'Connell,' said Joe. 'They haven't the heart to stay. They'll not get into the poorhouse and the relief work is coming to an end. Even if they could stay for a few months, then what? Out onto the streets. They won't refuse a chance of a voyage into the unknown and a stake of two pounds. That might be enough to get them a new start.'

Matt stood on the wagon and watched as the people began to follow Mr Carbury out past the hedgerows and up the pathway towards the manor house.

That night Matt told Lorcan and Annie about Grosse Isle in Quebec and about the doctor he'd met in Chicago. 'That was when I wrote to warn you not to think about leaving here.'

'We couldn't bring ourselves to leave, not while we still had a roof over our heads,' said Lorcan.

'You heard what happened in Ballinglass last year?' asked Matt.

They shook their heads.

'Joe Foley told me today. The whole village was turned out by the landlord. Roofs pulled from the cottages and the families chased from the ditches they tried to shelter in. Three hundred people,' said Matt.

'But the same thing is happening everywhere.' Lorcan

shrugged. 'You'll be evicted if you don't pay your rent.'

'That's the thing of it. They had their rents, ready to pay. The landlord decided that he didn't want tenants any more, he'd rather turn the land to pasture. The law was on his side. He owned the land, could do what he liked with it. Turned them all out, every man, women, and child. The soldiers ran them off.' Matt waited for the significance of that to sink in before he went on. 'The way I see it, the only chance of security in this country is to own a piece of land. Everything, every single law, is in favour of landowners.'

'You're not telling us anything we don't know already. Hasn't it been that way since before we were born?' Lorcan leaned back in his chair. 'If we're lucky enough to get another long lease, and with the seeds you brought, well, we'll be all right for another few years. There's no point in worrying now.'

'Jesus Christ, Lorcan, will you wake up!' said Matt. 'This is exactly the time to be worrying. Having a lease is no security at all. He can still put the rent up so high that you can't afford it. If not this year maybe the next or the year after that. He can decide not to renew it for whatever reason he likes. You can still end up on the side of the road on His Lordship's whim.'

'Why worry about what might happen in the future when we have no control?' said Lorcan.

'Listen — I have friends in America where I settled — an Indian tribe. They gave me money to bring to the famine relief. When I got to New York, I made the donation.'

'How very good of them!' said Annie. 'Was it much money?'

'It was one hundred and seventy dollars.'

'That's a lot of money,' said Annie, nodding. 'Well, it sounds like a lot of money to me. They would have been able to feed hundreds with that.'

'Yes, yes, I know, they would have. They did, I'm sure. What I'm trying to tell you is that my friends, the Choctaws, gave—'

'Choctaws? Is that their name?' said Annie. 'How strange!'

'Yes, yes, unusual, but what I'm trying to say is that they gave me more than that.'

'Much more?' said Lorcan and he sat up straight.

'Yes, my friend Awachima gave me beaver pelts worth a lot of money. Look, I was able to work my passage most of the way, so I didn't have to spend too much getting here. So with the money from the pelts that I traded and my savings I have nearly eighty pounds. We could buy the house and some acres and have enough to get more seeds to sow in the spring. We could do it.' He couldn't help the grin from spreading across his face.

Lorcan whistled. 'Eighty pounds? Eighty pounds? Are you sure you weren't hit on the head?'

Annie looked into Matt's face. 'What he gave you was to help feed the people, is that right?' she asked in a quiet voice.

'He said it was to "save my people" if that's what you mean.'

'The Choctaw —' Annie stood up '— they gave that to you so you could help the poor starving wretches that are dying on the roadside. You've had that money all this time and did nothing with it? For the love of God, you could have given some of it to those people outside the workhouse. You could have saved their lives. The children . . .' She turned away from them.

'Annie, I have wrestled with the morality.' Matt stood and put his hand on her shoulder. He felt her muscles tense and quickly took his hand away.

She turned to listen to him but would not meet his eyes.

'Don't think I do this lightly,' he said. 'Don't think I can close my eyes and ears to the horrors that are outside this house. I've travelled through the country and I can tell you that what's happening here is happening all over Ireland. This little part of the country is not unique. I know people are dying from want of food, and when winter comes . . . we can't know what hardship that might bring. All I can do is make sure my family is safe, and the people in this house are my family.' He closed his mind to the thought of his wife, alone for almost six months now. 'The only way we can survive is to take advantage of the low price of land and buy as much as we can afford. Then we might be in a position to help others, but for the moment we have to look after ourselves.'

Annie lifted her eyes to his. He could see her distress as she wrestled with her conscience. His heart broke a little at the pain he was causing and was about to cause, but he knew it was the right thing, the only thing. He would have to hammer in the final nail.

'I think Maguire has put in an offer on Abbeyfield,' he said.

Annie put her hands to her mouth and looked at him. He barely heard her say, 'No.'

'That feckin' Maud Sweeney,' said Lorcan. 'She always had a thing about living here, ever since she was

205

a young one. I think she had a fancy for you, Matt. Do you remember?'

'No.'

'Well, you never looked at her, though in those days she was a good-looking girl. I always thought there must have been someone else — but you never—'

'Look, Maguire is making money hand over fist. If he has put in an offer to buy the house, don't you think His Lordship will snatch it?'

'Yes, you're right,' said Lorcan. 'If there are no rents coming in, he'll sell to whoever will buy. Sorry, Annie, Matt's right. We can look to helping others when we're more secure.' He turned back to Matt. 'And would we both own the farm, is that it? You're going to stay?'

Annie sat down slowly. One hand still covered her lips.

'I can supply the money, but I won't be staying around to work the land with you,' said Matt. 'I'm planning on going back to America. Once we get everything sorted here, I'll go.'

'Whatever you want,' said Lorcan.

'What about the children?' said Annie.

Matt glanced at Annie. 'The land has to stay in the O'Connell name. If the worst happens, then I'll come back until Tomás is old enough to take over.'

'That seems fair enough to me. Isn't it, Annie?' said Lorcan.

She said nothing more, just watched the faces of the two men as they continued with talk of title deeds and legalities.

'We'll go to see Carbury tomorrow make an offer, or at least find out a bit more. What do you say?' Matt watched Lorcan's face absorb the possibilities of their new future.

'We'd own the land we work. *Own it*. Imagine that, Annie.'

Annie folded her hands in her lap and wouldn't raise her eyes to look at her husband.

'There is something else that I would ask you to think about though,' said Matt. 'It's like you were just saying about helping people, Annie. There is something else that's been on my mind these last few weeks.'

Annie lifted her head to meet her brother-in-law's eyes.

'The boy, in the workhouse,' said Matt uneasily. 'Do you remember him?'

She nodded.

'I can't get him out of my mind. I thought he was Éamonn, you see. I told him he was going to his mother. I'll never forget the look on his face when I told him I'd made a mistake . . . when he had to turn back into the workhouse and the door closed behind him.' Matt put his head in his hands. 'I have to find out what happened to him.'

'Fair enough,' said Lorcan. 'I don't remember much about the workhouse, only that I thought I would never get out of it alive.'

'We'll go when you come back from seeing Carbury,' said Annie. She seemed pleased that she might be able to help someone after all.

CHAPTER 29

Knockanree

1847

Matt waited in the wagon and watched patiently while Annie quietly issued instructions to Tomás and Seamus. It was a few moments before he realised that Lorcan was talking to him.

'. . . especially turnips.'

'Turnips?'

'Yes, especially turnips. Get as many as you can.' Lorcan smiled brightly at his brother and Matt decided not to encourage a repeat of the one-sided conversation they'd had the previous night when they'd returned from meeting Carbury and an excited Lorcan had become engrossed in explaining the benefits of turnips over beetroot.

'C'mon, Annie, you're making Matt tetchy.' Lorcan winked at Matt. 'Yeh'd think she was going to America, not Kildare town. I can't say I blame the boys for not wanting to go. Too many memories. But I hope you find that little lad and, if you do, well, we said it all last night. We'll be happy to put a roof over his head.'

'You're a good man, Lorcan,' said Matt.

Annie was coming, still calling instructions: 'And make sure you keep the goat tethered. Don't let him stray or we'll never get him back.' She took her place beside Matt and he steered the wagon out the gate onto the bohereen.

'*Don't forget what I said about the turnips!*' called Lorcan after them.

Matt caught Annie's eye and saw the question on her face. They both smiled.

'I don't know why that man's so obsessed with turnips,' Matt said.

The road to Kildare was as busy as the last time he'd travelled it.

'Where do you think they're all going, Matt? The workhouse won't let them in, not unless they're fit for work. And there's not many that look fit for anything.'

'Heading to the ports. There's ships going to America and Canada and England every day.'

'They don't look ready for a sea voyage either.'

'No, they've no idea what's ahead of them.' Matt's thoughts went to Katie McCauley and her family. That feeling of dread began to gnaw deep in his stomach. He worried that in his clumsy efforts to help, he'd harmed them, left them open to retribution. Whether or not Doherty had survived, he had put Katie and her family in real danger.

'Matt, are you all right?'

He was aware of her hand on his arm. 'Yes, I'm fine.' He turned his head to look at her and managed a half-hearted smile.

She patted his arm again. 'I hope you've been happy,' she said. 'Lorcan reads me your letters, but you never say if you're happy there.'

'I'm happy, Annie. Really, I am.'

'You could stay, Matt. Even if we don't get to buy the land, you could still take a tenancy somewhere near us. God knows there's lots of empty farmland.'

'I can't stay. There's someone waiting for me, back there.'

'Oh, I see. I'm pleased for you.' She turned her face from him and studied the flat landscape as though she were seeing it for the very first time.

Matt steered the horse and wagon through the mass of people toward the workhouse. He felt Annie's hand link his arm and hold on tightly. She stiffened in the seat beside him as they edged nearer the door. Crowds still surrounded the workhouse, desperate to get in. The pitiful cries of mothers watching their children grow weak and listless made Annie's eyes fill with tears. Matt would not allow himself look at the huddled crowds, but nothing could keep out the wailing of a child who lost his parents or parents who lost their child while they waited and waited.

He walked around to lift Annie down but as soon as her eyes met his he knew she would not go inside the building. Matt nodded and handed her the reins.

He approached the door and, as he had the previous time, rang the bell loudly and listened to it echo throughout the building. This time the footsteps came quickly. The master let him into the hallway.

'I'm looking for Billy Lawlor. I was here two weeks ago. You do remember, don't you?'

'Yes, I remember,' the master said sourly. 'What is your business with the boy?

'I am here to check on his well-being.'

'The boy is as one would expect. Both his parents have died. The boy doesn't appear to have any other relatives.'

Matt did not hesitate.

'I will take the boy to work on my farm. That's if he is well enough.'

'He appears to be free of fever, but we will see.'

They walked past a steamy washroom where the women worked, laundering the clothes for the inmates. Onwards to the dormitory, the lime-washed walls a poor barrier to the infestation of disease.

Matt saw the boy sitting in the corner, staring at the sky beyond the high window.

He turned at the sound of footsteps, scrambled to his feet and faced the men.

'Lawlor!' called the master. 'This man needs help on his farm. Are you willing to take the job for food and board?'

'Yes, sir,' he replied without hesitation.

'You may go with him now, so.'

'Yes, sir,' he did not move.

'C'mon, lad,' said Matt in a friendly voice, 'there's work to be done.'

'My mother said if anything happened that my aunt and uncle would come for me. I think I should wait for them.'

Matt looked at the master who shook his head slightly.

'Billy, I will leave my name and address with the

master, and if — I mean when — your relatives come looking for you, he will know where to send them.'

The boy hesitated briefly then nodded. He had no belongings to collect and in his bare feet followed Matt down the corridor out into the light.

Outside the workhouse Annie had grown anxious as she waited in the cart, surrounded by the people begging around her. They beseeched her, murmured ingratiating words: 'Will the lady spare a few coppers?' She had brought her purse, filled with farthings, so that she could give something to as many as possible. Even handing over a small amount lessened her unease. The purse was long empty but still the crowds surrounded the cart, bony hands outstretched. Unable to look at the faces any longer she closed her eyes and prayed that Matt would not delay much longer. Her intention had been to look at the grave near the fever hospital, but she feared that if she left the horse and cart unattended it might not be there when she came back. She felt frightened by the wild eyes of the people, and the horse began to move uneasily. She steadied him with the reins and prayed for Matt's return.

She heard the door open and felt relief flood through her when Matt came forward with the young boy. She briefly closed her eyes and said a silent prayer of thanks.

Matt lifted the boy into the back of the cart, took the reins and turned the horse slowly around. The people moved aside but still held their hands out towards them, pleading for a morsel. Annie was ashamed of the relief she felt when they were behind her. It was not long since she had been one of those people begging for a crumb. She tried to hide the tears that welled up in her eyes.

When they were clear of the town, Annie lifted her head and turned to the boy who was looking at her with concern. She rubbed her eyes with the edge of her shawl and asked him his name and his age.

'Billy Lawlor, ma'am. I think I'm ten.'

'You think?'

'I lost count. It's usually my birthday sometime around the harvest, but there hasn't been a harvest for a long time, so I'm not sure.'

Annie smiled weakly and ruffled his dark hair. 'Ten it is, so.'

CHAPTER 30

Knockanree

1946

Rosie struggled into the red-and-white polka-dot dress, aware that her name was being called from downstairs.

'*I'll be there in a minute!*' she shouted back. Let Connie manage the food for a change, she thought as she tried to do up the back buttons.

'You're not wearing that, are you? Where did you get it anyway?'

She hadn't heard Connie come up.

'I *will* wear it. Mam always said that red suited me. You don't recognise it, do you? It's one of Mam's old dresses. The one with the full skirt. I just made it narrower and took the sleeves out and—'

'And made the neckline lower,' said Connie. 'It's too tight on you. You have far nicer things.' She crossed to her sister's wardrobe and pulled open the door. 'There! The nice blue dress is always lovely on you.'

'No. This fits perfectly and anyway I don't want to be

"lovely". I want to be gorgeous and exciting. Do up the buttons for me.'

Connie went behind her sister and roughly fastened the buttons. When she finished, she sat on the bed while Rosie twisted to see how she looked in the mirror.

'What are you doing, Rosie? Why are you making yourself up like that? It's only the neighbours and the volunteers coming. Is there someone you're trying to impress?'

Rosie sat at the dressing table and pinned up her hair. 'You know there is. And what of it?'

'Rivers? I was afraid you'd get carried away. What exactly has he said?'

Rosie put her lipstick down and smacked her lips together. 'He doesn't have to say anything. I can see it in his face when he looks at me. He makes me feel special.' She hooked an earring through her ear. 'Not just special, he makes me feel important. He listens as though my opinion actually matters.'

'Rosie, he does that with everyone. You don't really think he'll ask you to go to America? Are you mad? You can't go off with a man you barely know, and what about Pádraig? What did you tell him about your son?'

'Mind your own business, Connie. I'm not asking for your advice. I knew well what you'd say. I knew you'd tell me to stay here and look after Dad and Grandad. Well, that's all very well for you, off in Dublin having a great time. You don't know what it's like to be here day after day, listening to Dad and the others talk about nothing but the land and the cattle. You don't know what it's like to walk down the street and not have one single person say hello to you. To have your son ignored.

215

To have everyone whispering about you, and sniggering.'

'I know it's hard for you, Rosie, but you don't have a choice. You must see that. It's just the way things are. Anyway, Rivers will never ask you to go away with him. He's an honourable man and he thinks you're a married woman.'

'I'll tell him tonight. I'll tell him the whole truth. I know he wants me. He might be the only chance I ever get to leave here. Don't ruin this for me, Connie, or I'll never speak to you again. I swear it.'

Connie went to the door. 'I won't say anything, but you haven't said that you love him. It seems to be all about what he can do for you. I don't think you're being fair to him. To him or to Tommy.'

Rosie pretended she wasn't listening — she was on her knees searching the bottom of her wardrobe for a pair of high heels. The door closed and she heard Connie's footsteps on the stairs. She stood up and took a deep breath. The pale-blue dress lay on the bed where Connie had left it.

'No,' she said aloud, 'those days are over.'

She smoothed out her dress, ran her hand around the neckline and slipped on the high heels.

'Yes,' she said to her reflection, 'I'd love to dance.'

Rosie went downstairs, out into the yard and called Pádraig's name. She knew that apart from the promise of cake, the party didn't hold much excitement for her son. He came out of the barn, hands deep in his pockets, and kicked a bale of hay as he passed.

'Mam, can I ask Rivers to help me build a wigwam? Why have you got a dress on?'

'It's my party dress. Do you like it?'

'You look different.'

I suppose that's as good as compliments get around here, she thought. 'Do you know where Rivers is?'

They both saw him at the same time, walking slowly back from the fields, head bent, lost in thought.

Pádraig ran to meet him. 'Rivers! D'yeh remember that you were going to show me how to make a wigwam?'

'I do.'

'Well, can we do it now?'

'It will be dark in an hour.'

'Just start it, *please, please*.'

Rivers looked to Rosie. She waited for him to make a comment on how she looked. She saw his eyes take in her dress and waited for a smile that didn't come.

'Can we, Mam, please?' Pádraig hopped from one foot to the other.

'If it's all right with you?' Rosie said.

Rivers nodded.

'Be back before it gets dark,' she said.

Pádraig whooped and ran on ahead toward the small meadow.

Rivers hesitated. 'You look very different.'

'That's what Pádraig said.'

Rivers looked down at his own clothes, borrowed from her father. 'I don't have . . .'

'Why don't you change into your uniform?'

He nodded as Pádraig ran back shouting for him to hurry up.

'I'll see you later,' he said to Rosie.

'Yes, later.'

Through the kitchen window Connie watched Rosie and Pádraig talk to Rivers.

She'll make a fool of herself, she thought. She has no sense whatsoever, never had. And that dress! She couldn't look at her sister, so she turned to count the cutlery for the third time. Connie had to admit that Rosie had worked hard getting all this food ready. Pots of stew and potatoes simmered on the range. The smell of roasting chickens and pork crisping in the oven wafted through the air and out into the yard. Baskets of bread, fairy cakes, rock buns, and slices of buttered tea-brack were ready. Stacks of shining plates and glasses waited to be filled. She'd made it all look so easy.

The sound of volunteers arriving brought her back to the window. Connie watched her sister greet them; she saw how at ease she was. Knew most of them by name, asked after their parents, their children, listened to their answers with real interest. Some had brought girlfriends and introduced them to her with obvious pride. They all wanted to talk with her. She'd never seen Rosie like this, at least not since before Pádraig was born. For the last few years, she'd hid in the shadows, and in truth everyone thought that was for the best. The old Rosie, or at least the younger Rosie, had always been the centre of attention, the younger, prettier sister.

I've always had to put her first, Connie thought. She remembered her mother's warning words when they were little: 'Don't run too far', 'Wait for Rosie', 'Hold Rosie's hand.' All my life I've had to hold Rosie's hand. 'Be careful, mind the baby, mind your little sister.' She did mind her, had slowed her running to match her little sister's pace, checked around the bend in case something was coming. Picked her up when she fell, let her win the race, the game, the prize.

Seán wandered into the kitchen, took a piece of bread and bit into it with obvious pleasure.

'It was a good idea to have the party outdoors, Grandad, wasn't it? We'd never have got everybody into the house. This is much better, isn't it?'

'It is, Maureen, to be sure. Whose wedding is this?'

There was no point in telling him she wasn't Maureen. To Seán every woman was Maureen. 'It isn't a wedding, it's the party for the volunteers, for getting the harvest in.' She looked into her grandfather's eyes to make sure he understood.

'Oh yes, very good.' Seán smiled and nodded. 'I forgot for a minute. Where's me pipe?'

Connie tried again to run a comb through his hair, but he put his hands on his head. 'OK, OK,' she said. 'I give up.' A brief search of the kitchen uncovered his pipe – in his slippers for some unknown reason. He wandered out to join the growing crowd.

He's really getting more forgetful, she thought, but she hadn't time to think about that now. There must be a hundred people there to feed.

She heard the sound of a car approaching. Fletcher, at last, she thought and was surprised at the pleasant feeling of anticipation that bubbled up inside her. Through the window she saw the car turn into the laneway. It was Father Geraghty's car, which came to an abrupt halt as Mrs Beattie, his housekeeper, held onto the door with one hand and a cake tin with the other. Michael Maguire and his mother slowly emerged from the back seat, and all four stood in the farmyard looking around at the chairs and tables, the bales of hay, strings of lanterns and lights from the house to the dairy.

Connie knew they'd all be in for a grilling from the postman and the priest's housekeeper, but tonight there should be enough people around to occupy their interest. Connie straightened her plain skirt and checked all the buttons on her blouse were done up. She stepped out to welcome the guests.

CHAPTER 31

Knockanree

1847

Lorcan returned with a clutch of rabbits he'd snared. Along with the rabbits he carried a circular piece of wood that he'd cut from a fallen bough.

Matt picked up the wooden disc and looked at his brother with raised eyebrows.

'For Éamonn,' said Lorcan. 'I'll carve a cross and his name on it and we'll find a place.'

Annie took the piece of wood from Matt's hands and looked at it. 'Yes, it will be good to have a marker for him.' She kissed Lorcan's cheek.

Lorcan spent many hours working on Éamonn's plaque. He carved a Celtic cross in the centre of the disc and etched Éamonn's name around the edge. When he was finished, he showed it to Annie and Matt.

'Where will we put it, Annie?' said Lorcan. 'We can't take it to the hospital grave.'

'Do you want to put it somewhere in the house?' she asked.

'I don't know.' He looked at the plaque, then at her.

'He was a great one for the small meadow,' she said. 'Do you remember him eating all the blackberries that time. Ate them until he was sick.' She smiled at her husband. 'He wouldn't even admit he'd done it. Remember him standing there, his hands as black as his mouth, and I chased him around the kitchen.'

Matt watched the couple laugh at the memory and he suddenly missed his cabin and his wife.

'There's a fine stout oak tree in the small meadow, near the blackberry bushes.' Annie reached across the table and took Lorcan's hand. 'And we can find a space in the wall near it for a little shrine to the Blessed Virgin so we can say a prayer for him there.'

Lorcan bent his head and pressed his lips to her hand.

The last weeks of August and into September the brothers, Annie and the children worked every day planting the crops that would get them through winter. Especially turnips. They planted the seeds Matt had bought in Kildare, but it was too soon to plant the Indian corn that was being imported since the famine.

He had always sown crops in his small patch of land at home, but it had been a long time since he'd had planted on a large scale, and every muscle and bone in his body complained. Trapping was a more leisurely way of survival he thought. Harsh work, and sometimes fruitless, but it didn't involve as much bending over.

Matt stretched his body and put his hands on his sides. The sun hung low on the horizon and gave the world a rosy glow. Billy Lawlor mimicked Matt's actions, stretched, and rubbed his aching muscles.

'I think that's it for today,' said Matt. 'You run on with Tomás and Seamus.'

'Ah, no,' said Billy and he watched the two boys work alongside their father. 'I'll wait for you.'

They walked back to the farmhouse together in silence. The birds sang their goodnight to the disappearing sun. As they neared the house, they saw the orange glow of lamplight appear in the kitchen window. Matt thought of the cabin far away. The comforting glow in the evenings when she lit the lamp. Was she still there? He could do nothing but wait.

They ate rabbit stew and wiped their bowls with soft fresh bread while they talked of the work they'd yet to do, but it was pleasing to them to contemplate the possibilities of their future.

Except for Annie.

Matt watched her fill two bowls with the leftover stew and put bread into her apron pockets.

'What are you doing, Annie?' he asked.

'I saw some of the Nugents. They used to live on the far side of Knockanree. I saw them look over the hedges to watch the planting. It was only when I went to talk to them that I recognised who they were. They look awful. They're sleeping near the bridge. I told them that if I could spare anything after the evening meal that I'd bring it out to them. They'll be waiting at the bottom of the lane.'

'Be careful, Annie. You know it's against the law to help people who've been evicted.'

'I told them to wait till it's dark. If there's any soldiers around, we'd hear them. I can't turn my back on the Nugents. We've known them all our lives.'

'There might a handful tonight, but what about tomorrow night, and next week. There'll be dozens. How are you going to choose who to save, Annie? Are you going to feed the ones strong enough to make their way to the front or are you going to walk among them and pick the ones who are going to live or die?'

Annie looked him in the eye. 'Matt, I have been in their place. I know what it is to sleep in a ditch with my children and husband clinging to life. If someone had come to me with a bowl of soup, I would pray for them every day for the rest of my life. I would send their name in my prayers to God Almighty.'

'God Almighty doesn't seem too concerned about the people in the ditches from what I've seen.'

'I'm going as far as the bridge,' she said firmly. 'If there's anyone there who needs food, I will give them whatever I have.' She put the bowls carefully into her wicker basket.

Billy came and stood beside Annie. 'I'll come with you.'

Matt looked from Billy's young face to Annie's determined one.

He sighed. 'I'll come too, just in case.'

The sound of the horse's hooves stopped them in their track.

'It's Carbury,' said Matt. 'Quick, hide the basket.'.

Matt opened the door as the land agent dismounted.

Carbury strode across the yard and Matt stood aside to let him in. Lorcan and Annie, a little flushed, stood by the fire. There was no sign of the children — or the basket.

'His Lordship had decided to sell you the house and ten acres at a total cost of eighty pounds.' He sat at the table without waiting for an invitation.

'That's four pounds an acre and forty for the house?' said Matt. 'That doesn't leave us much for seeds.'

'That's the offer — take it or leave it. Those are the instructions I have received.'

The brothers' eyes met over his head and Matt gave the smallest nod to Lorcan. He knew they could just about manage it.

'We'll take it,' said Lorcan and he banged the table with his fist.

'Indeed,' said Carbury. 'I will send the details to His Lordship's solicitors and they will be in touch with you.'

'How long will it take?' asked Matt.

'A couple of months, I should say.' Carbury got to his feet, shook hands with Matt and Lorcan.

They watched him mount horse and ride off into the night.

The brothers hugged and congratulated themselves on becoming landowners.

Annie retrieved the basket of food and, with Billy, quietly left to look for the Nugents at the end of the lane.

It was a Sunday afternoon and Toddy Maguire was enjoying a peaceful few moments dozing in the warmth of the late August sunlight. He had manoeuvred the armchair to that particular spot several years ago specifically to bask in the last sunrays of the day. It was because his eyes were closed that he did not see the rider coming, but Maud did.

The door to the tiny drawing room was flung open and Maud shouted Toddy's name startlingly close to his ear. He jumped.

'Get up, quick. It's Carbury. Tidy yourself up, Toddy, for God's sake.'

Toddy did up his waistcoat buttons and waved away his wife's attempts to brush his hair.

'It's all right, Maud, stop fussing,' he said, brushing crumbs from his lap.

The knock on the hall door froze them both.

'I'll go.' She snapped her fan open. Toddy left the drawing room door slightly ajar and watched Maud twirl her curls before she threw open the hall door.

'Mr Carbury, what a surprise! My apologies. The girl is on her half-day. I don't usually open the door myself.' The fan flapped excitedly. 'Do come in,' she said in the voice she reserved for the upper classes.

Toddy had noticed this accent had emerged at the social gatherings they often attended. The wives of all the merchants and traders seemed to have developed this affliction. Sometimes he hadn't a clue what they were talking about.

Toddy came from behind the door. 'Carbury, come in, come in.' He turned to his wife. 'Claret for our guest, sweetheart.'

The occasional thump from the children jumping around upstairs went unnoticed by Toddy, though several times Carbury looked to the ceiling, as though it might soon collapse on him.

'I felt obliged to let you know that the O'Connell's have made an offer for Abbeyfield and His Lordship has accepted it.'

'But you can't take it! It was a done deal. We shook on it,' said Toddy. He started to pace in front of the fireplace. 'This is unacceptable. How much rent is he willing to pay? Whatever it is I will pay more.'

'It was never a done deal. You were prepared to grab the tenancy of the house with only an indication that you would take it over at some point in the future,' replied Carbury in a cool voice. 'No money has changed hands, no documents were signed. You are no worse off than you were before.'

'I am very much the worse off for this, as well you know.' He lowered his voice. 'I've told Mrs Maguire that we would be the next tenants of Abbeyfield. Everyone knows it's the best farmhouse in the area. She's had her heart set on it for years.' He put his hand to his head. 'She's started packing,' he moaned.

'That was rather presumptuous of you,' said Carbury. 'We hadn't even agreed the rent. You were so sure that His Lordship had no other option that you strung out the negotiations. Well, it's to your own cost now, sir.'

'There must be something to be done about this. Tell me how much are they prepared to pay.'

Carbury poured himself another glass. 'As a matter of fact,' he paused as he sipped, 'The O'Connell's are not extending the lease, they are intent on buying the farmhouse, the dairy and some acres.'

Maguire was incredulous. 'I don't believe it. How could that be? Only months ago they sold everything they had. I know because I bought it all. Then she came back a few weeks ago and wanted to buy it all back. Where is the money coming from? How much? Tell me how much. If I can match it—'

'His Lordship has agreed to sell them the house and the land. As for where the money is coming from, I don't know. I suspect the brother made a small fortune in

America.'

'I knew he was trouble the minute I set eyes on him.? Just my luck that a ghost from the past would appear and interfere in my business.'

'A ghost with gold in his pocket,' said Carbury. 'Indeed, who would have thought?'

The children of Toddy and Maud Maguire hid behind the bannister of the stairs. They dared not move a muscle while the storm raged below them.

'*You imbecile!*' Mrs Maguire lent her full weight to the shout. '*You let it slip through your hands, didn't you? The only thing I ever asked of you. Fool!*'

'Dearest, it was absolutely not my fault.' Toddy was aghast at the accusation, but this was not the time to mention all the other things she had asked of him. 'We have been most severely treated by that blackguard, Carbury. Have a glass of claret, dear. You've had such a shock. Your nerves . . .'

Maud took the very full glass he handed her and sat on the end of the brocade-covered sofa.

'The O'Connells and Carbury are in it together,' Toddy continued. 'I tell you, dearest, we have been duped by that family. What should have been ours has been snatched from of our grasp. It is skulduggery of the very worst kind. I offered him a fair rent for the place, but they conspired to lead me up the garden path.'

Maud Maguire raised an eyebrow. 'And why, pray tell, would they do that?'

'Jealousy, of course, my dear. It's the only answer. He twisted the buttons on his tweed jacket and avoided his wife's eyes. 'Once they found out that it was our family, they couldn't bear to think of you living in that house. Why, they realised at once how much better suited you would be to that house than those pig-swilling . . . excuse me, dearest, my feelings have overtaken my prudence and my frank words may assault your delicate ears, but they are deserving of the utmost reprimand.'

'I should have been so happy there, Toddy.' Mrs Maguire sighed and snapped open her fan again. 'The O'Connells have done us a gross misdeed. I will never forgive them for this. I am wounded. I will take this injustice to my heart, and to my grave.'

The children's ears were to the door. They heard the quiver in their mother's voice. She was in tears and their father not far behind. They too swore they would never forgive the O'Connells for whatever it was they had done to upset their parents so.

CHAPTER 32

Knockanree

1946

Colin Lawlor suspected that he'd had maybe one too many slugs of his father's poitín. He stopped to sit on the low stone wall that surrounded the small meadow. I just need to gather myself, he thought. Just one more swig.

The voices of the boy and the Indian reached his ears before he saw them. The thought of hiding came to him, but his legs felt leaden though the alcohol burned in his veins. He stood up, swayed slightly, and waited.

'Hello, Colin! We're going to cut branches!' called Pádraig, his eyes bright. He went to stand beside Colin. 'We're going to make a wigwam. Do you want to help?'

'Great,' he replied. 'Are you moving into it?' he said to Rivers.

'I'm sorry things didn't work out well for you, Colin,' said Rivers. 'What are you going to do now?'

'What's it to you? I can look after meself.' He knew his words were slurred. 'It would have worked out grand

230

if you hadn't come along sticking your big nose into things that have nothing to do with you.'

'We did what we had to,' said Rivers. He started to walk past him.

The words Colin wanted to say had melted from his brain. When Rivers moved, Colin swung a fist at him. Rivers dodged it easily and caught Colin as he lost his footing.

'I don't think you should go to the party,' said Rivers. 'You've been drinking.'

'I haven't been asked to the stupid party.' He regretted the words as soon as they were out of his mouth. 'Anyway, I'm busy.' He saw the pity on Pádraig's face and felt his small hand on his arm.

'They must have forgot,' said Pádraig. 'That's happened to me a few times. Come to the party. There's loads of food. There'll be enough for you too.' He looked up into Colin's sweaty face.

'I'm busy, I told you. I've things to do.' He pushed Pádraig's hand away and strode off, crookedly, into the fading light.

'Will he be all right?' Pádraig asked Rivers as they watched him disappear down the track.

'He'll feel differently tomorrow,' said Rivers. 'Now we must work fast. The sun will begin to set soon. We promised your mother we would not stay past dark.'

Pádraig listened carefully to Rivers' instructions as he explained what they needed to do. He was glad to have Rivers teaching him how to make something. They worked silently, the boy and the man, each occupied with his own thoughts. They cleared a site near the wall so the structure would be protected from the wind, then walked around the meadow. Occasionally Rivers cut off a young supple branch and watched Pádraig carefully use his knife to sharpen the end into a point as though it were a giant pencil.

'I'll be the only person in Knockanree with one of these, won't I? I'll be able to bring some the boys from school to see it. If they're allowed come.'

'Why would they not come?'

'I don't know. Just not allowed. Mam says it's probably too far out of town for them.'

'I see, yes, that could be it.' said Rivers. He turned away to collect more saplings.

When they had a big enough pile, they drove the pointed ends into the ground to form a circle.

'Tomorrow we will bring some rope to tie them together. Then we need to find bark to cover it,' said Rivers.

Pádraig was disappointed. 'I can start collecting the bark now.'

'No,' said Rivers. 'It's nearly dark. We can do that tomorrow and bring some straw too.' Rivers started to walk in the direction of the farmhouse. '*Come!*' he called back toward Pádraig, who was still standing in the circle of saplings.

'*I'm just going to clear the stones out. I won't be long!*' Pádraig shouted after him.

The sound of fiddles and flutes drifted on the light wind.

'*Five more minutes!*' he called back to the boy. '*Then come to the house! Don't make me have to come back for you!*'

Pádraig finished clearing the stones from the ground and surveyed the flat surface with satisfaction. I can make the floor from hay, he thought. There's still loads of it in the barn.

He pulled the neck of his jumper away from his body and looked inside. I'll fill up my jumper if there isn't a sack around.

He raced along the path till he got within sight of the barn, then crept along its edge until he could slip through the open door. Perfect, he thought. He clearly heard the music from the party, then another sound. Footsteps.

Probably Mam coming to look for me.

He shot up the ladder to the loft and hid himself under the loose hay.

He heard someone shuffle about below.

I'll wait here for a while. Just a few minutes.

But the person below was in no hurry and Pádraig snuggled into the warm hay and waited.

He was asleep when the barn doors at last closed below.

This time there was no mistake — she was certain that the car coming up the bohereen was Fletcher's. She looked at her watch. Can he ever be on time? Connie excused herself from Mrs Beattie's questions and walked toward the laneway. The car had come to a halt further up the bohereen. Serves him right for being so late. Fletcher got out but instead of coming toward her he went to the passenger's door and yanked it open.

Connie heard the giggle as Fletcher helped the blonde curly-haired woman out of the car. She was small and slender and, even in her high heels, barely came up to Fletcher's shoulder.

'Hi, Connie! Sorry we're late!' he called as they neared the gate. 'This is Nuala. You remember I told you we met when we both volunteered.'

'What I remember is that you didn't exactly volunteer, Fletcher, did you?' Connie took Nuala's proffered limp hand. 'You're very welcome, Nuala.'

'I worked extremely hard that day, didn't I, Nuala?'

'Of course you did. Fletcher, remember what I said.' She smiled sweetly up into his beaming face then turned to Connie. 'We have another engagement to go to, haven't we, dear?'

Connie glared at Fletcher.

'I'm sorry, Connie. Nuala wants me to go to meet some of her friends. I'd said yes before I realised it would clash.'

'There, you see, I told you she wouldn't mind.'

Nuala took Fletcher's arm and steered him expertly toward the centre of the crowd.

Connie heard her say, 'One quick drink and then we'll go.'

Who the hell is she to think that I wouldn't mind, thought Connie. She bit her lip. Fletcher just let himself be dragged away. Really! She's not even his type, not at all.

She found her eyes drawn again and again to the couple, unable to quite believe this version of the Fletcher she'd known for years. He seemed besotted with Miss Curly Top. She saw the way he bent his head to catch what she was saying., the way he laughed at her story. I can make him laugh too, she thought. It doesn't bother me at all, really it doesn't. Why should it? We're just good friends. Would Nuala allow a friendship such as theirs to continue? No. She knew, without a single doubt. Nuala wouldn't stand for it — never in a million years.

The band were not really what you might call a band, more a collection of musicians, fiddle and accordion players mostly. Flynn had brought his bodhrán, and others had assorted flutes, tin whistles, and spoons. The group grew and spread by the porch door, and after a few tuning issues they launched into a lively jig. Some of the volunteers gave a loud whoop at the sound and clapped along with great enthusiasm, if not timing. Rosie walked through the crowd with plates of sandwiches. Neighbours and villagers she hadn't spoken to in years returned her greetings a little stiffly, but they were guests of her father and would not dare snub her in his home. She knew the dress would raise a few eyebrows and probably be a topic of conversation in the days to come, but she felt it was a risk worth taking. As the beer and poitín flowed, the mood grew warmer and there was talk of the old times, of gatherings and harvests of days gone by.

'Sing one of the old songs, Rosie,' said a neighbour. 'Sing the one your mother used to love, God rest her!'

Rosie knew the one he meant. Everyone had 'their' song, a party piece, and of course she knew her mother's song. She sought her father's face. He was leaning against the door frame as he listened, sipping from his glass. He nodded, eyes already watery. The mention of her mother's song had swept memories into her heart and tightened her throat. She knew she would not get through the whole thing without help.

Then she saw him. Rivers. She walked toward him and held out her hand.

'You'll have to help me with this, please, Rivers? You know it.' She had heard him play the air on the flute one day.

He nodded, took her hand, and let her lead him to the centre of the crowd. She bent her head so that her eyes would not show the struggle within, but he had already seen the flash of sadness cross her face. He took out the flute and raised it to his lips.

'*This better not be a rain dance, Chief!*' shouted someone in the crowd.

Even Rivers smiled.

The fiddle player started the slow melody. Rivers joined in. He had learnt the air as a child — another melody passed down from Matt O'Connell's time. Rosie began to sing 'The Lark in the Clear Air'. Her voice lifted effortlessly and blended with the music. It was a song of hope and joy and love.

And when the song ended, there was complete silence for a few seconds. Then people said, '*Maith an cailín! Good girl!*' and clapped. A few neighbours old enough to remember her mother singing the same tune tried to discreetly wipe away a tear.

The fiddle player started a jig, others followed his lead and some energetic dancers were soon twirling in the darkening light.

Rosie and Rivers moved toward each other. 'Thank you, Rivers,' she said softly and smiled into his ebony eyes. 'I couldn't have got through that without you.'

'We should help Connie with the food,' he said.

'Yes, we should,' she said and was thrilled by the feel of his hand on her back as he guided her toward the house.

CHAPTER 33

Knockanree

1946

How could I have imagined that I could do it, get through an evening like this without Maureen, thought Jack. I might have managed if I hadn't heard the song. It was like she was just behind me, singing softly into my ear. He blinked hard several times, but it was no use. The tears slipped from his lids, down his cheeks as he searched his pockets for a handkerchief. There seemed to be no escape, people everywhere. He wiped his face with the back of his sleeve, murmured something about checking the sheds then skirted around the edge of the crowd through the small gate at the end of the yard.

He caught a whiff of smoke on the wind. A cigarette? No, more than that. He quickened his step. He could see the haybarn. As he watched a man in a long coat opened the doors and ran inside.

'*No!*' Jack shouted too late and too far away. He heard the whoosh of flames as they met the oxygen.

Jack broke into a run. The man hadn't come out. What's he doing?

'*Jump, I'll catch you!*' Jack heard the man shout.

He glimpsed him through the smoke. The flames leapt from bale to bale but he did not move.

'*Jump!*' he shouted again.

'*Come out!*' Jack shouted and edged forward.

Something fell from the loft into the arms of the man, who wrapped his coat around it. He struggled out toward Jack, face blackened. When he was clear of the door he fell to his knees. A child fell from his coat and landed hard on the ground. He didn't move.

'Oh Jesus, no! Please, God, no!' said Jack.

The man turned the child over and thumped his back. Nothing. He tried again.

A harsh choking cough came from the child.

'*Thank God, thank God!*' said Jack, oblivious to the lines of people who had formed to hand along buckets of water.

Some surrounded Jack and the man and the child. 'That's it, get that poison out of him.' They scooped handfuls of water on his head and face.

'You were just in time, Jack. A few more minutes and you'd never have got him out.'

'It wasn't me, it was . . .' Jack turned to find the man who'd saved his grandson.

The stranger had disappeared.

CHAPTER 34

Knockanree

Winter 1847

The family continued to take soup to the end of the laneway every evening and turned a blind eye to anyone they might find sleeping in the barn.

On a damp day in December the brothers travelled to Kildare together to conclude the purchase of Abbeyfield with His Lordship's solicitor and Lorcan was put on the title deed to the house, the dairy and ten acres of land. There was no talk of celebration, not with the devastation that was evident in Kildare and in Knockanree.

The winter crops they'd sowed flourished and the harvest that year had been good. They even managed a small crop of potatoes, planted more in hope than expectation. The only problem was that they'd planted too few. Lorcan and Matt had many a late night discussing how the sowing would be spread. They'd opted for the safety of the crops they were sure of and risked just one field of potatoes. Their neighbours had planted none at all. Please God that's the end of the blight, they'd said, after they'd waited and prayed decades of the Rosary during the night as they kept watch for the early signs of rot they'd come to dread.

The long, dark evenings weighed heavily on Matt. Although he joined Lorcan in making drawings of the fields and planning the crops for next spring, he was restless. He knew he would not stay to harvest them.

He sat in the corner of the dark kitchen and watched Annie lean over Lorcan's shoulder as he pointed to the different parts of the plan. He saw her eyes shining as she listened to her husband.

Only the weather prevented him leaving now. The winter had come early, and though some ships were prepared to travel in the winter months — foolhardy, he said to Lorcan — he didn't feel comfortable with that idea. Even if the ports on the other side were not ice-bound, the chance of making it safely across the wild Atlantic Ocean were not in his favour.

'I've made that crossing twice now,' he said to his brother. 'I'd be pushing my luck trying to escape the sea a third time. Better to wait till the spring. I'll go in March.'

'Why are you looking out the window all the time,' asked Billy, fear in his voice. 'Is someone coming?'

'No, Billy, not at all. Nothing like that. I'm thinking that it's nearly time for me to be on my way. That's all.'

'I'll come with you,' said the boy.

'No, Billy, you've got to stay here. It's a long, long journey. Lorcan and Annie will need your help with the sowing in the spring. They wouldn't be able to manage without you.'

'But you'll be back, won't you?'

'If I'm needed, I'll be back.'

Lorcan caught the last few words as he came into the kitchen. 'Don't tell me you're still thinking of leaving. Why would you go back there? We did well together this year. We make a good team, don't we? Why not work the land together? If everything turns out as good as it did this year, we might be able to buy a few more acres, build a cottage for you, if you want.'

'And live there by myself? No, thanks. Lorcan . . . I have someone waiting for me in America. I'm married. Her name is Mina. She's from the Choctaw people. My life is there, with her. I'll be going as soon as the weather warms a little.'

'Annie said she thought there was someone waiting for you over there. Why didn't you tell us you were married?'

'I don't know. There are some things I prefer to keep to myself. The world over there is very different to here. A different way of life.'

'Are you trying to tell me she's not a Catholic?'

'She's a good Christian, better than I am. She's better than I deserve.'

'I'll make something for them, for the Choctaws, when you're going. I'd like you to take something with you, for them.'

'All right, but nothing too big. I'm not dragging a set of chairs across the ocean.'

'I'll think of something small. What about a flute? Do they have anything like that? Would they know how to play one?'

'They have pipes, but yes, I'd say they'd like it. If they

don't know how to play, sure, can't I show them?' A smile lit up Matt's face as he thought of Awachima trying to play an Irish jig on the flute.

'Show me some of those symbols you were telling me about. Like the one about your neck there.'

'This one is for protection, but there are others from the time before they were Christians. Here, I'll show you.'

Matt went to the large timber mantelpiece and carved some of the Choctaw symbols: arrows, crosses, animals, and woodpeckers. Peace, friendship, love and happiness were etched into the wood.

Lorcan watched carefully and over the next few days studied the symbols and reproduced them on two flutes he carved from rosewood. When he was finished, he handed one of them to Matt and stood back, waiting to hear his brother's opinion.

'Wonderful,' said Matt. 'Look, boys. Look what your father did. See here, these are the Choctaw markings, and see what he's done? He's put them next to our own Celtic symbols — the crosses, harps and circles. Genius. Lorcan, you must add those Celtic symbols to the ones I carved in the mantelpiece.'

Lorcan smiled and rocked back on his heels. 'I will — I'll do that. Give the flutes a blow, Matt. Let's hear if I got the tone right.'

Matt blew into the mouthpiece, placed his fingertips over the holes and began a soft Irish air that he'd forgotten he even knew.

'I'll need a bit of practice before I can show them how to play it.' He turned away so that they would not see the emotion in his eyes. 'I can't think of anything they'd like better,' he said, running his fingers over the holes and blowing into the mouthpiece again.

Lorcan beamed with satisfaction at his brother's praise and carefully wrapped the flutes in clean linen, ready for their journey.

The winter passed slowly. It was a dark cold time and the stench of death and decay was everywhere. Matt had noticed that there were fewer and fewer bedraggled people walking the roads. He knew that many had gone to America or to England, and those that remained had no chance of finding food or shelter, except what was given secretly under cover of dark. He dreaded going to the barn each morning for fear of what remains he might find in the straw. There is only so much horror that my eyes can take, he thought. The time will come when I can no longer look and stay a sane man.

He became impatient at the slow passing of the days and watched the sky and the earth for a sign that spring was near. He wanted release from Abbeyfield, from Ireland.

Matt sat alone by the dying embers of the fire. He looked around the empty room committing it to memory. It was time for him to leave this place. He knew this was the last night he would sit in this room, knew he would never come back to Abbeyfield. There was one final task to complete before he left. He took out the quill and ink and wrote to his brother.

Dear Lorcan,

It's past time for me to go back to America. I know I should have waited and said goodbye to you and

Annie, but I know, we all know, that we shall probably never see each other again and it would be the hardest of partings. I have left you one of the pipes you made. I will take the other one with me. It will give me pleasure to think of you here playing the old tunes on your pipe while I am teaching Awachima and his family how to play a jig and a reel on the other.

Please say goodbye to Billy for me, tell him I will never forget him. I know you will both do your best for him.

Forever in my thoughts,

Your brother,

Matthew

He quietly pulled the door closed and walked across the yard. As he turned to secure the wooden gate, he stared at the house one last time. A shadow passed an upstairs window. It was either Lorcan or Annie. He quickly looped the rope over the gatepost and turned toward the small meadow. He wanted to say goodbye to Éamonn's cross and then pay a visit to Gráinne's grave before he started his journey back to his home.

CHAPTER 35

Knockanree

1946

Jack lifted the boy and carried him back to the house. Rosie and Connie came running toward him.

Rosie screamed and put her arms out to take him.

'I've got him, I'll carry him!' Jack clutched the boy to his chest. 'Send for the doctor, quick!'

Father Geraghty could move quickly for a large man. He was gone in his car before as Jack reached the house.

The fire in the barn still smouldered and the blackened tin roof glowed with heat. Smoke hovered over the farm like an evil spirit.

After the doctor arrived Jack walked back to the smouldering barn. Helping hands had thrown bucket after bucket of water onto the structure until it cooled and the hissing stopped. The neighbours and volunteers gathered around him. It was a blessing, they said, that many bales of hay and straw had been taken out. If the barn had been piled high, the boy wouldn't have stood a chance.

Jack turned to the crowd.

'Where is he?' he called out. 'Where's the man who got him out?'

The crowd looked around. No one stepped forward.

'We were trying to fill buckets and form a chain,' said one of the volunteers. 'The smoke was so thick . . . the man just disappeared. I didn't see him go. I'm not even sure I'd know him if I saw him again. Is the boy all right?'

'The doctor's with him now — I think he'll be all right. I'll let you know.' Jack raised his voice. '*Thank you, everyone!* There's no more to be done with the barn tonight. Come back to the house. You must all have a fierce thirst. There's plenty of food and drink still.'

He strode away and the crowd began to drift towards the farmhouse.

'How could it have started, though?' Jack paced the kitchen, waiting for the doctor to come downstairs. 'No one was over there. Wasn't everyone in the house or in the yard?'

'Yes,' said Connie. 'Well, I think so. What was he doing in the barn anyway?'

'He was with me in the small meadow,' said Rivers. 'I told him to come home, but he wanted to finish clearing away some of the stones. We talked about getting hay to cover the floor tomorrow. I'm sorry. I should have waited.'

'That explains what he was doing there,' Jack said. 'Could he have started it himself, by mistake? An accident?'

'He had nothing with him to start a fire. It might have

been an accident, or maybe not,' said Rivers. 'But I don't think Pádraig did it.'

'Who would do such a thing?' said Connie. 'Who would put a child's life a risk?'

'Well, maybe he didn't know Pádraig was in there,' said Rivers.

'He? Who are you talking about? Do you know something?' said Jack.

Rivers looked uncomfortable but went on. 'Colin Lawlor was around earlier. He was very angry. He said he'd never forgive you for making him leave his home place.'

'*The spiteful bastard!*' roared Jack. 'He did this and nearly killed Pádraig! Even if he didn't mean to harm him, that makes no difference. If that man, whoever he was, hadn't got there in time this would be a very different story.' He continued pacing the kitchen till he could quiet himself no longer. '*I'm going up there now to have it out with him!*'

'No, Dad!' said Connie. 'It might have nothing to do with him at all. Let the gardaí talk to him.'

People sitting in the yard outside could hear what was being said. As soon as Jack emerged from the farmhouse, they were on their feet. They waited for him to move. He knew they were ready to follow him. They wanted justice done as much as he did, and they wanted it now.

Connie turned to Rivers. 'Please go with him! Please! Before someone gets killed.'

The Lawlors' cottage was just a few fields away and the crowd covered the ground quickly.

Old Sean followed the movement of the crowd at a slower pace. 'Are we in the Corpus Christi procession? I like a good procession,' he said.

Jack led the way with long strides, anger sharp on his face. Rivers caught up with him. Jack didn't slow down.

'Jack, wait. This isn't a good idea. I've seen angry mobs before, in towns across France and Holland after the Germans had left and the Allies took control. Mobs turned against anyone they thought had collaborated. Innocent people will get hurt.'

'Stop talking, Rivers. You said yourself it was him. He's no innocent.'

'I didn't say that!'

Jack turned up the laneway leading to the cottage. The door was already open. Mrs Lawlor watched the approaching crowd. Whatever she was feeling, she stood her ground. She called to her husband to come out. He edged up behind her and watched from over her shoulder.

'I've no gripe with you, Mrs Lawlor.' Jack stopped at the front door. 'It's your son I want to talk to.'

'Talk to?' said Mrs Lawlor. 'And ye need all these with you to talk, do you?' She cast a cold eye over the crowd and stopped at Jack. 'What business do you have with my son? You didn't want to talk to him these last few months. You were willing to pass over him when he wanted to talk, so you and your mob can shag off! The cheek of you coming up here waving sticks and stones. Be off with you now!'

'It's all right, Ma, I'll talk to him.' A dishevelled Colin Lawlor brushed past his parents and came out of the door to face Jack. 'What's going on?' He looked around the crowd of people. Some had trampled through the cottage vegetable patch.

'You know damn well what's going on,' said Jack. 'You set fire to the barn, didn't you, you bastard?'

The crowd murmured and inched closer.

'What are you talking about?' Colin looked toward the farm. The smoke hung in the air. 'I wasn't near the barn.'

Rivers stepped forward. 'You were, Colin. You spoke to me at the meadow.'

'Yeah, so what?'

'You swore you were going to get even,' said Rivers.

Colin frowned. 'Maybe I did say that. What of it? It's a free country.'

'*You nearly killed Pádraig!*' shouted Jack.

'What are ya talking about?'

'You set a fire in the barn. Pádraig was in the loft. He was trapped there. He nearly died.'

'Jesus, no! I didn't go near the barn. Is he all right?'

'No thanks to you. He was saved by one of the volunteers. You're not going to get away with this. You have to answer for it.'

The crowd agreed. A slow murmur and shuffling rippled through the mob as the circle tightened around them.

For the first time Jack saw fear crossing Colin Lawlor's face. Jack felt blood thundering through his ears. He was mad with rage. He felt like a man who could commit murder.

Colin's mother went to her son's side and tried to pull him back through the door. In trying to save her son, her movement triggered a ripple through the crowd. Someone picked up a stone and threw it at the house. Hands reached toward Colin.

Jack was no longer in control. He looked toward Rivers who tried to intercede but was cast aside as Colin was pushed to the ground. His mother screamed for mercy.

A single gunshot stopped everyone in their tracks.

A man in a long overcoat stood at the back of the crowd, holding a revolver.

'*Leave him alone*,' he said. He glared at the faces in the crowd. '*Leave him. He didn't do it.*'

Jack recognized the man as did some of the men in the crowd. The whisper went through the mob — it was the man who had saved Pádraig. But they didn't let go of Colin Lawlor.

Jack went to the stranger and held out his hand.

'I can't thank you enough. You saved my grandson's life.'

'Your grandson?' said the man. 'Is he all right?'

'Yes, I think so. The doctor is with him now.'

Colin Lawlor pulled away from the grasping hands as his mother rushed forward to put her arms around him.

'*Bastards!*' she cursed them. 'You could have killed him. He told you he had nothing to do with it.'

'How do you know that?' Jack asked the stranger. 'How do you know it wasn't Colin Lawlor?'

'I saw who it was. He came out of the barn a few minutes before the fire took hold.'

'Who was it?' asked Jack, looking around.

'Him.' The man pointed at Old Seán.

'*Dad?*' Jack was horrified. '*Dad, were you in the barn?*'

Seán looked around at the crowd, mystified at the sudden attention. 'Maybe. I couldn't find my pipe. I don't know where I left it. Have you got it? Has Maureen put it up somewhere?'

The men in the crowd looked at the old man, then at Jack. They began to dissipate like ghosts in the twilight.

Rivers approached Colin. 'I'm sorry,' he said. 'I think I have done you a great wrong. It is my fault.' He held out his hand to him.

Colin's eyes blazed with the anger of injustice. 'It's not the only wrong you've done me. You took my job, my place, you've left me nothing.' He pushed past Rivers open hand, shouting over his shoulder, '*Rot in hell! Rot in hell, the lot of you!*' Going into the cottage, he banged the door closed.

Rivers stood looking at the closed door for a few moments before he turned away and walked back to the farmhouse. There was nothing he could do.

Jack turned to the stranger. 'Jack O'Connell,' he said, holding out his hand.

'Farrell,' the man replied, 'Tommy Farrell.'

CHAPTER 36

Knockanree

1946

Pádraig sat on the side of the bed while the doctor listened to his lungs through the stethoscope. He didn't seem to be hurt. In fact, he was quite animated. But his voice was hoarse. Rosie could barely understand what he was saying.

'*Mam*,' he croaked, '*it was him!*'

'Who was him, love?' She knelt by the bed, unable to take her eyes from her son's face.

'It was the guardian angel who saved me. I couldn't see him, only hear him. He was shouting '*Jump, jump!*' But then he came nearer, and I could see who it was, and he opened his arms and I jumped.'

'You could see his face? Who was he, Pádraig? One of the volunteers?' She smiled at the doctor over Pádraig's head.

'No, Mam,' he rolled his eyes. 'He was the real angel, the one in your photograph, the guardian angel with the long coat.'

'*Jesus!*' said Rosie.

'Not Jesus. It was the angel,' said Pádraig.

Rosie gripped Pádraig's hand. 'You must have imagined it, son. With the smoke in your eyes . . .'

He shook his head. 'It was him, Mam, honest it was.'

'Oh, dear God,' she said, just as Jack tapped softly at the door.

'Rosie, there's someone downstairs to see you. It's . . . the man who saved Pádraig . . . it's . . .'

'I know.' She got up from her knees. 'I know who it is.'

Connie handed Tommy a damp cloth to wipe his face and hands. Then she gave him a cup of tea and asked if he'd like something to eat. He didn't seem to hear. His eyes travelled around the room as though he couldn't quite believe he was there.

Old Seán sat in his chair by the fireside, blissfully unaware he'd nearly been the cause of his great-grandson's death.

'Maureen,' he asked Connie for the tenth time, 'have you got my pipe?'

'Look, it's beside you, Grandad.'

Rivers sat opposite Tommy. He looked at the overcoat the man wore. 'Army?' he asked.

Tommy nodded but didn't seem inclined to continue the conversation.

'The gun you fired at the Lawlors' cottage, can I see it?' said Rivers.

Tommy took it out of his pocket and placed it on the table.

Rivers picked it up. 'It's a Luger, isn't it? Where'd you come across this?'

'It's mine,' said Tommy. 'I found it.'

'No one is saying it's not yours. I asked where you got it, that's all,' said Rivers evenly.

'Poland,' said Tommy.

Connie saw the way he nervously pulled at his fingers as he watched Rivers handle the gun.

'Or it might have been Germany. It was near the end.' He stood up as though to leave.

Connie went to him and put her hand on his shoulder, pushing him gently back into the chair.

'Tommy,' she said, 'stay where you are. She'd kill me if I let you get away again. You might want to say goodnight to your son. After all, you've just saved his life.'

'*My son? He's mine?*' A huge smile spread across his pinched face. 'I hoped, when I saw him, but then I didn't know if she'd married someone else. I've been gone an awful long time.'

Rivers looked up quickly from the gun. His eyes went from Connie to Tommy. He pushed the gun across the table toward the other man.

'You have been gone a long time,' said Connie. 'She was starting to think you weren't coming back at all.'

Rivers sat for a few moments, then got to his feet and said he would check the damage to the barn.

'I'll see you tomorrow?' he asked Tommy.

'Maybe,' Tommy replied without lifting his eyes.

Connie watched Tommy fidget with the gun before returning it to his pocket. He stood at the sound of footsteps coming down the stairs. The footsteps stopped at the other side of the door. Tommy put his hand on the back of a chair as though to steady himself.

'Come on, Grandad, time for bed,' said Connie.

Seán tried to shrug her off, without success.

The handle turned and the door opened. Rosie stopped to let Connie and her grandad pass. She met Connie's eyes briefly as she closed the door behind them.

Rosie and Tommy regarded each other silently.

'Is it really you?' she whispered. 'You look so . . . different.'

He bent his head. 'I know I look different, maybe not the same man you remember, but it is me.'

His voice was unchanged, but he was not the same as she remembered. The twinkling eyes of the boy she knew were now the brooding eyes of a man with a past, a haunted past.

He held out his arms to her.

She went to him and felt his arms close around her. He smelled of smoke.

'Tommy, I thought you weren't coming back. I thought you were dead.'

He cleared his throat. 'I nearly was, more than once. Is he . . . Pádraig . . . is he all right?' He released one arm to steady himself on the chairback.

'Yes. You saved him.' She hugged him again.

'I heard him calling. Anyone would have done it.' He smiled as he removed her arms from his neck and stood back to look at her properly.

It was she who spoke first.

'Look at you. Your coat is scorched, and your poor hands.' She turned over his bony blackened hands. They were covered in old scabs and welts. 'I'll get the doctor to look at you when he's finished. He'll just be a minute.'

'Don't worry about me. I've been worse. I've seen plenty of doctors since I got back.'

'What? How long have you been back?'

'A few months . . . yes, about three, I suppose.'

'Jesus Christ. You couldn't write a letter to let me know you were still alive?'

'I was in hospital for months, in England and then in St Brigid's in Ballinasloe. I started to write to you, so many times, but I could never find the right words. How do you start a letter like that after six years? I'm not much at letter-writing anyhow. I thought I would wait until I was better, until I was able to talk to you face to face, you know?' He looked at her hopefully. 'I came here and found a party in full swing but when I saw you, surrounded by so many people, I couldn't just walk up and start talking. I didn't know how to go about it.'

The doctor's footsteps registered heavily on the stairs. They waited in silence until he came into the room.

'We'll need to keep an eye on him. He's inhaled a fair bit of smoke and sometimes it takes a day or two to get rid of it, but he'll be all right. His voice will be hoarse for a few days. He'll probably cough a fair bit too.' The doctor nodded toward Tommy. 'Are you the man who saved him?'

'Yes, doctor,' said Rosie, with a smile. 'This is my husband, Tommy. Could you take a look at his hands, please?'

'Yes, of course. Well done. Let me see.'

Tommy held out his hands and the doctor glanced at them back and front, then rummaged in his bag and gave him some cream.

'I'll need to listen to your chest,' said the doctor as he put the stethoscope in his ears.

Tommy hesitated for a moment then removed his coat. The doctor pulled up Tommy's shirt. His torso was riddled with faded red scars and lumps and when the doctor turned him around to listen to his lungs, the same evidence of torture was visible there too.

'I'll check you again tomorrow when I call in to see the lad.' The doctor didn't ask about his scars and Tommy remained silent. 'You should get a good night's rest.' He closed his bag. 'Goodnight,' he said and moved to the door. Then, almost as an afterthought: 'You'll be here?'

'Yes, of course he will. Goodnight,' Rosie answered, and she went to close the door behind him.

'Did I miss something?' Tommy said.

'You could say that,' said Rosie. 'You've missed the last six years.'

'I know, but did I miss our wedding? You told the doctor I was your husband.'

Rosie raised her arms in the air. 'Well, what was I supposed to do? You'd fecked off to England and I was left having to sort out everything . . . the baby . . .' She started to cry. 'I didn't know what to do.'

'Oh, my poor darling!' He put his arms around her.

She pulled away from him and sat down. 'You lied to me, Tommy.'

'I'm so sorry, Rosie. They told me you came to the shop.'

'But why, Tommy? Why would you make that up? You told me your parents owned the greengrocer's, not your aunt and uncle. Why didn't you tell me? I went to see them. They told me you were a prisoner of war. They were awful to me. Well, she was. Called me a gold-digger and said any money due to you would come to them as next of kin. She was horrible. Why did you lie?'

'Because of this.' He waved his hand around the room. 'Because of you. I could see the moment we met that I wouldn't have a chance with a girl like you. I had no one. Well, my uncle and aunt, but you know now they've no time for me. They have their own children. I'm only an inconvenience to them. How could I tell you that I slept in a fold-up bed at the back of the shop? I wanted to impress you, that's all. I wanted you to think I could be somebody someday, otherwise you'd walk away. Well, I thought you'd walk away. That's why I had to join up. I told you the truth about that. I thought I could earn a bit of money to give us start. Though if I'd known then what was ahead of me, I'd have listened to you. If you knew the number of times I swore at myself for not listening to you. But I've paid the price. I'm so sorry. Can you forgive me?' He took her hands in his. 'Tell me about Pádraig. I didn't know who he was, not until your father told me. I couldn't believe it. You must have had an awful time of it.'

Rosie nodded. 'Mam tried to help. She gave me Granny's wedding ring. Said I couldn't be walking around like that without a ring on my finger. You'd be amazed at the difference a gold ring makes. People smile at you and offer you a seat on the bus. It's like a magic wand that changes everything. Dad wouldn't be moved. He said I could never come to Knockanree with the baby, that I had to put it up for adoption. I told him you'd be back soon. I really thought that you'd be back in a few months. The time went on and there was no choice but to go the nuns. Mam began to tell people in the village that I'd got married and gone to England with my husband. Dad was furious, but Mam was trying to help. I'd convinced her that you'd come back and we'd get married and who would know the difference then? So I had to work for the nuns in the laundry to pay off the debt. They said I couldn't leave until the two hundred pounds was paid in full.' She folded her arms tightly across her chest and let her head drop. 'They tried to make me give him up for adoption, but I wouldn't. They were in my ear day and night, saying, "What kind of a life can you give him? How will you provide for the child? He'd be better off with a proper family." I was terrified every minute I was there. Some girls' children went for adoption without the girls even saying they could, but who'd listen? I think the only thing that saved us was Connie and Fletcher. They visited me on Sundays — every Sunday for nearly three years. Brought clothes and presents for Pádraig. The nuns knew that I hadn't been completely abandoned by my family. They knew that there would be questions asked. Connie made sure she told them that she worked for a newspaper. I really think that's what made the difference. The nuns wouldn't take the chance.'

Tommy took out a packet of cigarettes and she took one. He held the match and watched her face as she lit the cigarette.

'So, did you get the money from someone?'

'Mam got sick, really sick. She knew she was . . . didn't have very long. Connie told me Mam begged Dad to let me come with the baby, she said she couldn't go to her grave without seeing me and her grandson.' Tears filled her eyes. She wiped them away with her fingers. 'Dad couldn't refuse her. He was heartbroken. They'd been together more than thirty years. I think he would have done anything for her. Even so, he wouldn't come himself. He sent Connie and Fletcher with the money to get us. You should have seen Mam's face light up when we came, Tommy. It revived her. She lasted nearly six months and, not only that, she was happy. I looked after her, did everything for her. But do you know what the really cruel thing is?'

He shook his head.

'If Mam hadn't got sick, I might still be in that awful place. It was like a terrible trade – my freedom, mine and Pádraig's, for her life.' She smiled a little shakily and Tommy took her hand again. 'Dad said he could see some improvement in her for a while, but it didn't last. Neighbours and villagers came. She was often too weak to see anyone. Sometimes I thought they were really coming to gawp at me and ask me questions. I told them nothing of course. I had the ring on my finger and called myself Mrs Farrell. With Dad behind me it worked. Nobody would say anything to my face, or my father's. But I know by the way they looked at me that they didn't believe you existed. As far as they knew, I'd been in England all that time. They asked me what part I'd been in. They all seemed to have cousins or brothers or someone in every part of the country. I told them that you were working in a factory in Liverpool and with the war on you couldn't get back so easy.'

'You called yourself Mrs Farrell.' His face beamed with pleasure.

'I had to. Mam had told them I was married. I couldn't

let them know she'd lied to their faces. Anyway, it was easier than telling them the truth. None of them had the guts to even question Dad. Or if they did, he never told me. He barely spoke to me at first. But he couldn't resist Pádraig who followed him everywhere. He couldn't sit down without the child trying to climb up into his lap.' She smiled again. 'Dad is tough nut, but Pádraig is as stubborn as him. He softened toward him, bit by bit. Sure, he loves the bones of him now.'

Tommy leaned over and coughed. She heard it rattle through him.

'Are you all right? You don't look very well.'

'It's been a long day,' he said. 'I'm not as strong as I was. I need to rest. I'd better go.'

'Go where? Have you a room in Foley's?'

'No, I brought a tent. It's probably still near the barn somewhere. Don't worry about me. I'm used to sleeping outdoors.'

'Oh Tommy, I've been going on and on, and you haven't even got a chance to tell me what happened to you.'

'It'll keep. I'll go and find that tent.'

'You will not. The doctor's coming tomorrow. You have to be here. I've told him you're my husband. I'll get you some blankets. You can sleep in the parlour.'

He nodded, too tired to argue, and she led him to the parlour. They stood in the doorway, uncertain how they should behave.

He lifted her chin and kissed her gently on the lips. It had been a long time since she'd been kissed. She enjoyed the feeling of his soft lips on hers but pulled away after a few seconds.

261

She whispered goodnight and left.

Rosie knelt at the end of Pádraig's bed and listened to his breathing. She joined her hands. '*Thank you, God, for saving him. Thank you for sending Tommy back to me.*'

For the last six years she'd thought that everything would be all right once Tommy came home. But this wasn't the way she'd imagined it would happen. She'd thought that first there would be a letter from him, then she'd go to meet him in Dublin, in the Gresham or the Shelbourne Hotel. He'd be older and wiser, and better dressed. They would see each other, and Tommy would hold out his strong arms and would hug and kiss her and tell her that she was the most beautiful girl in the world. They would celebrate with bubbly champagne and be the envy of every other couple in the room.

The reality was so completely different — his tired face, smeared with soot, eyes red-rimmed from the smoke. He was Tommy, her Tommy, but not the boy she knew from the past nor the man she would have liked him to be in her dreams.

Tommy had come back and was now asleep in the front parlour. Is it possible? she thought. She climbed into her familiar bed. Where do we go from here? Certainly not for champagne in the Shelbourne.

CHAPTER 37

Knockanree

1946

Connie found Rivers sitting on the gate to the laneway smoking a cigarette. He didn't appear to notice her approach.

'What a night!' she said, climbing up to sit beside him. 'I didn't know you smoked.'

'So that's Tommy?' he said.

'Yes, that's Tommy, all right.' She took the cigarette he offered. 'I only met him once before, briefly. Rosie talked so much about him I feel like I know him well.'

'How come no one recognised him?'

'He was never in Knockanree before.'

'Jack never met him before tonight?' He raised a questioning eyebrow.

'They eloped. They ran off to England. When Rosie realised she was pregnant, she came back on her own. Tommy was already gone to war.'

'Why are you lying to me, Connie?' he asked in a low voice.

263

'What do you mean?' She didn't turn her head to look at him.

'Tommy thought that Rosie might have married someone else. How could he think that if they were already married?' He got down from the gate and stubbed out the cigarette with his foot. 'She's not married to him, is she?'

Connie put the cigarette to her lips and slowly drew the nicotine into her body. 'All right. They're not married.' She looked around to see if anyone was within earshot. 'Don't say that to anyone.'

'Why did you not trust me with the truth?'

'It's not my secret to tell. If she didn't tell you herself then how could I say anything? We just don't talk about it at all. If people here thought she was an unmarried mother she'd have to leave for good. Not to mention the fact that he fought for the English.'

'He fought for the British army. Why should he suffer for that? It was the right thing to do.'

'Look, Rivers, things are very different here. I know you have strong feelings about Ireland being neutral, but you must realise that we've had to put up with a lot from the English for hundreds of years. It goes against the grain for us to hop-to-it when they whistle. Things are better now, a bit better, but for our parents' generation, well, it was their lives, the lives they lived every day. Being able to say no to England was hard fought and hard won. We'll never forget. When Dad heard that Tommy was gone to join the British army, in Dad's eyes he might as well have burned the tricolour. There'll be many places he won't be welcome now. It certainly won't be easy for him, or for Rosie.'

Rivers shook his head.

'Don't shake your head like that! It's true that you know about war, the horror of it. The human sacrifice, blood and guts and marching behind the flag of liberty. Yeah, that's all very well, but Americans don't know what it's like to lose a war, to have everything taken from you, to beg for every little thing. Have your land, your home, stripped from you and foreigners walk your fields, live in your house, spit on you in the street, murder you at will with no consequence.'

Rivers had watched her steadily. When he spoke, she could hear the low anger in his voice.

'I know, and every Native American Indian knows, what it is to lose our land. To have strangers take what was ours and use it as their own. To be kicked and spat at and have our women and children cower in fear. *We know, Connie. Believe me, we know.*'

Connie bit her lip and turned her head, cursing the foolishness of her outburst. She watched Rivers walk away into the darkness. She wanted to run after him, to apologise, but she knew an apology wouldn't be enough. She didn't know what would be enough.

Early next morning Jack was passing the open kitchen window when he heard Rosie and an unfamiliar voice. It took him a moment to realise it was Tommy.

'. . . a few weeks, that's all the training I got. Only fired a gun once, at the firing range. Next thing I knew I was in France driving a truck. A few weeks later we were trapped behind the Germans at Dunkirk, couldn't get to the beach. Only there a month and I was captured, couldn't believe it. I got mixed in with all the Dunkirk lads. We just had time to scribble a message to our next of kin on the Red Cross postcards to say we were all right before the Jerries loaded us onto the trains. Packed us in standing up.' Tommy's voice broke for a moment — then he went on. 'We couldn't sit down, couldn't move, couldn't breathe with the door locked. They threw in some food, bread, I think. Only the ones at the door could get it. Anyone near the back, like I was, got nothing. The longest four days of my life.'

'Oh, Tommy! I thought you'd be all right in a camp. Were they awful?'

'I got moved around to different work camps in Poland. For the last couple of years before the war ended, I was mining coal mostly. Worked in shifts, we did, fourteen hours at a time. I don't know how I lasted. We were hardly fed enough to keep us alive. If they thought we were slacking, they'd beat us. They beat the living daylights out of anyone for no reason. I've seen men kicked to death for stopping work to cough. If they thought a man was sick or weak, they had no hesitation in finishing him off. Work or die. The only thing I had to cling on to in the work camps or down the mines was the vision of you in my mind.'

Jack heard the sound of tea being poured.

'I had this,' said Tommy.

'My photograph,' said Rosie.

'I had it with me when I got captured. I hid it in the lining of my coat. Whenever I was sure I was alone, I'd take it out and look at your beautiful smiling face. Do you know, Rosie, it was only that photograph and the coat that got me through the war? You gave me a dream of a future. The little house, the garden, the food on the table. Us, together.'

'Oh, dear God,' said Rosie quietly.

'Then near the end things got a bit better. There was a change. We prayed it was nearly over, but we had no way of knowing. We never got any news, nothing. They were rattled, though, the guards I mean. They marched us to new camps every couple of weeks. We thought the Russians must be advancing from the east and the guards had to march us deeper and deeper into Germany. About five hundred miles, I reckon. I thought we wouldn't make it, thought they'd just pull the trigger on us. Whenever they'd stop to make camp, I was sure they were going to just finish us off. I don't know why they didn't. Maybe they just followed the orders they were given. We were starving most of the time. If we stopped at a farmhouse, the guards would take whatever the people had, and if there wasn't enough to go round, they took what they wanted first and gave us the scraps. If they had pigs we'd go to their trough and rummage through the slop and eat whatever wasn't too rotten. It was life or death. It's all right. It's over now. The only thing is people say, "Oh, you were nice and comfortable in a POW camp sitting out the war". But it wasn't like that. Wasn't like that at all.'

Jack heard Tommy strike a match.

'I ended up in Bergen-Belsen, about a week before the Americans came and opened the gates. The Germans weren't killing people in that camp by the time I got there. There were no gas ovens. They just left everyone to die of starvation or disease. Rows of us lying there in filth. When the Americans came, they lifted us out and put us in the guards' billets. We were lucky we hadn't been there too long. Most of the civilians were too far gone, couldn't be saved. I was one of the lucky ones.'

There was a pause, and Jack smelt the tobacco smoke

through the open window.

'They had to burn the huts. Hundreds of dead lying everywhere, too many to bury. The living like walking corpses. It was too late for them. Even after the soldiers came and started to feed everyone, they were too far gone. I still see their huge eyes and hollow cheeks.' He paused. 'I don't sleep very well.' Tommy's voice trembled and the cup and saucer rattled again.

Jack had heard enough. Maybe too much. He'd been comfortable in his belief that Tommy was no good. Getting his daughter pregnant and then disappearing without marrying her was the worst thing that a father could imagine. He'd thought he had the right to be angry and he'd nursed that anger over the years until it lived on his shoulders like a comfortable blanket that he could pull around him, confident that he was in the right. He'd taken it out on Rosie. Even when she came back to nurse Maureen, he let her know in a million tiny ways that he was still angry and that she was the cause.

Maureen's death might have been a time for us to come back together, to being a father and daughter but I didn't let that happen, he thought. I never comforted her in the way I did Connie. It went too far, maybe too deep to change. Even found myself snapping at poor Pádraig. Without Tommy Farrell there'd be no Pádraig. That thought brought an ache to his heart. And the fire. Without Tommy, Pádraig would probably have been burned to death. That was reason enough to be in the man's debt. I suppose I'll just have get over it, he decided. That's what Maureen would say.

'I know, Maureen, I know,' he whispered to the air. 'I'll try.'

CHAPTER 38

Cobh, County Cork

1848

Matt stood on the stern deck and watched Ireland recede until it was just a thin dark-green line on the horizon. When he returned his attention to the main deck he found Dixon, in charge of stores, calculating the rations per person for the ships company and passengers. The steerage passengers queued and watched. They were used to queueing. Their eyes fixed on Dixon, who calculated, measured out and distributed food and drinking water and told each one that this was their ration for seven days. Two fire grates were assigned on either side of the deck for the cooking of the food, and there was much argument and squabbling among the passengers over pots and pans and other utensils needed. There was a great deal of jostling around the grates; only when the fires were quenched in the evening did the noise level drop as the passengers returned to their cramped berths below deck.

Matt had paid five pounds for a cabin and food for the crossing. As he handed over the fare, he wondered what Annie would say of this extravagance. He had no doubt that she would have taken a berth below and fed everyone on the ship. He felt guilty, just a little, as he sat at the captain's table and enjoyed the food and company.

On the second day, the passengers began to form a queue again. Dixon shouted at them, *'I told you it was to last for seven days. I told you.'* He flung his hands in the air as the passengers, carrying their bowls and bags, looked at him with blank, wide eyes.

Matt realised that they were Gaelic-speakers, with little knowledge of English. He went to the deck and spoke to them in Gaelic, telling them what the quartermaster had been trying to explain about the rations. The passengers cried and begged for more food. When the captain came from his cabin demanding to know 'What the hell is going on?' Matt explained that most of the passengers would not have understood the English quartermaster's instructions.

'I have to say, captain,' said Matt, 'that even if they had understood the instructions, they are so hungry they would have eaten everything anyway.'

'God damn Irish! Why can't they speak the Queen's English like everyone else? Sort it out, Dixon,' he barked. Then he turned to Matt, 'Eh, thank you for your assistance. Eh, much obliged,' as he disappeared up the steps to the bridge.

Matt and Dixon came to the conclusion that the only way to make the rations last for the duration of the journey was to distribute the portions daily. Matt conveyed this information in Gaelic, and once the passengers knew that food was to be had that day, their good humour was restored. When they realised the amount of food was much less than they had received the previous day, the murmuring began. Whispers went round that they had been done out of their fair share. No matter how many times Matt tried to explain the mathematics of the situation, they did not seem, or even appear to try, to understand. Some turned on Matt for interfering and getting their rations reduced.

The journey stretched before them, but Matt saw each day as a day nearer home. He took his meals with the captain and Dixon and in the evening he walked about the main deck, music and song drifting up from the steerage quarters. Occasionally an Irish person would address him. He realised he was an object of curiosity to the other passengers and they would not believe he was Irish, convinced that he was, in fact, an American. He did not tell them the story of Knockanree, but he did tell them he had travelled in America and had a house and a wife there. They asked him how many more days they would be at sea, convinced that they should have arrived by now. They questioned him about life in the new country. Sometimes he could answer, but often he could not, because they enquired whether he'd ever met this or that person, a relative who'd emigrated in the past. He tried to explain about the enormous size of the new country, the millions of people there. They nodded, but their understanding of America and of what awaited them in New York was scant. He tried to warn them of people who might look to take advantage of them. They laughed this off and told him 'not to be worrying'. That it couldn't be any worse than what they'd come from.

Should I have waited for a ship to Boston? he wondered. He watched the cloudy sky and felt the black sea heave beneath him. Thoughts of his last night in New York came to him and his dreams were haunted by Shay Doherty's shocked face. Did he live? I have to find out. I won't spend the rest of my life wondering if I took a life.

The excitement of drawing close to land and finally docking was short-lived. Even though it had escaped with just a few cases of illness, the ship was to be quarantined for several days at Staten Island. Those with sickness and fever were removed to the hospital on the island, and the remaining passengers and crew were told to remain on board until, eventually, after one of the longest weeks of Matt's life, the pilot came out to direct the ship into the dock in New York.

Matt watched the activity of the people ashore as the harbour drew near. He could see the movement of workers and people milling about the quayside, waiting for news of passengers. He hung back from the sides of the ship and looked for the two-faced men who persuaded passengers to come with them to boarding houses. He studied them, but it was no use. He would not have recognised any of the men from that night.

The crowds on the quayside had thinned out and Matt could not remain on the ship any longer. He negotiated the unsteady gangplank and made his way through the last straggles of his fellow travellers on the quayside. They looked disorientated on their land legs, confusion compounded by the shouting and noise of workmen and crowds of people searching the faces of the new arrivals.

As a group moved away, he saw her. He was sure it was the same girl. Older, but he couldn't mistake that red hair and the way she stood, her eyes watching everything that was going on. She didn't notice Matt. He observed her for a few moments, glad to see she looked much healthier than the last time he'd seen her. Her clothes and shoes were well worn but clean. Her shinning red hair was neatly tied up with green ribbons. As he made his way through the crowd, he saw her move toward a young family and start to talk to them in Gaelic. Her restless eyes passed over Matt, but her face did not register any sign of recognition. He stopped in his tracks, unsure if he should approach her. As he watched, he caught snatches of her voice on the wind.

'Only six pence for a hot meal and a bed, and your luggage will be stored free. You won't get any better than that,' she said, smiling and picking up one of the bags.

The young family spotted a relative running toward them, waving his cap in the air.

They took their bag from Katie and rushed off. Matt tapped her on the shoulder, and she turned to him with a scowl on her lovely face.

'How are you, Katie?' he said.

'Do I know you?' she asked him, unsmiling. 'I've seen you before somewhere.'

'I met you at the docks the day you arrived. We only spoke for a minute or two.'

'It's you! Yes, I remember. That was our first day here, that day. How could I ever forget it?' She looked around the docks, now almost empty. 'It's not safe for you here. I know it was you that killed Shay Doherty.'

'He died? I wasn't sure.'

273

'Oh, he died that night, all right. They tore up the town looking for you. They asked me about you. I told them I didn't know you, didn't know where you lived. It wasn't a lie – I couldn't remember where you said the boarding house was. I knew it was you.' She looked around and pulled his arm toward a shady alleyway. 'How did you get away so quick?'

'Ship. It doesn't matter. Are you all right, Katie? What happened to your father? Is he all right?'

She pulled her shawl around her. 'Me father's grand,' she said and tossed her head. 'Other than the nightmares, he's not got a care in the world. Sure, he spends all day asleep in the bed and all night in the bar drinking the brandy. Even if he were ever sober, I don't think he would be fit enough for a day's work.'

'But if you could leave here, get away from the city?'

'We can't go. We owe too much money to them now. The first night, when Shay Doherty brought us there, we met his brother, John. He owns everything. They couldn't do enough for us. Gave us a cellar to sleep in. We thought it was grand. There was bedding, and we had a bit of dinner and we thought everything was going to be all right. I soon found out they were only out for what they could make from us. Instead of the sixpence they had told us it would cost, they said it was three times that, even for the children, and that we must not have heard right. It was a huge amount out of what me mother, God rest her, and father had saved. I said to me da to just give it to them and we'd move on. I didn't trust them, not an inch. If we'd got away, then it might have been all right, but they got me father a few drinks and played cards with him. I begged him not to play, but he couldn't see the harm and he was happy with the drink and the company, and they slapping his back, telling him he was a great fella. In a few days every penny we had was gone. They'd locked all our bags away and said it cost a shilling a day to mind them. Sure, we didn't have a thing, and no way of making any money and the little ones still had to be fed and clothes got. He said I could . . . work off the debt.' She twisted the ends of the shawl through her fingers and bent her head. 'I have to do whatever he wants or we're all out on the streets.'

'Jesus Christ, what kind of man would do that?'

'Well, if there's ships coming in and I can get a few new people to come with me, back to the house . . .'

'He gets his claws into them, is that it?'

She nodded.

'And if you can't? Get anybody to come back, I mean. Then what?'

'Don't look at me like that. You've no idea how it is. The only way I can help me family is to bring other people. Doherty thought he'd do better with a girl, respectable dressed. He thought the Irish coming off the ships would be more inclined to be persuaded by a smile and a soft voice than the rough ways of some of the other runners. He was right, you know. They look at me and think I must be doing all right to be dressed like this.' She threw her head back. A sore laugh came from her throat. 'They follow me like lambs to the slaughter.' She tilted her chin. 'I'm not proud of what I do, but it's not my fault. I don't twist their arms. It's the only way I can take care of me family. He'll get every penny out of them and then throw them out when they're no more use to him. Sometimes he makes them work.'

275

'Doing what?' Matt was almost afraid to ask.

'All sorts. He has places skinning horses and boiling bones for glue and the like. Horrible dirty work. Some he sets to making that drink he sells in the bar. They're packed into cellars to sleep at night and given a bit of food. Doherty charges them whatever he likes for bed and board. If they run out of money and can't work, then he makes them a proposal. Well, the women. You know what I mean.'

Matt nodded but avoided her eyes. He wanted her to stop talking. He didn't want to hear what was coming next. Though he knew before she said the words.

Her voice dropped even lower, as though she were in a confessional. 'He owns a house.' Her eyes darted from side to side as though the picture of it was in her mind. 'Some girls even younger than me.' She bit her lip. 'I have to go there if I can't get anyone to come from the ships.' She searched Matt's face for a sign he understood.

He nodded.

'I have to keep me sisters going to school. They might get a chance of a proper job in a shop or sewing or something clean and decent.' She wiped her eyes with the corner of her shawl then pulled back her shoulders resolutely and looked him in the face. 'This is the life we have now, sir. This is where we'll stay and make the best of it. Maybe if me mother hadn't died, well, it might have been different, but I'm young and strong and I can see the others right.'

'I understand that, Katie, but would you not all be better getting away from here? What sort of work did your father do at home?'

'We had a smallholding, sir. It was enough to feed us

until the potatoes failed. It's all he knows how to do, handle a shovel, but there's not much call for that here.'

Matt thought for a moment. 'There's farms in New Jersey, maybe looking for help,' he began, but she shook her head impatiently.

'Do you not understand anything? We don't know anybody in New Jersey. We only know the people in our neighbourhood. Me father won't go elsewhere.'

'But you, Katie, you could leave, start a new life.'

Again, she shook her head. 'I told you I can't go and leave me father and sisters here at the mercy of Doherty.' She looked around and lowered her voice. 'There's a lot of evil goings-on here, sir. I would be afraid of what they'd do to him. He owes a lot of money and no way to clear it. And the young ones — there'd be no one to look out for them. I can't walk away from them, sir.'

She was so sure of her words that Matt suspected she'd thought about it in earnest many a time.

The wharf was empty of immigrants now, the deserted ship at rest by the quayside, with no sign of another ship on the horizon. Matt was glad he would not have to witness the charade again. Facing the evening sun, they watched occasional waves lick the harbour wall. It seemed oddly peaceful. Slowly it dawned on him: Katie hadn't managed to persuade any of the immigrants to come with her. He knew what the night ahead held for her.

'Katie,' he said, 'come with me, away from all this. You can find a decent life for yourself and your sisters.'

She smiled. 'You're a kind-hearted man and I'm glad to have met you, but I must be on my way.'

'No, wait.' He took a pound note from his pocket.

277

'Take this — take it to a bank. It's worth five dollars.'

She hesitated, then took the note.

He wrote the name and address of Mrs Jansen on a piece of paper and handed it to her. 'It's the boarding house,' he said. 'There might be work . . .'

She took the piece of paper without looking at it. 'That's very kind of you, sir.'

'Call up in a day or two. I'll speak with Mrs Jansen.'

'I will, of course. Thank you, sir,' she said, but without conviction.

They shook hands and parted, going in opposite directions. Matt walked away but turned to wave. It was too late. She'd already disappeared back into the maze of streets. Back to her life.

CHAPTER 39

Knockanree

1946

'There's nothing like a near death experience to increase your popularity,' Jack had said that morning as more visitors arrived.

Rosie had been tempted to turn them away, but Tommy had taken her arm and said, 'Let the boy have his moment.'

Two nights had passed and things had calmed down. The gaggle of visitors to Abbeyfield bearing cakes and sympathy had subsided for the moment.

Connie took advantage of the quiet and commandeered the kitchen to type up some of her stories. Neat piles of scribbled notes lay in a line along the table. Every now and then she rummaged through them, scratched out lines and pencilled in new ones. She kept the pencil tucked behind her ear.

She was aware of the sound of a car driving up the laneway, and even when it turned into the yard she didn't look up. She already knew who it was.

Fletcher came into the kitchen, white as a ghost.

'I'm sorry I couldn't get here sooner. Is he all right? Where is he?'

Connie poured him a glass of water. 'Keep your voice down. He's asleep, and I've packed Rosie off to bed for a few hours — she's barely closed her eyes since it happened. You can see him when he wakes up. The poor child is exhausted. The coughing has died down now — it was awful to hear him cough and retch during the night — but I think the worst is over.'

'Thank God,' Fletcher flopped onto a chair. 'If only I'd stayed, but . . .'

She looked behind him. 'You on your own?'

'I am . . . is he really all right?'

'He's a bit hoarse but loving the attention. Says the only thing he wants to eat is jelly and cream.' She pulled the page from the typewriter and handed it to him.

'What do you think?'

Fletcher sat and scanned through the article.

'Jesus, you mean the man who saved him was Tommy?' He sat up straight. 'Are you sure it's OK to print that? What did Rosie say?'

'Nothing. She hasn't seen it yet. I wanted to show it to you first.'

He read it again, more slowly.

'It's good, but . . .'

She stiffened.

'I don't think this is a story you can use in the paper. It could cause a lot of problems for Rosie, and your family.'

'Yeah, you're right, I know, but I wanted to write it.

I wanted to see it on paper. Maybe I can use it another time.'

'A very long time into the future. How are they getting on?'

'Rosie and Tommy? They're still a little awkward with each other, but I suppose that'll pass. As for Dad and Tommy . . .' She took the pencil from behind her ear and twirled it in her fingers. 'It's hard to say. I haven't heard them talk except for "pass the salt". Probably not much in common — a farmer and a soldier.'

'It'll take time. What do you make of him? What's he like?'

'Like the weight of the world is on his shoulders. Like he's afraid to talk in case he says the wrong thing. Like the stuffing has been knocked out of him. He's a fish out of water here. You'd think he would talk to Rivers, but he didn't seem to take to him at all. He's going soon, Rivers I mean — in a couple of days, I think.'

Fetcher picked up the glass and sipped, but even that couldn't hide the pleased look on his face.

He put the glass down and looked at the line of paper scraps on the table. He selected one.

'What's all this?'

'Thought I'd have a go a writing some fiction. Well, not exactly fiction. Stories, I suppose, based on things that have happened. I've written a couple already. One is about a woman called Doris — I met her in Parnell Square one day. She was a suffragette, knew Hannah Sheehy Skeffington. I spent the whole afternoon with her, talking about her experiences. I was thinking that maybe I could turn it into a short story. Or maybe a long story. I don't know yet.'

'What on earth's happened to you, Connie? Human interest stories? I thought you were only interested in analysis — facts and figures. Only myself to blame really, haven't I? Should never have bought you that typewriter.'

Connie laughed at the memory. 'And then you had to carry it all the way to Waterloo Road!'

Fletcher stood up suddenly. 'You're not thinking of leaving the paper?'

'Of course not. I have to eat.'

He sat down again and smiled at her across the table. 'That's all right, then. Will you marry me, Connie?'

'Won't Nuala mind?'

He shook his head. 'It was never going to work. I was dazzled momentarily by her platinum hair. But the night of the party she read me the riot act for making a fool of her. She thought I'd only brought her here to make you jealous. I swore I didn't but she pointed out, quite correctly, that I hadn't stopped talking about you from the time I collected her until we got to her friend's house. I didn't mean to talk about you all evening, it was just that every conversation seemed to twist itself towards you. Didn't even know I was doing it — that I've been doing it for years. You're my point of reference, Connie, my centre of gravity, my North Star. Yours is the opinion I look for on everything from the colour of my tie to who the next president might be.'

'But you've be really off with me lately. If I didn't know you better, I'd say you were sulking.'

'Yeah, I'm sorry about that.' He bent his head. 'It was Rivers, the way you talked about him. I began to think you'd fallen for him. I suppose I overreacted.'

'Fletcher, you were jealous?' Connie threw back her

head and laughed. 'I told you why he was here. I told you about the medallion. Did I mention the gift that the Choctaw people gave to Ireland during the famine?'

'The famine? How on earth . . .?'

Connie stood up, took his hand, and pulled him to his feet. 'I'll tell you later. C'mon, I'll take you up to Pádraig.'

He pulled her toward him. 'Connie. If you marry me, I promise I'll never propose to another woman again.'

'Fletcher, that's all very well, but couldn't we start a little lower down the scale.'

'What do you mean?'

'Couldn't we start with, maybe, dinner?'

'We've had lots of dinners.'

'Yes, with half the reporters from the paper. Fletcher, it has to be different.'

'I get it. Like a date, you mean. You want to be wined and dined — you old romantic!'

'I'd call it practical to see how we get on without bringing the latest headline into the conversation. Those are my terms. Take it or leave it.'

'I'll take it. Dinner, Saturday night. And then, will you finally accept my proposal?'

'Fletcher, you've never said you love me.'

'I thought you knew that. Of course I love you. Have done for years.' He took a step back. 'And you. You feel the same?'

'We'll talk about that on Saturday.'

After they'd had lunch Fletcher was in a rush to get back to Dublin — he had a deadline — as usual. Connie worked on her story about Rivers' visit to Knockanree and the

Choctaw's donation a hundred years before. It seemed to have fallen out of the collective memory, but she was determined to bring the story back to life. She said she needed to think and get some air. She put on her raincoat, just in case, and went in the direction of the small meadow. It was mother's favourite place to sit and think and she had a lot to think about. Not only the story she wanted to write — that could wait. What she really needed to be absolutely sure about was her feelings for Fletcher. Sure that what she felt was a good honest feeling and not something brought on from the jealousy she experienced when she saw him with Nuala.

She sat on the wall and twirled a blade of grass through her fingers. I never thought there was a chance of losing him until it nearly happened. If he had fallen for that woman I'd have been devastated. What he said, about me being the first person that he goes to tell, that's the same for me. He's the first person I talk to and probably the only person I listen to. But is that enough, is that love? Who knows? All I feel is that my world without him would be a sad lonely place. If that's not love I don't know what is.

CHAPTER 40

Indian Territory

1848

'All right,' Abe de Boer said, beckoning Matt to follow, 'let's get you stocked up. Here, you will need coffee. And let me see . . .' He ran around the shop putting some supplies together. 'You should have let me know you were coming. I could have got word to Mina.'

'You haven't seen her?'

'Not since before the winter.'

Matt borrowed a horse from Abe and rode out of the Fort, taking the trail toward the cabin. A new moon was rising, but it was still light enough, and he knew the road well. He began to whistle an old tune as he rode along, the gurgle of the river keeping him company the few miles to his journey's end. To home.

He rode for more than an hour in the creeping darkness until, in the distance, he saw a light. He sniffed the air. Smoke? He dismounted and led the horse the rest of the way, keeping to the shadows. The treetops waved in the breeze and night creatures watched him draw near. The door was open, and there was a figure moving inside. He wasn't sure until her voice reached him. It wasn't a song he'd ever heard her sing before, but it was definitely her. She stopped singing and began to speak in her native tongue. She wasn't alone. His heart thumped in his chest.

She was singing the tune again, a quiet, soft song. What is it? Matt thought. He stepped nearer the door and a twig cracked under his foot. The singing stopped. He stood for a moment, then softly called her name.

Her small figure was framed in lamplight as she peered out into the night. He called her name again, but still she waited, her eyes growing used to the darkness. Matt moved nearer the cabin as she came through the door, and he opened his arms for her to fill them. They stood entwined until, out of the corner of his eye he caught a movement in the cabin. She stood back and allowed the child to crawl towards them. She bent to pick him up and turned his face to see his father for the first time.

'Chaytan, this is your father,' she said.

Matt looked from the face of his wife to the face of the child, whose blue eyes shone and reflected the smile of his father.

For a moment Matt thought he'd fallen asleep in the grass on the riverbank in Knockanree. He woke slowly without opening his eyes and became aware of the soft breathing of the body beside him. He released his breath slowly. He was back where he belonged.

He eased himself from under the blankets and went to the window, looking for the waters of the Arkansas River racing past the jetty. There was always something calming about the river, even when it was running fast. He brewed himself some coffee, went outside and sat on the porch and thought about the things he needed to do. First go to see the Choctaw people and tell them of his journey and how their gift had saved many lives. The door opened behind him and he turned, expecting to see Mina, but instead he saw the baby, who regarded him uneasily. Matt wasn't sure how to deal with this little person but he thought a smile would never be the wrong thing. He sat down in his chair and beckoned to the child to come and sit with him. His son toddled unsteadily and clambered up to sit on Matt's knee. They looked at each other with serious faces until one of them smiled and the other found he couldn't resist an answering grin.

Mina came out to find her son and husband dozing in the morning sun. She couldn't take her eyes from Matt's lined face. He seemed to have aged more than the two years they'd been apart. She found a little room on the chair beside them and squeezed into it, sorry that she was waking him, but hungry for his attention.

She started to look in his pockets, causing Matt to laugh out loud and hold her wrists.

'Where is it?' she asked, smiling into his face.

'Where's what?'

'The medallion, the one I gave you before you left. Where is it?'

Matt looked at his wife a little apprehensively. 'I'm sorry. I gave it away in a moment of great need. I've left it at home, I mean in Knockanree. I gave it to . . .' He paused. 'I gave it to someone who needed protection.' He reached into his breast pocket and pulled out a small box. 'But I brought you this from New York. Open it.'

He watched as she opened it. Inside was a chain holding a silver cross embellished with turquoise beads.

Mina's eyes narrowed. 'It's beautiful,' she said. 'But why did you give my necklace to someone else? Was it a woman?'

He laughed quietly. 'A lady, yes.'

'But why?" Her hand tightened into a fist.

'Well, I wanted her to protect someone — and I reckoned she needed all the help she could get.' He smiled and kissed her. 'Let's have some coffee and I'll tell you all about it.'

After a few days they rode to the settlement in Scullyville. As they drew near, the Choctaw people turned from their work in the fields and faced Matt, raising their hands in recognition. They rode slowly, and some of the people followed along on foot. Awachima came to meet them and Matt dismounted and greeted his friend. Loma now had a wife and a child. More and more people surrounded them as they walked toward the chief and elders, who waited quietly. When the greetings were over, Matt sat and told them the story of his journey.

'I travelled across the great stormy ocean to the land of my people. In Memphis I gave your one hundred and seventy dollars in the name of the Choctaw Nation to the Quakers. This has been recorded in writing. It was used to buy the food that was sent to Ireland to be given to those in need. The people of Ireland thank you very much for sending them food.'

He paused while the Choctaws took in this information and nodded in understanding. Matt thought they seemed pleased, but it was hard to tell with these stoical people.

He continued the story. 'I went to my home place and found my brother and his family near to death,' he continued. 'I was able to save my brother and his wife and two of their children, but their other two children I could not save. My brother and his family are now safe and well. They are secure on their own land and in their own dwelling, which can never be taken from them.'

Matt looked at the faces surrounding him, and they appeared to approve. He took the flute from his bag and presented it to the chief.

'My brother would like you to have this. He made it himself. It is his way of thanking you.'

The chief held up the flute so that all could see and there was nodding and many smiles. They passed it around and admired it, tracing the carvings with their fingertips.

'Before I left, I carved some of the old Choctaw symbols for peace and friendship in the fireplace where they gather around. There will always be a place in Ireland that is linked to the people here and you will always be remembered and prayed for in Abbeyfield, Knockanree.'

The chief arose and said that they were greatly pleased with his news and with the marking of Matt's home place with the sacred Choctaw symbols. He examined the pipe and said it would be best left in the hands of Loma. He already knew how to play the pipes very well and would best use the gift. Loma stepped forward and took the pipe as a sign of friendship between the two tribes of Choctaw and the Irish.

Matt, Mina and Chaytan stayed with Awachima and his family for several days. When he was alone with Awachima, Matt told him how he'd sold the beaver pelts for two hundred dollars and that he'd used that money to pay for the farm.

'Is that all right with you, Awachima? Perhaps you would have preferred me to distribute the money among the people.'

'If you had done that, your brother might not have survived. I cannot say that I would have acted differently. In the choice between saving a brother and saving a stranger, who can say what is right?' He looked around at his family. 'If I could have saved my brother, I would have.'

Many times Matt was asked by Choctaw people, who came to sit by their fire, to recount his odyssey to Ireland and the saving of his people. The story of the house of the Choctaw markings in Abbeyfield, Knockanree, was told and retold around campfires by the people for many months and years.

Matt spent hours teaching Loma the melodies he remembered from his youth. Loma turned out to be a good student and he played very well. Matt often thought of Lorcan and Annie when he listened to Loma, and he looked forward to the day that he would teach Chaytan to play.

CHAPTER 41

Knockanree

1946

Pádraig was much better now and the arrival of his father seemed to have brightened his face, though it was still a little pale for Rosie's liking. The doctor had declared him fully recovered but Rosie still watched her son closely, an ear cocked for any sign of a cough. He sat at the table eating mashed egg from a cup, his favourite breakfast, while firing questions at Tommy who considered each one thoughtfully before giving an answer. Everything from 'Did you shoot anybody?' to 'Do they have horses in France?'. Answered 'No' and 'Yes' in that order.

Rosie watched her father gloomily stare out the window. It wasn't raining. Not that it mattered, the harvest was in. A poor harvest it had to be said, but it could have been a lot worse.

She knew he was worried about the meeting with the bank manager next week. She guessed it wouldn't be an easy meeting, but she believed her father would reach some agreement with the bank. She patted Pádraig on the head as she put more toast on the table. Yes, it could certainly have been an awful lot worse.

She smiled at Tommy, hoping he would relax a little. She'd told him her father's grumpiness wasn't because of him, but he didn't seem able to accept that. 'He just doesn't like me, he's never going to like me.' The silences grew and lengthened between them and Rosie tried to fill the emptiness, but she couldn't think of anything the two men would be interested in. Except Pádraig, they both loved Pádraig. Maybe that's enough to start with, she thought. The child's chatter filled the space between them. That and the wireless. She thanked God for the wireless.

This was Rivers' last day. He was to catch the four o'clock train from Knockanree. Tonight he'd be on the ferry to Liverpool. She'd barely seen or spoken to him since the fire. He'd been up and out before anyone else, probably out roaming the fields and searching the out-buildings one last time. Looking for a sign that the medallion was hidden somewhere in Abbeyfield.

Jack cleared his throat. 'Tommy, would you like to take a walk across the fields?'

Rosie kept her surprise to herself and smiled encouragingly at Tommy.

'Yes, I would, sir,' he said. 'But I have to warn you that I can't walk very far, or very fast. Not yet anyhow.'

'Fair enough,' said Jack. 'We'll walk as far as the abbey and back. We can take it at a slow pace. We're in no hurry.'

Pádraig was on his feet. 'Can I go, Mam? Please. I'll be good. I promise.'

Tommy smiled at her. 'Don't worry. I won't let him out of my sight.'

Pádraig punched the air and ran to the porch to find his wellingtons.

Rosie watched her father pull on his jacket then turn to Tommy to help him into a spare raincoat. He produced a pair of wellingtons for him, and when Tommy rolled up his trouser leg, she saw her father turn away from the sight of the scars on his legs. Nobody mentioned them, as though they didn't exist. Perhaps better not to say anything, she thought. It would only lead to talk of the war. Best not to have that conversation. Tommy eased his feet carefully into the wellington boots and the scars were hidden.

Through the window she watched them cross the farmyard and saw her father slow to Tommy's pace. A small sign, she thought. But he's trying. They're both willing to try. She was about to turn away when she saw Pádraig reach for his father's hand. Tommy took it as though it were the most natural thing in the world. Like they belonged together.

Rosie heard Rivers come into the kitchen and felt, rather than saw, that he had crossed to where she stood. Too close. She could feel the heat from his body. She wiped her hands on her apron as she turned to him.

'Are you OK? Have you got everything? There might be some socks belonging to you on the line.'

'Rosie, I wanted to ask you.' He hesitated. He seemed unsure of the right words. 'Are you . . . all right?'

'I'm grand, thanks.' She avoided his eyes. The radio crackled in the corner.

'No, I mean do you think that you and Tommy will

stay together?' He took a breath. 'Look, I know you're not married.'

'Did Connie tell you?' Rosie's eyes narrowed to slits.

'No, not exactly,' he said. 'I want to say . . . I would have said something before, but I realise that it's too late now. Tommy is a good man, but you know there are other choices you can make?' He looked into her eyes and moved even closer to her. Almost touching.

'Other choices?' Her voice had dropped to a whisper. 'No, Rivers, for a woman like me, in real life, in my life, there are no choices. It's very clear what I must do.'

'Are you sure, Rosie?' A beat passed. 'It's a big world out there. You don't have to stay here forever.' He gently brushed a stray hair from her face.

She swallowed hard and felt his hand in her hair, on her neck. She drew closer. It seemed right to lift her head.

Neither of them saw Maguire cycling up the laneway.

'I do,' she whispered. 'I'm sorry. I know I gave you the wrong idea.'

'Why is it wrong? You're not married,' said Rivers.

'In everyone's eyes I *am* married. If I do anything else other than leave here with Tommy then the lie I've lived for years will be exposed to the world. Not only my lie, but my family's, my mother's, God rest her. I'm as tied to Tommy as if we had really stood in front of an altar and made vows. And I want to be tied to him, to the father of my child. There is no other way, Rivers. I'm sorry. I was selfish to have led you on. I was wrong. I've waited all these years for Tommy to come back, but now he has . . .'

The latch on the porch door rattled and Rosie turned quickly from Rivers, her face burning.

Maguire came clattering into the kitchen, took off his bicycle clips and landed his bag on the kitchen table.

'There you are, Rosie, the very woman I've come to see. How is the boy? Terrible thing to happen. I didn't see it myself. I couldn't run to help at the barn, you understand, couldn't leave Mother on her own.' His smiled displayed his tobacco-stained teeth.

'Yes, we were blessed.' She acted as though she was engrossed in the contents of the pot. 'What can I do for you?' she said over her shoulder. She heard voices and through the window she saw her father talking to Tommy as they came across the yard.

'Excuse me,' said Rivers. 'I need to have a word with your father before I go.'

What is he up to? Rosie thought. She watched him through the window, saw him stop to talk to her father and then both of them turned and walked back to the fields. Tommy limped toward the house with Pádraig firmly holding his hand.

She realised that Maguire was saying something to her.

'It's about your son's birth certificate.' Maguire took a single cigarette from his pocket and struck a match on the range. He pulled on the thin cigarette until its tip blazed. 'The school is opening next week and, as I informed you some days ago, we'll need Pádraig's birth certificate.'

'Well, I don't have—' she began.

'Is it all right for me to tell him, Rosie?' Tommy stepped out of the shadows and held out his hand. 'Tommy Farrell.' He smiled at Maguire. 'We haven't met, have we? I'm Rosie's husband.'

Maguire shook Tommy's hand limply, unable to move his eyes from the younger man's face, which bore an unmistakable resemblance to Pádraig's.

"*Dad!*" called Padraig from the porch. "*We have to take our boots off out here!*"

'Yes, in a minute, son. Mr Maguire, we'll be moving soon. I've been ill for a while, but I'm on the mend now. My wife here has been so patient with me.' He put his arm around her waist and squeezed her to him.

'Moving?'

'Yes, to Dublin. I've been offered a job there.'

'Well now, Mr Maguire,' said Rosie. 'if that's all, myself and my husband have a lot to organise.'

'Of course, of course,' said Maguire. 'Can I ask who you'll be working for, Mr Farrell?'

'Guinness. I'll be delivering the barrels. I've experience with that sort of work. I'll start as soon as I've built up a little more strength.'

Maguire stood up to leave. Smoke drifted from his forgotten cigarette. He mumbled something about deliveries and went out the back door, leaving Tommy with his arm still around Rosie's waist.

Rosie saw the look on Pádraig's face. 'Go up and get some dry socks on,' she said before he could speak.

'But—'

'*Now!*'

He frowned and looked like he was about to answer when Tommy spoke.

'Do as your mother says. I'll be up to you in a minute.'

Pádraig thumped up the stairs.

'It's the truth, you know — the job and everything.

296

They're willing to take on ex-servicemen and I can start whenever I'm ready.' Tommy's face lit up with excitement.

'Are you ready, Tommy? Might it be too soon?'

'If I have you beside me, I can take on anything. Do you think we can take up where we left off? We could get married straight away. I know it's a lot to ask. I'm not in as good shape as I was, but I'm getting better all the time.' He stood, swamped in the borrowed raincoat, his heart in his eyes.

She hesitated. She didn't know why. Isn't this what I've wanted, she thought, what I've waited for all these years? She saw his face crumple with disappointment.

He looked away and searched his pockets for cigarettes. His voice shook when he tried to go on. 'So it's no, is it? Yes, of course, it's been such a long time. Things change. People change.' He talked slowly, dragged the words out, stretched the moment, watched her face for a sign. His hands trembled as he lit the cigarette.

Something about the way his eyes had shone with hope went to her soul. His sad brown eyes just like Pádraig's. Just like his son's eyes.

'I'm sorry. I don't know why I hesitated, Tommy. I must be still in shock. But we can't take up where we left off — we've gone way past that. There's our son to consider.'

'Our son, our own family. It's all I've ever wanted,' he said. 'You are all I've ever wanted.' He paused. 'Do you think that you could want that too?'

Rosie smiled. 'Yes, Tommy, I do. We've waited long enough. It's time for us to move on. All of us. Together.'

CHAPTER 42

Indian Territory

1848

Matt had been back in Indian Territory for several months before he sat at the table and began the letter to Lorcan and Annie. Abbeyfield seemed so far away but he could picture Lorcan reading the letter out to Annie and the children. The door to the cabin was open, a warm breeze ruffled the writing paper. He wanted to write of his journey home, of arriving back to Fort Smith, but all of that would take too long to go into.

The page lay open before him. He knew what he wanted to say — to tell his brother about Chaytan. He pictured Lorcan reading the letter, what his reaction to his news would be. He'll worry. He will immediately think I want my share of Abbeyfield. I must make it clear from the start that that's not what I'm looking for.

He gave the wording a lot of thought, and when he was happy he wrote it down neatly on the page. Then he moved on to the favour he wanted to ask of his brother:

'*There is another matter that I hope you can help me with. I have made an error in leaving . . .*'

Matt looked up from the page. A noise outside. A rider was coming close to the cabin. He picked up his rifle and went outside to the porch. He couldn't believe his eyes. Abe de Boer, who hardly ever left Fort Smith, was riding towards him.

Abe began waving and shouting before Matt could even hear what he was saying. Then he heard.

'*Matt! Matt, I have the good news for you!*'

Abe dismounted and took off his hat to use as a fan.

'Calm down, Abe, you'll give yourself a turn.' Matt laughed and led him toward the shady porch, pointing toward the rocking chair.

Mina poured Abe a cup of water while Chaytan peeped from behind her skirt at the red-faced man.

'I got a letter, Matt,' Abe said, pulling off his coat and looking in the pockets. 'Here it is!' He triumphantly pulled out an official-looking letter. 'It's from the US Geological Survey. They're going to survey the Indian territory.' Abe looked at him expectantly.

'So? What's that got to do with me?'

'Oh, ya, ya, I forgot to tell you. When you were away they came to the Fort. They say they would be coming back in a few months to start the survey. They asked me —' he looked around, eyes wide, '— right there in the shop, to recommend a guide.'

He sat back, then realised that Matt still had no idea what he was talking about.

'*You!*' he said, slapping Matt's leg. 'I said you'd be the best person to take them.'

'But what do they want, Abe? What the hell does the

US Geological Survey do anyhow?'

'They look for what's in the ground and on the ground, they measure the river, the hills. They find anything worth mining — gold, silver, copper, you name it. They find all the stuff and write it down so there's a record kept.'

'I don't know, Abe. Could lead to a whole lot of trouble.'

'How could that be? They don't go to mine it, just to find it. It will be good for the Indians to know if there's anything valuable on their land, same as anybody else.' Abe shrugged then leaned forward. 'It's easy money for you, Matt. You just got to take them around. They're from out east, terrified they're going to be scalped in their beds here. They don't know the Choctaws are friendly. Well, sort of friendly. I told them about how you speak the Indian language and know the country like the back of your hand. They sure are keen for you to be their guide. Coming tomorrow, they are. If you won't do it there's plenty who will.'

'All right, all right, I'll take them to see the chief and elders. If they say it's OK with them, then I'll take them wherever the hell they want to go.'

When the US Geographical Survey group met with the Choctaws, the chief agreed to let the surveyors sample and measure the land. Matt explained that they would also look for precious metals and minerals, and Mr Oliver Weldon, who was leading the survey, assured the Choctaws that they would retain rights to whatever the survey uncovered.

It was a larger party than Matt had expected. A total

of nine men. Weldon, the chief engineer, had two assistants who helped with taking the measurements and soil samples. Four labourers drove the wagons carrying supplies: equipment, tents and everything they would need for the months travelling around the territory. There was also a cook and a helper, who had their own chuck wagon and prepared all the meals for the party.

Five weeks into the survey they reached the rich Three Forks lands, the clear waters of three rivers rushing along, colliding haphazardly and separating like quarrelling sisters. It was an area seventy miles from Fort Smith but Matt knew it well — he'd often hunted and trapped here.

Cook had set up camp on the edge of a mixed-oak forest and the smell of cooking meat signalled the end of the working day. It was an hour till sundown. Matt sipped his coffee and absently looked into the white-hot fire. He was thinking about Mina and Chaytan, but a job like this was, as Abe had said, easy money. The labourers were in the process of taking down one of the skeletal wooden structures the surveyors used to gain height when taking measurements of the land areas. Mr Weldon and his two assistants sat engrossed in their work at the large table near the wagons, transferring figures from their notebooks onto graphs and map outlines. The labourers joined Matt at the campfire and poured themselves some coffee. He got along with most of the men, but he tried to avoid Hutchins, who was probably about the same age has him. Maybe if he smiled a bit more he wouldn't have that sullen set to his mouth, Matt thought. He knew the type – a complainer if ever there was one, always checked the plates to make sure he had as much, if not more, than anyone else, always put his saddle and blanket nearest the fire. He was what they would call back home a begrudger. He hated anyone else to have a bit of good fortune. He didn't talk about himself, never said where he was from, and Matt could never figure out his accent.

Matt raised his cup to his lips as he watched Hutchins come toward the fire. He knew there would be words if there was no coffee left in the pot. He could feel himself relax when he saw the labourer fill his tin mug, but the reprieve didn't last for long.

'Is that true what I heard today about the Choctaw?' Hutchins directed his question to Matt.

'Depends what you heard.' Matt didn't raise his eyes.

'You should know. Well, you should know better than anybody.' Hutchins' face looked like he'd just sucked a lemon. 'You being "*married*" to one of them. Is it true that you get to own the land that they own?'

'Something like that,' said Matt.

'I wondered why you took a Choctaw, that's all. I mean why else would you go marrying into them if there weren't nothing in it for you?'

Matt rose slowly to his full height and looked down on Hutchins. 'I think you've said enough.' He tossed the dregs of his coffee to the ground and turned away.

'Maybe she's good in the sack, is that it? I noticed her straight away when we called by your place – she's a fine-looking woman, for an Indian, I mean. I hear them squaws will do anything you want them to. Is that right?'

Matt started to walk away but Hutchins went on.

'I wonder how she's getting along without you in that cosy little cabin you got there on the Indian land. Just her and the boy there now, is that right? Suppose you gotta take care of any half-breeds that they pop out, but there's always the river for that. Not like it's a white kid coming outta them.'

Matt didn't think twice. He swung his right fist straight into Hutchins' jaw and watched him land heavily on the ground. The other men didn't interfere. Matt knelt down beside the man on the ground and pulled him up by his hair.

'*You say one more thing to me, ever, and you'll be parting company with this.*' He pulled back Hutchins' hair by the roots and put his knife to his scalp. 'You got that?'

Hutchins, white-faced, nodded and Matt let go of his hair with a final push of disgust. As he walked away, he rubbed his hand on his trousers to rid himself of the greasy oil from Hutchins' hair. It smelled vaguely familiar. It smelled of apples and bear fat.

CHAPTER 43

Knockanree

1946

Jack and Rivers walked the fields for the last time.

'I'm sorry you didn't find what you came for.' Jack looked across the brown fields and sighed. 'I'll miss you when you're gone. I'll never forget how you helped us. I know I didn't exactly give you a warm welcome, but it was the timing. Everything seemed to be against me.' He took his handkerchief from his pocket and wiped his nose. "I think there's a fear of losing the land bred into us. The land is part of what we are. It holds us together. When things around us start to change and shift, the fear of losing it takes over. People in our lives grow and leave and even die. The only solid thing in life is this land, these fields, and the house. Everything else changes, but these are the furrows that my father and his father before him worked. These fields are the threads to our past and our future. Without the land we're nothing. I know Rosie will probably go now. Connie's life is in Dublin. It certainly isn't here. Don't get me wrong — can't blame either of them. They have their own lives to live. But it makes me wonder what I'm doing all this for, with no one to take over. I bought too much land. Don't ask me why. It was after Maureen died. Maybe I was trying to comfort myself, somehow make up for the loss of her. I don't know. But anyway, I owe money to the bank. I thought I'd be able to repay it this year but I won't. We did what we could with the crops, and it could have been a disaster — we were lucky to get anything out of it at all. It'll be an uncomfortable meeting with the bank manager, but next year might be better.'

They fell into step and walked the edge of the field. The autumn sun shone into their eyes.

'Maybe Pádraig will take over when he's older?' said Rivers.

Jack hesitated. 'Maybe. We'll see.'

'You can get in touch with me, Jack, if ever you need help. I'll come back.'

Jack's smile was genuine. 'That's a comfort to me. I might take you up on that.'

'You're going to need more than my help Jack. You know that as well as I do.'

Jack stood straighter. 'What are you talking about?'

'Colin Lawlor. He knows this land, has worked it all his life. You owe him, Jack. You know you must put things right with him. Especially after what happened the night of the fire.'

Jack growled in his throat and then spat into the nearest bush. 'I'll take on who I see fit. I won't be coerced into taking someone back who went against me like he did.'

'He was doing what any man would do to feed his family. Then he was accused in the wrong. He's owed an apology, Jack, at the very least, and his job back.'

Jack spat again. 'I don't know about the job, but I suppose you're right about the night of the fire.'

'I will come with you,' said Rivers. 'I need to make things right with him before I go.'

CHAPTER 44

Indian Territory

1849

Awachima, Loma and three others made their camp near enough to the surveyors to keep an eye on what was going on but not near enough for the white men to know. Matt knew the signs. He had expected that the chief would send some of the tribe. From time to time over the weeks he caught a fleeting glimpse of one of the watchers, over a ridge or in the meadows of tall grass, but said nothing. No point in worrying anyone unnecessarily.

The group had headed west, and Matt was aware that Loma had watched them set up their new camp, unload their wagons and release the horses from harness to wander the virgin fields. Matt organised the camp then remounted his horse.

'Mr Weldon, I'm heading to those foothills. I'll be back by sundown. Might be some boar, or if we're lucky a wild turkey, in the woods there.'

Matt took off his hat, wiped his brow, and pointed toward the foothills. Anyone watching would not have taken any notice, but Loma knew what that meant. He watched Matt leave camp and was just about to mount his own horse when he noticed another man lead a horse away from camp, then mount it and quietly follow Matt's trail.

Loma followed discreetly at a distance. For two or three miles he kept the man in his sights until they came to a series of stony hills divided by crossing canyons. Loma sought high ground, and when he reached the highest bluff, he caught sight of Matt not too far distant but on the other side of a canyon. He was about to call when he saw the other rider was almost behind Matt. It was a narrow passage around the outcrop and Matt was concentrating on steering his skittish horse around the edge.

Then Loma saw the other man take his gun and fire. The shot went just over Matt's head. For an instant Loma was relieved, then the rocks and stones above Matt began to tumble and Matt's startled horse lost its footing. In that instant everything seemed to slow down: the wild cry of the horse, Matt's desperate scramble to free his feet from the stirrups, the rising ball of dust from the disturbed boulders. He saw Matt release himself from the back of his horse and cling to the edge of the precipice. The horse fell headlong into the canyon. The sound of the animal hitting the canyon floor echoed around the white rocks.

Loma raced back down the track he'd come.

'*You! What are you doing here? Get a rope!*' said Matt.
Hutchins lay down on the very edge of the canyon

within touching distance of Matt, but he didn't stretch out his hand.

'You don't remember, do you, what I told you that night in the alleyway?'

Matt wasn't listening. He focused on the rock he was clinging to. A small rock jutting from the side of the canyon wall. He could feel it moving under his weight.

'*For the love of God, get the rope!*'

'The night you killed Shay. He was only nineteen years old. His whole life ahead of him. Maybe you didn't know he was my brother when you left him to die in the dirt. I swore I'd find you. Did you know there was a price on your head? Well, Katie knew what you were worth to me.'

Matt tried desperately to find a foothold. His fingers gripped the rock. He was barely able to catch what Ike Hutchins said.

'*What the fuck are you talking for? Get the rope, Ike!*'

'Ike's not my name. I invented Ike when I went to see Mrs Jansen. Lovely woman, that Mrs Jansen. Told her I was a cousin of yours and had lost your address. She told me about Fort Smith. A piece of luck arriving just when old Weldon was looking for help. Everything fell into place. Just had to bide my time, and now here we are.'

Matt watched in horror as the other man crawled toward the ledge and picked up a sharp, ice-white stone. Ike leaned over the precipice and hammered the stone into Matt's fingers. The pain was excruciating. His bleeding fingers slid along the side of the rock. He found himself falling backward. He screamed as he fell away from the grinning man on the precipice. It was the last thing Matt heard as he disappeared into the canyon.

CHAPTER 45

Knockanree

1946

The nearer they got to the cottage, the more Jack dragged his heels. Why did I let Rivers talk me into this? he thought. I'm going soft in the head. Apart from the night of the fire, it had been years since he'd taken the trouble to visit the Lawlors' cottage. Never any need to. He saw Colin every day and his mother was in and out to Maureen all the time.

The sound of logs being split came to them as they neared the cottage. Colin Lalor swung the axe rhythmically, splitting the logs with clean, steady strokes. He may have seen the two men approach but made no sign of acknowledgement.

'Colin, can we talk?' said Rivers.

'Talk all you want. I don't have to listen to you, though.' He selected another log.

'Stop acting the eejit and listen to what the man has to say to you,' growled Jack.

Rivers watched as Colin put the log on the plinth.

'I'm sorry, Colin,' said Rivers. 'I know that you have suffered because of my actions, and I hope that you can accept my apology for causing you . . . for the damage done to you.'

Colin leaned on the axe and met his eyes. 'Is that it? You're very sorry, are you? Well, that's of no use to me.' He swung the axe and split the log.

'Well, you weren't exactly blameless yourself, the way you treated the volunteers,' said Jack.

'I lost my job, my livelihood, because of the two of you. Lost everything. I was nearly lynched for something I didn't do. Something you accused me of. As if I would ever hurt Pádraig or set a fire like that! You think you can wipe that out with a handshake?' He shook his head.

Jack looked toward the ruined vegetable patch. 'I'm sorry. I lost my head that night, and I regret what happened. It was my fault, though. You can't hold Rivers responsible.'

Colin leaned on the handle of the axe and looked at Jack. 'That's the first time I've ever heard you apologise for anything, Jack O'Connell.'

'Well, I mean it,' said Jack, aware of Rivers eyes on him. 'And I think we might talk about you coming back.'

'At what rate?'

'The same rate.'

'Well, you know my answer to that.' Colin picked up another log.

'Maybe you can talk about it?' said Rivers.

Colin paused and then nodded. He was a stubborn man, but not stupid. 'Come inside,' he said.

The three men filled the small, gloomy room. Jack took in the meagre furnishings, a bed in the corner and a large pot containing what he thought must be their dinner. It hung precariously over the open fire.

Colin's father was sitting at the table.

'Mr and Mrs Lawlor,' began Jack, taking his hat off, 'I've apologised to Colin, and I'd like to apologise to the both of you, too, for the, eh, upset, the other night. I'll get that vegetable plot put to rights and replace anything that was damaged.'

It was obvious that Mrs Lawlor had been watching at the window and had seen their approach. Several bowls were on the table and she was in the act of slicing soda bread.

'It's in the past,' she replied. 'Sit down and eat.'

Jack was mortified by the hospitality. 'Not for us. No, we're grand,' he said, flustered.

Rivers sat at the table and thanked Mrs Lawlor for the hot soup. She smiled at him and waited for Jack to sit. Jack, abashed, sat down, and took the offered bowl.

Mrs Lawlor sat opposite Rivers and nibbled on a crust of soda bread. 'And what brings you to this part of the country?' she asked him.

'Mam, will you leave the man alone and let him have his dinner,' said Colin.

Jack looked into the thin soup and wondered how it could be considered dinner.

'I came to find something that was left in Abbeyfield house or farm many years ago,' Rivers said, smiling. 'I hoped it would be easy to find, but I have not succeeded.'

'What is it?' said Mrs Lalor. She leaned forward on her elbows.

'A silver medallion — which would fit into the palm of my hand. It was probably hidden, but I'd hoped there would be a sign to show where it is. But I was wrong.'

'A sign? What kind of sign?' asked Mrs Lawlor.

Rivers took a notebook and pen from his pocket and made a quick sketch of an arrow within a circle. 'This sign — which is also engraved on the medallion itself.' He showed the drawing to Mrs Lawlor.

She glanced at it and passed the notebook to her husband.

Mr Lawlor stared at the paper in his hand. 'Colin,' he said as he passed it over to his son.

Colin Lawlor stopped eating and looked at the drawing, then at his father.

Rivers watched the two men keenly. '*You know where it is?*' he said.

Colin hesitated.

'Colin,' said his mother, 'you must do the right thing.'

'Yes, I've seen a carving like this. An arrow in a circle. I haven't looked at it for years — since I was a boy."

'*Where? Where did you see it?*' said Rivers.

'The small meadow.'

'*Can you show me?*'

Colin looked from Jack to Rivers. He stood, lifted the bowl to his lips and quickly drained the contents.

'Oh, all right. Come on,' he said. 'I'll show you.'

CHAPTER 46

Indian Territory

1849

Mr Oliver Weldon and his assistants picked over the remains of the poor meal that Cook had managed to put together. The men around the campfire talked in low voices of the disappearance of their guide. Hutchins had returned to camp in high spirits and said he'd tried his hand at hunting but didn't have any luck. He said he'd seen Matt head toward the hills but that he wouldn't go there.

'Too many places for snakes to hide,' he'd said. 'Headed back towards the river. Tried to catch a couple of fish but didn't have any luck there either. He'll probably be back by morning,' he said, putting his blanket nearest the fire.

They set out at first light, all of them, even Mr Weldon. Hutchins brought them to the place he said he'd last seen Matt, then hung back. He didn't want to be the one to find him. They rode through the winding canyons, steep white stone on either side as high as cathedral walls. They could see something up ahead and as they neared the brown outline, they recognised Matt's horse, his neck broken in the fall. Matt's body must surely be near, but they could find nothing. They left the canyon to search on higher ground, thinking he might have fallen into a small ridge or onto a ledge. But they found nothing of him. Hutchins looked over the edge. He knew where Matt's body must be — he'd watched him fall. But apart from the dead horse marking the spot and some fallen rocks, the floor of the canyon was undisturbed.

'Maybe he's OK. Maybe he's walking back to camp,' said Mr Weldon, without conviction.

They searched for hours, until there was no place left to search. Hutchins was last to leave. 'He has to be here somewhere,' he repeated. He checked over his shoulder frequently as they left the canyon. The other men took his persistence for concern, even though it didn't make sense. Everyone knew there was bad feeling between the two.

They broke camp two days later, having repeatedly searched the area. They took Matt's saddle off his dead horse and packed it with the other supplies before they headed back towards Fort Smith. Mr Weldon would need to recruit another guide for the Indian territory and that was the most likely place to find one.

It took them several days to complete the journey, and when they entered Fort Smith, Abe de Boer was perplexed to see them return so soon. Mr Weldon told a distraught Abe about Matt's disappearance.

'Hutchins is on his way out to see Matt's wife.' Mr Weldon told Abe. 'He's taking her the money he was due, and his belongings. Says he wants to pay his respects to her. He was very keen to be the one to do that. Said he owed it to Matt.'

Sure is a nice part of the country, thought the man known as Ike Hutchins. Yeah, that Matt O'Connell knew what he was doing marrying a Choctaw squaw. Well, now she was all alone, out there in the cabin, miles from anywhere and anyone.

He didn't feel the need to hurry or to be quiet as he rode right up to the cabin. He watched for a sign of the woman. Sweat ran down his back. He took off his hat and bandana and wiped his eyes as he looked around. He'd been here once before when the survey group had met up with Matt O'Connell. He knew there was the cabin and barn and a jetty with a small canoe tied to it. Now, where could she be? he thought. The only sound came from the river. Maybe I'll just go right on in and make myself at home.

He checked his belt to make sure his hunting knife was handy and led his horse to the empty barn, out of sight.

She must be in the cabin. Maybe she's hiding. I like that in a woman. Time for a little fun. He ran his fingers through his hair, remembering Matt's threat to scalp him. He climbed the three steps to the porch and gently pushed the door open.

'Hello, Missy Squaw,' he called. 'I have a message from your man.' He walked into the silent cabin, his knife in his hand. It took a moment for his eyes to adjust, and he could barely make out the buckskin clothes of an Indian across the room. Before he could say another word, the door slammed close behind him. He wasn't alone anymore.

A few days after the survey group returned to Fort Smith, Abe rode toward the cabin by the river. He could smell the smouldering timber.

'*Mina*,' he called, '*are you here?*'

He walked around the remains of the barn and cabin, kicking over the ashes. Everything been burned to the ground.

Maybe this is what the Choctaw do when there's a death. Who knows? thought Abe. He sat on a tree stump, took his handkerchief from his pocket, wiped his tears, and loudly blew his nose. 'I'm so sorry, Matt,' he said to the trees.

He decided it was best not to disturb this sad place. He mounted his horse.

Am I just imagining it or can I smell wild pig? he thought. Must have been an animal caught in the fire.

Abe faced his horse toward Fort Smith and never returned to that spot.

CHAPTER 47

Knockanree

1946

The three men quickened their pace as they neared the meadow. Jack saw Connie standing outside the wigwam.

'Rivers,' she began as soon as he was within hearing range, 'the wigwam is amazing!'

'Colin knows where it is!' said Rivers.

'Oh, dear God! Where is it, Colin?'

Colin pointed to the big oak tree. 'It's there on that tree.'

Rivers rushed over and pulled the brambles away from the tree trunk. 'I've looked already. There's nothing there.'

'It's hidden,' said Colin, pointing. 'It's behind that cross.'

Rivers saw that the top of the wooden cross was fixed to the tree by a single large nail. He pulled himself up on a low-hanging branch to reach its level and found he was able to swing the cross sideways without dislodging it.

Underneath, cut into the bark, was the sign he'd been looking for.

'*It's here!*'

He ran his hands around the cross and the tree trunk, looking for a gap or hole that the medallion might be hidden in.

'*But no medallion!*' He raised his hands, despair and frustration written on his face.

'Rivers, it could be anywhere around — we must keep looking!' said Connie.

'Wait!' said Colin. 'Let me see that arrow again.'

Rivers swung the cross sideways once more.

'Look! Do you see?' said Colin. 'The arrow is pointing over there — to the old shrine in the wall.'

'My God, so it is,' said Rivers.

Colin stood back as Rivers leapt to the ground.

'A shrine — a religious place!' said Rivers. 'There was something about a religious place in Matt's story! Jack, you thought it meant the abbey.'

'And it was always told in our family that the shrine in the small meadow would protect us,' said Colin quietly.

They all gathered around the shrine.

'You can't touch that,' said Connie. 'It would be a sin to disturb the Virgin Mary.'

'A woman,' said Rivers. 'He said he gave it to a woman, for protection.'

The three men knelt in front of the statue in its recess and swept away the dead leaves around its base. The Virgin Mary smiled steadily from her cracked face. The men exchanged glances, not sure who should make the move.

'Maureen wouldn't like me moving the statue,' said Jack. 'I don't think I want to touch it.'

Connie knelt beside them, made the Sign of the Cross, and apologised aloud to the Blessed Virgin. She reached in and gently lifted the statue, laying it carefully on the grass at her feet.

Jack removed the flat round stone that had supported the statue for a hundred years. Beneath it was a small hollow between the stones of the wall and in the hollow was a soft leather pouch.

As Jack handed it to Rivers, he felt the weight of something inside it.

Their eyes met.

Rivers pulled open the leather string threaded through the pouch and emptied the silver medallion into the palm of his hand. The silver had tarnished a little but the arrow was visible.

'I can't believe it,' said Connie.

Rivers brought it to his lips and kissed it.

'C'mon,' said Jack. 'This calls for a drink!'

On an impulse, Connie put her hand on Rivers' arm. 'I'm sorry, Rivers, for what I said, and didn't say. I hope you can forgive me.'

Rivers picked her up and swung her around. 'Today I can forgive everybody everything.'

When he put her down, he looked more carefully at the medallion. One side had the arrow within the circle. The other side was smooth.

'*But there is no map! Look!*'

He held it out to them. Disbelief in his eyes. He rang his fingers across the smooth surface.

Connie took the medallion from him. 'It's very

tarnished. Maybe when we clean it up it will show the map.' She ran her fingertip across the surface. She could feel nothing.

'Is that not what you wanted?' Colin asked.

'Yes, it is,' said Rivers. 'Thank you for your help. I just expected more. Perhaps the story was not completely correct.'

Colin declined the offer of a drink and returned to his family's cottage. Before he left, Jack asked if he could come to see him later. They still had things to talk about.

Rivers, Jack and Connie started back down the pathway toward the farmhouse. Connie carried the small statue of the Virgin Mary, meaning to wash some of the dirt from it. They walked toward the farmhouse in high spirits, eager to share the story with the others.

They came down the lane past the blackened barn and saw the horse and cart in the yard. Beside it, Rosie and Tommy were engrossed in conversation.

Jack saw the embrace. Then the kiss.

'Well, I suppose that's to be expected,' he said.

Connie watched Rivers from the corner of her eye. He didn't appear to notice the kiss.

When they got to the house, Pádraig and Seán were in the kitchen.

'Where have you all been?' said Pádraig indignantly. 'I was looking for ye! And what are you doing with Éamonn's statue?'

'Look what we've found, Pádraig,' said Rivers, putting the medallion on the kitchen table.

'Your treasure!'

'Yes, the Virgin Mary was minding it,' said Connie as she placed the statue on the table.

Jack told Rosie, Tommy and a wide-eyed Pádraig how they had found it.

'Rosie, where's the stuff for cleaning silver?' said Connie.

Rosie brought what was needed and, sitting at the table, opened the bottle of cleaning liquid. Dabbing some onto a cloth, she rubbed it into the blackened silver.

They all watched intently, waiting for the map to appear.

Rosie lay the silver circle on the table. The reverse side gleamed without a mark.

'*Aw!* No map!' said Pádraig.

Rivers picked it up and examined it.

'Thank you, Rosie,' he said. 'It's beautiful but I'd hoped for more. I will bring it back to the elders. They will be disappointed. They were so sure there was a map.'

'Why did you bring the statue here, Connie?' said Rosie.

'She looks like she needs a bath. Seemed the least we can do,' said Connie.

'Is that the pouch the medallion was in?' Rosie picked it up. 'That could do with a wash as well.' She pulled at the stiffened leather strings holding it together.

'Be careful, Rosie, it's coming apart,' said Connie. 'I don't think you can wash something like that.'

But, as Rosie tugged at the withered leather, the pouch opened out to a square patch of cloth.

'*Rivers!*' she said. '*Look!*'

He bent over the table. '*The map.*'

The inside of the pouch had ink markings. Long and

short lines, wavy lines, squares, arrowheads and crosses.

'It looks like a drawing of a town.' Connie pointed. 'That wavy line looks like a river. Where do you think it is?'

Rivers stared at the map. 'I don't know. I can't say exactly where, but the crosses could mean it's a burial ground.' He looked up at Rosie. 'I didn't think to look inside. Thank you.'

The clock in the hall struck two.

'I must leave soon,' said Rivers, 'but there is something else that I need tell you. I'm sorry, I should have told you sooner.' He sat at the table. With both hands he indicated the other chairs. 'Please sit down, all of you.'

They sat, Pádraig on Rosie's lap. All stared at Rivers, waiting.

He turned to Old Seán. 'Your grandfather, the man who made the flutes, his name was Lorcan, yes?'

'Yes,' said Seán. 'That's right, Lorcan was his name.'

Rivers produced an old tobacco tin from his inside pocket and carefully placed it in the centre of the table. Some of the green paint had eroded, and the corners bore the signs of rust.

Jack raised his eyebrows.

'Open it,' said Rivers.

Jack leaned in an picked up the faded green-and-silver tin. He prised open the lid and turned out the contents. A letter fell onto the table.

'Matt O'Connell wrote this to his brother, Lorcan,' said Rivers. 'It was not sent. I give it to you now.'

Jack leaned over the yellowed paper and read the words "*To Lorcan O'Connell, Abbeyfield*".

'It came to light very recently,' Rivers went on. 'When some of our burial grounds were . . . appropriated. We moved the remains to a new site, and it was at that time that this was uncovered. It's what led me here.'

It looked old, the edges a little frayed. Rosie could see an inky fingerprint on the corner of the thick paper. The writing was faded but legible.

Jack took his glasses from his pocket. As his fingers reached toward the page, he paused.

'Why wasn't it sent?' said Jack.

'We don't know why it was not sent then, but it is here now,' said Rivers. 'We can only guess that he died before it was complete.'

The letter lay on the table between them, the lines made by the original folds were embedded into the paper. Her father's eyes were glued to the unsent letter.

He's afraid of what's in it, I know, Rosie thought. She knew her father's face better than her own, knew what every line and twitch and flicker of an eyelid meant.

Jack unfolded the page. It smelled faintly of tobacco.

Rosie shivered though sunbeams sliced through the room.

They waited while Jack read.

Seán banged his stick on the floor. 'Out loud, Jack, for the love of God!'

Jack looked up. He began again.

Dear Lorcan,

I have returned safely to the Choctaw people and they are greatly heartened to hear that you are all well. They are pleased with the pipe, especially the carving on it. I've told them that I've made Choctaw carvings in the hearth of Abbeyfield and they feel we are bonded by this.

Lorcan, when I returned to Indian Territory I found that Mina had given me a son. We have named him Chaytan. You may be worried that I now expect my son to have a share in Abbeyfield. Our agreement was that Seamus and Tomás would inherit, and I will not go back on my word. I know that if my son ever visits Knockanree you will welcome him into your family.

There is another matter that I hope you can help me with. I have made an error in leaving

Her father turned the page over. Only Lorcan O'Connell's name and Abbeyfield were neatly written on it.

'What does it mean?' said Jack. He scanned the page again. 'It isn't finished.'

'He said he made a mistake in leaving. Did he mean leaving here or leaving America?' said Rosie.

'We don't know,' said Rivers. 'I suspect he meant he'd made an error by leaving the medallion but we'll never know. The reason I'm showing this to you is that you said I came as a stranger. But that's not completely true.'

'Well, it was true when you came,' said Jack.

'There is a reason that I am here, a reason besides the medallion.'

'Well, spit it out.'

Rivers pushed the letter back toward Jack. 'There is a reason that I have the letter, a reason that it was I who came to Abbeyfield. Read it again, Jack. Read about Mina and Matt and their child. Their child's name was Chaytan. When he grew up, he married and had daughters, their names were . . .'

Rosie put her hands to her mouth. She saw the nerve in her father's forehead began to twitch as Rivers listed the descendants of Matt O'Connell and Mina, name by name, generation by generation, all the way down to Redmond Rivers, of the Choctaw Nation of Oklahoma.

'*You're* Redmond Rivers!' Rosie exclaimed. 'You're related to Matt O'Connell. Oh my God, that means you're related to us!'

'Why the hell didn't you tell us that when you got here?' said Jack.

'From the moment I came into the house I felt it would come between us. The fear of losing the land is strong within you. If you thought there was any threat, no matter how remote, to Abbeyfield, you would not have let me stay. Part of me loved this place even before I saw it, but I knew it was never meant for me. Matt says in the letter that the children of Lorcan would inherit the land. Either way it's not about the land.'

'Then what is it about?'

Rosie spoke softly. 'It's about belonging, isn't it, Rivers? It's about finding where you belong in the world. And who you belong to.'

'It is, Rosie,' said Rivers. 'That's exactly what it's about."

Connie reached for her notebook. 'What does that make you to us? A cousin, maybe a third cousin? This will make a great story. I'd say we're the only family in Ireland with an American Indian cousin.'

'That may be true, but I am not your only cousin. I have family who are also your cousins.'

"That's incredible,' said Connie.

Rivers stood. 'When I get home I'll tell them about you all.'

'Wait till I tell Fletcher!" said Connie. 'Oh God, do

you really have to go now? I have so many questions.'

'He'll be back. Won't you, Rivers? Maybe next year,' said Jack, a note of hope in his voice.

Rivers shook his head. 'Not next year, but perhaps sometime in the future. Don't worry, Connie, write to me.' He took her pen and notebook and scribbled his address. 'I'll let you know what happens and I'll answer your questions — if I can.'

Rivers hugged Connie, then Rosie and shook hands with Jack and Tommy.

Pádraig was a little tearful. 'You can't go now, Rivers,' he said. 'We have to finish the wigwam.'

'I've finished it for you already — you can show it to your father when you are well.'

Pádraig turned to Tommy. 'I'm well already — can we go now, Dad?'

'I'm taking Rivers to the station,' said Tommy. 'I have the horse and cart ready. You'd better come with us in case I get lost. We'll go to see the wigwam when we come back.'

Rosie, Connie and Jack watched the cart disappear down the bohereen and then went inside to the quietness of the kitchen. For a moment or two they were uncertain what to do next.

'Well, put the kettle on anyhow, Rosie,' said Jack. 'I need to sit down. There's too much happening. I can't take it all in.'

'Can you believe Rivers is a cousin?' said Connie as she scribbled notes. 'We have cousins in America that we never knew existed. Would Rivers be a third cousin, is that right?'

'He never even hinted,' said Rosie, putting cups on the table. 'Never a word.'

'He probably couldn't get a word in edgeways,' said Old Sean as he settled himself into his armchair.

An hour or so later they heard the rattle of the returning wagon.

'I suppose you'll be making things official now?' said Jack to Rosie.

'Soon. But it'll be in Dublin, somewhere quiet. That's if you can manage without me. I don't want to leave you on your own. I mean, who's going to cook and clean after I've gone?'

'I've been wondering that myself,' he replied. 'Mrs Beattie is a fine cook. I could see if she'd do a few hours here.' He laughed at their outraged cries. 'Joking, only joking. Sure, we'll sort something out. I might ask Mrs Lawlor or one of her daughters. We'll figure it out somehow. Don't you worry. You've your own lives to lead. Both of you.'

CHAPTER 48

Knockanree

1946

A few weeks later Jack sat at the kitchen table listening to the thumps and bangs of suitcases being dragged from the tops of wardrobes. Tommy had returned to Dublin to arrange the small wedding and every day Rosie rang to hear the progress and issue instructions. She and Pádraig were to stay with Connie until everything was settled.

Pádraig ran excitedly from one room to the next, shouting 'Are we taking this?' every few minutes. Jack wanted to escape the turmoil, both in the house and in his heart. He pulled on his overcoat, made the familiar trek to the churchyard just outside the town and followed the worn path to his wife's grave.

'Well, you were right after all,' he said to Maureen. 'Tommy came back and they're going to make a go of it in Dublin.' He picked a few dead leaves off the grave. 'Connie will be married next spring. I'll miss them both,

Maureen. But more than that, I'll always regret the way I treated Rosie. But I've been making up for it. Well, trying to. It's so much harder without you to tell me when I'm being an eejit. I'll talk to her before she goes, try to make amends. I'd hate it if they didn't come back to see me, especially Pádraig.'

He leaned on the stick he'd forgot he was carrying and smiled at the sudden thought: 'Maureen, you'll never guess what was in the small meadow.'

Epilogue

Knockanree

1847

He gently pulled the door closed and walked across the yard. As he turned to secure the wooden gate, he took a long look at the house, one last time. A shadow passed an upstairs window. It was either Lorcan or Annie. He quickly looped the rope over the gatepost and turned toward the small meadow. He would say goodbye to Éamonn's cross and then pay a visit to Gráinne's grave before he started his journey from Knockanree.

He had just turned the bend in the path toward the small meadow when the silence of night was broken by the squeak of the gatepost opening and closing. Someone was coming after him. His heart sank, not wanting to talk to his brother or to Annie, not wanting to face them and say the words that would break all their hearts.

He listened for the footsteps but could hear nothing. It was only when he stood under Éamonn's cross that he could feel the eyes of someone on him.

'Come out!' he called.

The brambles rustled and a small body stepped forward.

'Billy! What are you doing out here?'

'I want to come with you,' said Billy, taking a few steps toward him.

'No, no, Billy. You'll be safe here. It's too dangerous a journey for you. Lorcan and Annie will look after you.'

Billy dropped his head. 'What if something happens? What if we have to go back to the workhouse? There'll be nobody to save us if you go.'

'That's not going to happen, Billy. Everything is taken care of. The family will look after you.'

'They might forget, and I'll have no one.' A sob escaped him.

Matthew looked at the small boy, his heart sore at the fear in the child's eyes. He knelt on one knee and beckoned Billy toward him.

'This is a special medal,' said Matt, taking the medallion from his neck. 'It has a magic that protects whoever owns it. I am giving this to you. It's yours.' He placed the medallion around Billy's neck. 'You own it now, and it will protect you.'

Billy held the medallion and looked at it carefully.

'What if it's taken? What if it's stolen? There's bad men . . . they might take it from me.' Billy's worried eyes looked into Matt's face.

Matt nodded solemnly. 'That's true. That's very true.' He looked around the meadow, still on bended knee. 'The very place,' he said. He moved to the small shrine to the Blessed Virgin Mary. Taking the medallion from Billy's neck he lifted the statue and placed it gently on the grass. Then he lifted the flat round stone that Lorcan had brought from the river as a plinth for the statue. There was a small hollow between the stones of the wall beneath it. Perfect. He felt in his pockets. Yes, I still have it, he thought. He placed the medal inside the doeskin pouch that Mina had given him and pushed it into the hollow. I'll buy her a new medallion and a new purse in New York, he decided. He replaced the stone and the statue, making sure it stood evenly, as though it had never been touched.

'Now,' he said, turning back to Billy. 'It's there for you. Whenever you need it.'

Matt climbed to the first low branch, where Éamonn's cross was fixed to the tree. Carefully he moved the cross and, with his knife, carved a circle surrounding an arrow into the bark.

'In case you ever forget where it is,' he said. 'That's what the Choctaw people do. They leave a marker in case they can't get back for some time. You see? The arrow is pointing to the shrine. You can climb up here and sit on the branch beside Éamonn's cross — and you'll be the only one who knows there's a secret behind it.'

Billy nodded. 'I won't tell anyone.'

Matt returned to the ground and placed his hand on Billy's thin shoulders. 'You must keep it safe and it will keep you safe.'

Billy nodded solemnly. It was enough to know the magic medal was there, hidden, watching over him with Mary, the Blessed Virgin.

Matt pushed him gently back toward the house and, as soon as he was out of sight, turned and began his journey back along the road to his home.

THE END